A PIONEER OF
AMERICAN FOLKLORE

A PIONEER OF AMERICAN FOLKLORE:

•

KARL KNORTZ AND HIS COLLECTIONS

•

Eleonore Schamschula
Foreword by Alan Dundes

University of Idaho Press / Moscow, Idaho
1996

00 99 98 97 96   5 4 3 2 1

Library of Congress Cataloging-in-Publication Data

Schamschula, Eleonore.
    A pioneer of American folklore : Karl Knortz and his collections /
Eleonore Schamschula ; foreword by Alan Dundes.
        p.   cm. — (Northwest folklife)
    Includes bibliographical references and index.
    ISBN 0-89301-185-1 (alk. paper)
     1. Folklore—United States. 2. Knortz, Karl, 1841–1918. 3. Folk-
lorists—United States. 4. Folklorists—Germany.   I. Title. II. Series.
GR105.5.S337   1996
398'.0973—dc20   96-3879
                                                                      CIP

To Walter and Marius

CONTENTS

FOREWORD

In the fall of 1988, approximately 700 folklorists from the United States and abroad gathered in Cambridge, Massachusetts, to celebrate the centennial of the American Folklore Society, which was founded in that locale 100 years earlier. Several of the charter members of the society were singled out for special praise—William Wells Newell, who more than any one individual deserves credit for the establishment and flourishing of the society, and Franz Boas, the stimulus for the study of native American folklore and a longtime editor of the *Journal of American Folklore*. The first list of members of the American Folklore Society, published at the end of the initial issue of the *Journal of American Folklore*, included some illustrious names: Oliver Wendell Holmes, John Fiske, Francis Parkman, S. L. Clemens, Edward Eggleston, J. W. Powell, Joel Chandler Harris, and Andrew Lang.

One name also found on the membership list was Karl Knortz, but he was not mentioned during the centennial meeting of the American Folklore Society, and his name remains largely unknown among professional folklorists. If one looks in standard works dealing with American folklore, one finds little or no notice taken of the folkloristic contributions of Karl Knortz. His name does not appear, for example, in Richard Dorson's *American Folklore* (1959), nor in Jan Harold Brunvand's *The Study of American Folklore*, 3rd edition (1986). He is not discussed in Rosemary Levy Zumwalt's *American Folklore Scholarship: A Dialogue of Dissent* (1988), and he rates only a single sentence in Simon J. Bronner's *American Folklore Studies: An Intellectual History* (1986). From this, one would be forced to conclude that either his contribution to American folklore study was unimportant or that his contribution, whatever it might be, has been largely ignored.

It will therefore no doubt come as a surprise to most American folklorists to learn that Karl Knortz (1841–1918) was one of the first important collectors of American folklore and that he published more books on folklore than did any of the other individuals whose names appeared on the initial list of American Folklore Society members. Moreover, his considerable collecting activity included a wide variety of folklore genres—rhymes, riddles, proverbs, superstitions, customs, and legends—and the range of his informants ran the gamut from school children to Native Americans. His 1905 book *Zur amerikanischen Volkskunde* seems to be the very first book devoted to American folklore as a whole.

If Karl Knortz was such an important early collector of American folklore, why then is his work so little known? The answer is quite simply that he published almost exclusively in German (although many of the texts that he collected he left in English) and his books were published in Germany, not in the United States. As most American folklorists did and do not read German, his valuable collections remained largely ignored. German folklorists could obviously read Knortz's works, but they tended to be more interested in German folklore, not American or even German-American folklore from the United States. So it seems that Karl Knortz, despite his indefatigable collecting and publishing activity, fell between the cracks into academic oblivion. It is worth noting that the only American folklorists to make use of Knortz's collections were themselves professors of German. Archer Taylor, for example, made ample reference to Knortz's collections of riddles in his *English Riddles from Oral Tradition* (1951), and Wayland Hand referred to Knortz's assemblages of superstitions in volumes 6 (1961) and 7 (1964) of the *Frank S. Brown Collection of North Carolina Folklore*. Taylor cited the riddles contained in *Streifzüge auf dem Gebiet amerikanischer Volkskunde* (1902) (Explorations in the Domain of American Folklore), while Hand referred to *Amerikanischer Aberglaube der Gegenwart. Ein Beitrag zur Volkskunde* (American Superstition of the Present: a Contribution to Folklore) (1913).

In an attempt to put together under one cover a large sampling of the American folklore gathered by Karl Knortz, Eleonore Schamschula has read nearly everything written by this prolific writer. In those instances where Knortz translated American folklore into German for his original German audience, she has retranslated that folklore back into English. She has also grouped Knortz's collected data conveniently into listings by genre. Accordingly, this book has sections devoted to riddles, to rhymes, to superstitions, etc. Knortz often bothered to indicate that he had elicited a particular item from oral tradition. However, just as often he did not do so. He was also prone to reprint folklore items from newspapers and from other early collections of folklore. With respect to the latter borrowing, one must remember that he saw his role in part as presenting American folklore to a German popular readership. The point is that sometimes he was careful to give sources for his data; sometimes he fails to give any source. Generally speaking, Schamschula has sought to include here primarily materials which came from American oral tradition. There seems little point in reprinting items which came from other early collections of American folklore, but in any given instance it was just not possible to ascertain beyond all doubt whether a particular item came from a printed source or was collected independently by Knortz.

What we have then in this unusual book is the American folklore data collected during the late nineteenth and early twentieth centuries by Karl Knortz which has hitherto been largely unavailable to American scholars. Knortz's books were not only in German, but were not easily found in American libraries. With this folklore now accessible, the reader will frequently find the first recorded occurrence of a particular item in the United States among Knortz's collectanea. Many of the items are still very much in oral tradition and the recognition that some of the current rhymes and superstitions go back at least one hundred years in the United States should be of interest to many readers.

It may be belated praise, but this volume should serve to demonstrate the genuine important contribution to American folklore study that Karl Knortz made. We owe a debt to Eleonore Schamschula for bringing this contribution to the attention of folklorists and students of American culture.

Alan Dundes

PREFACE

This volume represents the first study of the legacy of one of the earliest American folklorists, Karl Knortz, who has not made his way to general recognition. It also offers the first comprehensive bibliography of his scholarly works.

Karl Knortz's views and in particular his rich recordings of folklore data from the late nineteenth and the early twentieth centuries, are barely known to the English reading public since they were written in Karl Knortz's native German tongue. It is the intention of this book to make an important part of his folklore collections accessible to the non-German speaking audience. This selection of Knortz's American folklore data in English translation thus performs a service to the community of American folklorists that has long been overdue. It has become particularly interesting following the 100th anniversary of the American Folklore Society, which passed without taking much notice of this prolific collector and student of folklore.

It should be noted that Knortz, in his theoretical writings on folklore, used the German term "Volkskunde" in a way that encompasses fields beyond folklore: anthropology, prehistoric archeology, ethnography. The English term "folklore," in his view, represents merely one section of "Volkskunde." Whenever "Volkskunde" was used by Knortz as a theoretical notion, it is left untranslated.

I wish to express my gratitude to Prof. Alan Dundes who brought Karl Knortz to my attention and who encouraged me to further explore the work and biography of this prolific writer. I am especially indebted to him for the interest he took in the progress of this project and for contributing his foreword.

Eleonore Schamschula
Berkeley 1994

Part 1

•

Introduction

• O n e •

KARL KNORTZ:

HIS LIFE AND HIS WORKS

Karl Knortz may be regarded as one of the earliest scholars of folklore in America and one of the most prolific. He was deeply dedicated to this new and budding field of study, and his methods of collecting data were quite progressive in the 1870s when he started his work. The extensive collected information he provides, his way of documenting it, and his ideas on the theory of folklore genres make it worthwhile to the folklorist at the end of the twentieth century to take a closer look at these collections.

In America, Knortz's achievements were long obscured by the fact that, as a German immigrant he wrote almost entirely in German and that his works were published in Switzerland and Germany. As a result, his writings have remained almost inaccessible to potential American readers.

In Germany he was hardly a household name either, since he never traveled back to his native country to promote his books or to get acquainted with European folklorists. This, and the fact that Europeans showed little interest in the folklore of emigrants and in the degree to which those people kept their traditions and customs, prevented him from reaching a large German audience as a folklorist. The time has come to present to the American community of folklorists, in English translation, at least that part of Knortz's material collected in America.

On August 28, 1841, Karl Knortz was born out of wedlock in Garbenheim near Wetzlar (Germany) in then Rhenish-Prussia. In 1850, his mother, Wilhelmine Knortz, married Johann Jakob Waldschmidt, a butcher and innkeeper in Wetzlar, who seemed to have helped the boy get a solid education (Menges 1980, 226–27). Knortz attended elementary school in his native village. He remembered that time well, later writing about Garbenheim in connection with the great poet, playwright, scientist, and politician Johann Wolfgang von Goethe, who had often walked there from Wetzlar (1894a, 42–53). After elementary school, Knortz attended the Royal Prussian Gymnasium (high-school) at Wetzlar from 1852 to 1860.

There are only few sources available for biographic data on Knortz and their sparse information often does not agree on specific details. Knortz's studies in Heidelberg may serve as an example for this.

We read: "He was educated at Heidelberg University"(Appleton 1887, 564). "He graduated at Heidelberg 1863 (Ph. D. 1863)" (*Who's Who* 1899–1900, 408).[1] ". . . [A]nd for three years thereafter studied philology, philosophy and theology at Heidelberg University" (National Cyclopaedia 1900, 358). "Gymnasium (high school) in Wetzlar, Heidelberg" (*Wer ist's?* 1906, 608).[2]

Peter Assion reports in an introduction to the translation of *Zur amerikanischen Volkskunde* (1988, 4) that according to information he had received from the Heidelberg University Archives, Knortz was never registered there. Of course, this information might have been lost. After all, there is no entry in the local church chronicles for Knortz's birth, either (Hartert 1976, 302).

In 1863 Knortz emigrated to the United States. In *Amerikanische Skizzen* (1876a, 1–45), he gave a vivid description of a voyage from London to America on a crowded ship full of Irish, German, and Dutch emigrants who had to provide for their own meals, pretending to use the notes of a friend for his story. He certainly experienced similar adventures, if these were indeed not his own. The circumstances in the story fit the time frame of his own voyage. In the story the ship left London on May 12, 1863 (1876a, 3). When the "friend" arrived in New York, he began at once to look for work as a teacher, a task which proved to be more difficult than anticipated. Finally, a pastor offered him a teaching position at a newly founded German school in his parish. He had become interested in the young man after reading an essay of his, published in an American newspaper. In the form of his friend's diary, Knortz gives a detailed report describing the difficult life and the problems a teacher faced in a poorly funded, small school at that time. The young man in the story left this school in April 1864. The only difference between the adventures of this "friend" and Knortz is that Knortz did not move on to another teaching position in New Jersey (1876a, 20–42). Instead, Knortz found work as a teacher of German language and literature in the German-American Seminary in Detroit, Michigan in 1864. But he was restless and moved on from there after only a few years.

In 1868 Knortz went to Oshkosh, Wisconsin, and taught Latin and German at the local high school until 1871. During those years Knortz was also a contributor to *Deutsch-amerikanisches Conversations-Lexicon* (1872). His biography and the title of some of his works were included in this encyclopedia. It was noted therein that Knortz had published articles in many periodicals and that he had translated poetry not only from English but also from Spanish and Dutch sources (236).

From 1871 to 1874 Knortz was a faculty member of the normal school in Cincinnati, Ohio, and became the director of the school's German department. It was probably for a school performance there that he dramatized *Little Snow-white and the Dwarfs* (1873).

During those years he also began his lifelong preoccupation with American literature and his attempt to make it accessible to German readers. His translation of Henry Wadsworth Longfellow's *Evangeline* (1867) was published 1871 in *Der Deutsche Pionier* (1871b), and in 1874 *The Courtship of Miles Standish* (Longfellow 1858) was printed (1874b). In the course of his life, Knortz would again and again return to Longfellow's works.

As soon as Knortz had arrived in America in 1863, he was confronted with the bitter struggle over slavery. He was liberal minded and strongly sided with the abolitionists. Since one of the more crucial problems after the Civil War was the question of equal rights for Blacks, he dealt with it in his own way at school. Most Germans in Cincinnati supported equal opportunities for Blacks, so a Black girl was sent to their school to learn German and thus test the possibility for Black children to be accepted in a White school. Everything went well until there was a picnic, and the father of the White girl who walked beside her on the way to the park angrily grabbed his child and left. Knortz at once took the child's place beside the Black girl. This gesture was appreciated among her people, and some time later, on a trip to Lake Superior, several Black sailors recognized him, remembered what he had done, and made his life on board the ship as comfortable as possible (1884a, 166).

From May 1873 to February 1874 Knortz also briefly edited the journal *Der Deutsche Pionier* (*Die deutschsprachige Presse der Amerikas* 1973, 441), in which he had published his translation of Longfellow's *Evangeline* in 1871. Knortz, however, was soon asked to leave his job as an editor, since he had tried to change the journal to a literary magazine, contrary to the intentions of the Pionier Verein. After his dismissal, a letter appeared in the *Washington Journal* accusing the members of the Pionier Verein of censoring an article Knortz had allowed to be published and attacking them on religious grounds. The members of the board suspected that Knortz himself had written the article in the *Washington Journal* (*Der deutsche Pionier*, March 1874, 35–37).

Knortz later described American life in general and many of his own adventures during those early years in *Amerikanische Lebensbilder* (1884a). This book gives a good insight into current affairs, since Knortz was very interested in the everyday problems of his time and in the people he met. He had an open mind and reflected on all kinds of daily events. He was always eager to learn, to experience something new, and to take part in whatever happened around him.

In 1875 Knortz devoted himself to journalism again and became the editor of *Indiana-Deutsche-Zeitung* in Indianapolis, Ind. (Menges 1980, 226). In *Amerikanische Lebensbilder* he complained about the difficulties his Republican paper had with American newspapers during political elections, vividly describing the way opinions were formed and manipulated (159–62). He also wrote about his problems with a star reporter and with that man's verbal aggressiveness. He continued explaining how he himself soon left the newspaper, in order not to be held responsible for the paper's downfall (167–70).

After this experience, Knortz began to remember the "little theology" that he still retained in his memory from his "studies in Heidelberg," and, being in Pittsburgh without a job, accepted invitations from several pastors to preach in their churches on Sundays. When a pastor became ill, he substituted for him (1884a, 65). Soon he made preaching his vocation and became the pastor of the German Independent Protestant Congregation in Johnstown, Pennsylvania, for six years (*The National Cyclopaedia* 1900, 358). Franz Brümmer states that Knortz was the spokesman for the independent German community in Johnstown as well as the principal of its school (1913, 34). Several little stories in *Amerikanische Lebensbilder* are devoted to the memories of his time as a pastor and to his experiences with colleagues, members of the church, funerals, folklore of the Pennsylvania Dutch, and superstition, (1884a, 65–89).

In 1877, while he was in Johnstown, Knortz married Anna Singer, with whom he had a daughter in 1879 (*Wer ist's?* 1906, 608).[3] During that time he also became an American citizen. He mentioned this event humorously in *Amerikanische Lebensbilder* when he described how he traveled to Ebensburg with a group of people who wanted to become citizens. But when the future Americans and their witnesses finally were called into court in the afternoon after long hours of waiting, many of them were too drunk to answer any questions (176–81).

A few years later, in 1882, Knortz moved to New York City and became a teacher for the "Freie Gemeinde" in Melrose, a suburb of New York (Brümmer 1913, 34). After 1886 he devoted himself solely to literary work. But writing books seemed not to have provided enough of an income for him and he felt the necessity to look for a steady job again. In 1892 Knortz returned to teaching. He became superintendent of the German department of the public schools of Evansville, Indiana, and worked there until his retirement in 1905.

During his lifetime Knortz was acknowledged by several biographical publications. In *Deutscher Litteratur Kalender* he was recognized for his work as an "ethnograph, cultural historian, clergyman and superintendent of schools" (1901, 731).[4] His eminent role as a folklorist, however, was only rarely noticed.

Yet, during all his years of teaching, he had been interested in folklore and had collected rich data in the field, including many songs, rhymes and riddles which he had learned from school children, e.g., children's rhymes in New York (1896a, 59–73) and Indiana (1896a, 74–87) and riddles in Indiana (1902b, 210–40). In addition to orally collected data he also had looked for folklore in literature, and had published numerous books on the subject.

After his retirement, folklore remained one of his main interests and he kept collecting data. Knortz had always espoused a broad concept of folklore that included all kinds of people: American Indians, Africans, Asians, and Europeans and their cultures, lore, and beliefs. Knortz studied survivals, but he also looked into the everyday life of immigrants (e.g. 1876a, 20). He wrote about their cultural and acculturation problems, about interethnic relationships, and about simple people in general. Thus he described growing and harvesting strawberries in Quakertown, Connecticut, or growing cranberries in New Jersey, and he wrote about lumberjacks in Minnesota, Wisconsin, and Michigan and about moon shiners in the Blue Ridge Mountains (1900b, 60–7).

In 1908 Knortz moved to North Tarrytown, New York,[5] where he spent the last ten years of his life compiling enormous amounts of folklore, which he published in several books. He also kept writing on various other subjects, e.g., on writers (Sudermann), philosophers (Nietzsche), religion, peace, and the growing hostility towards Germans in America, which was the topic of his last book (1915). In all, he published another 23 works before his death on January 27, 1918.

Although Knortz is presented here as an early American folklorist, in Germany he was better known for many of his other publications and for an almost encyclopedic interest in the culture around him. Folklore plays a substantial, but by no means an exclusive, part in his scholarship.

Knortz was also a German poet and translator and took great interest in German culture and tradition. He gave talks in literary clubs and tried to preserve the German heritage for the second generation of immigrants. Even though he realized that there were many Germans who wanted to forget everything that reminded them of their past—customs as well as language—in order to become completely American (1882a, 2), Knortz still hoped the children of German immigrants who grew up in America would learn German songs, folk tales, games, and riddles. He wished they would cherish the customs of their forefathers, even if they felt American and spoke English.

Knortz knew that the immigrants' children would soon forget the language of their ancestors. He admitted he no longer believed that the German language was rooted so firmly in America that it could hold its own without a steady stream of new immigrants[6]. In addition he thought it was better for a country to have only one common language (1889a, 8). A few years earlier, he still had opposed those Germans who thought English was enough, fearing that Germans who were born in America would get rid of their parents' language as soon as possible. "We oppose this opinion, since we believe that the Germans have to fulfill a cultural mission here," he said (1884a, 206). Experience taught Knortz otherwise, and he decided translations had to familiarize interested Americans, even those of German descent, with the great works of German poets and philosophers. In a talk to the Literary Society in Morrisania, New York, Knortz expressed his hope that those works would help to realize the humane ideals that were found in German art and science, thereby softening the prevailing materialism in America (1889a, 6–8).

Since Knortz was a poet and a writer in his own right, he was very interested in German as well as in American literature. If he had ever had any hopes for a German-American literature, they had soon disappeared, and Knortz realized it would be better for German-American authors to become an integral part of American literature. Although he admired the successful young American literature, he was convinced that Germans could contribute much to it by offering their own rich literary tradition. Since Knortz noticed an eager interest in German science and literature among educated Americans, he encouraged them, as well as German immigrants, to read German poets and thinkers and to make those known in public life (1889a, 11).

But Knortz also wrote about American literature, poets, and writers. As an author, he felt obligated to introduce Germans in Europe to a literature which had been widely unknown to them. Along with studies about American literature (1880c; 1902a; 1909f) and several American writers, e.g., H. W. Longfellow (1879a), Walt Whitman (1886d; 1899b; 1911c), Washington Irving (1909h), he translated works by American poets (1871b; 1872b; 1874b; 1879b; 1883; 1887a; 1889b; 1889d). Among Germans, however, he was best known for his history of American literature, which was highly praised and which soon was considered a standard work in Germany (1891c).

As an author Knortz wrote poetry (1875a; 1877; 1878; 1884b; 1884c), detective stories (1889c), and a mystery novel modeled after Nathaniel Hawthorne (1893b). He also wrote and edited books on German (1885b; 1885c; 1896b; 1896c; 1897b; 1897c; 1898d; 1905a; 1908b) and British authors and their works (1872a; 1875b; 1876b; 1882c; 1886c; 1888; 1911a).

Since he loved his new country, Knortz wanted to share his affection for his American home with the people he had left behind in Germany. Thus he wrote many books, sketches, essays, anecdotes, epigrams and travel stories about every day life in America. Some reflect personal experiences, excursions to tourist attractions, life among the immigrants, or his impressions as a teacher and as an observer of various religious communities, especially those with Christian-Communist ideals like the Rappites in Pennsylvania. Others describe just curious or interesting episodes. Many of these books also contain folklore topics (1876a; 1882a; 1884a; 1891a; 1892b; 1892c; 1892d; 1893a; 1894a; 1896d; 1898c).[7]

Some of his writings were on political ideas and social theories (1880b; 1885a; 1886a; 1892a; 1907b; 1910c; 1911d), others on philosophical themes (1898b; 1899a; 1906b; 1909c; 1913c), and others dealt with religious questions (1882d; 1891d; 1892c; 1904c; 1909a; 1909g). He frequently appeared to be extremely anticlerical and critical of many Christian denominations, a fact which is not consistent with his own history as a preacher. He often scorned religious customs and even proposed for elementary schools the teaching of moral values without any religious connotations (1909e).

Being a dedicated teacher, another of his favorite topics was education. He not only wrote about the problems and goals of elementary schools or high schools, but also about the kindergarten system, which he introduced in some places. He often dealt with the teaching of German in America and also prepared several anthologies and some readers for schools (1895; 1896b; 1897a; an essay on the American elementary school in 1898c; 1900a; 1904a; 1904b; 1909e). He reflected on the role of Germans in the U.S. and on their reception in this country, (1894b; 1895; 1898a; 1898d; 1906a; 1915), on freethinkers (1910b), and various other subjects (1865; 1874a; 1886b; 1892e; 1908a; 1909b; 1914). His philosophical ideas were those of enlightenment and rationalism. He emphatically spoke out against racism.[8]

Knortz loved his new country and felt at home among Americans, who enjoyed a life free from suppression by an autocratic ruler. But he also remembered Germany and critically examined the problems of German immigrants and their integration into America, admonishing his former countrymen to be interested in their new country, its history, and its laws and to learn English rapidly in order to be able to participate fully in political life, since they now were Americans (1884a, 40). He was convinced that a German-American who traveled back to his native country would feel like a stranger there, and upon his return to America he would no longer be homesick. He would be proud that his children had become citizens of a free country, and for that reason he would give his best to his new homeland. In Knortz's opinion, the best a German immigrant could give were the works of his nation's philosophers and poets (1889a, 8).

Although Knortz lived in America and participated actively in the American way of life, he certainly was influenced by his cultural background and his German experiences before his emigration, be they political, social, or educational.

In the beginning of the nineteenth century, patriotism had spread in Germany after her wars against Napoleon, who had invaded the country. While Knortz was growing up, the political situation was volatile and the hope for more freedom and political stability resulted in the revolution of 1848. At that time, a parliament was elected in Frankfurt, which began to prepare a constitution for a united Germany. But only three years later the parliament broke up again and the German Confederation was re-established. Many prominent people had been members of the parliament. One of them was Jacob Grimm, who, together with his brother Wilhelm, was well known for the scholarly work he had done in many fields, e.g., in linguistics, historical research, literature, law, and politics. But the young Knortz may have known the Brothers Grimm mainly for their books of children's and household tales, which they had collected from friends and from storytellers and people who lived in villages around Kassel in Hesse, not very far from where Knortz grew up. The first tales had been published in 1812, and more volumes and editions had been printed during the following years. Although there had been publications of fairy tales before that time, for example, in the 18th century by Johann Carl August Musäus, none had applied the basic idea of publishing the stories as they were told by storytellers, with as little editing as possible. The Grimms wanted to preserve for Germany a work of traditional literature created by the people, and they recognized many tales as survivals of an ancient German religion. The tales collected by the Grimms were enthusiastically accepted by their readers and soon became part of children's readings.

At the same time other writers and poets within the Romantic movement, like Ludwig Tieck, Johann Gottfried Herder, and Clemens von Brentano, were interested in their nation's past, in folklore and legends, and generally in the creativity of the people. They collected tales and songs and theorized about the way these data should be presented. Knortz's ideas might have been influenced by the Romanticists, who looked back from the industrialized, mechanized, and commercialized present to remote and faraway places, to the more quiet past, and to folklore, nature, and the lifestyle of the common man. In his books Knortz often mentioned the Grimm brothers, the folk song collections by C. Brentano, Achim von Armin, Ludwig Uhland, Johann Joseph von Görres, Heinrich Heine, Friedrich von Schlegel, and Ludwig Tieck, and the works of many other members of the Romantic movement. He also mentioned the works of Wilhelm Mannhardt, Karl Simrock, Adolf Wuttke, and J. G. von Hahn, who contributed to German folklore studies during the nineteenth century.

Whereas these poets and collectors of folklore looked back to past societies, to the history of their nations, and to ordinary people and their lore and way of life, others used natural science to explore the past of humankind and its evolution. Charles Darwin published *The Origin of*

Species in 1859, and soon evolution was studied in many fields. It was used in anthropology and folklore when scholars tried to understand how primitive societies developed into nations with modern technology, or when they looked into superstitions and religious beliefs, customs, and cultural attitudes. In short, scholars were eager to research the slow change in culture and civilization from primitive beginnings to the present. At the same time folklorists hoped to explain the similarities of folklore and folklife in different areas of the world, often very distant from each other. Many of them ascribed those similarities to the psychic unity of mankind.

While all these exciting new developments went on in the world, the twenty-two-year-old Knortz was living in Germany, where he was very critical of the political situation and the restricted opportunities awaiting him. He was restless and adventurous and longed for a country where he could grow personally, find work and a financial future, and be able to live in a democracy and express himself freely.

In America, Knortz not only took great interest in the social development of the newly united country, he also closely followed the industrial, technical, and scientific progress around him. Early in his career he was interested in the use and possibilities of stenography and published an article on its history and literature (1865). In 1870 he wrote an article on the literature of phonography (1874a). He later used both techniques extensively in his fieldwork when he started to collect folklore.

Knortz's cultural background and his appreciation for the ideas of the Romantic movement might have persuaded him to learn more about people who seemed to have upheld their ancient ways, who lived in harmony with nature and her forces, and who still remembered their tribal legends and songs and acted out their heritage. In America he found those characteristics in Indians, and soon after he arrived he became actively interested in the habits, tales, and myths of American Indians. It is quite possible that he had read stories about their culture and way of life before he came to America or during the first years of his stay in the new country. At that time there were many stories available that described the cultural clash between the native inhabitants of the land and the settlers or frontiersmen, like James Fenimore Cooper's *Leatherstocking Tales* and the books and paintings of George Catlin, who had studied various tribes and recorded information about their customs and habits, and there were collections of Indian myths such as Henry Rowe Schoolcraft's works. Knortz soon realized that the way American Indians had been portrayed in Europe and the way they were shown in circuses and exhibitions conveyed a picture far from reality. He wanted to provide his German countrymen with a different view of the Indians, one that showed they were not uncivilized savages but had their own culture and a wealth of tradition.

His interest in native Americans moved Knortz to collect Indian tales and legends from missionaries, travelers, translators, Indian agents, and English and French books. He translated them into German and published them in 1871 as *Märchen und Sagen der nordamerikanischen Indianer* (1871a). In the introduction he stressed the fact that his collection consisted of original tales which expressed the ideas, beliefs, and cultural attitudes of the Indians, and that those tales were different from the usual stories which speak of battles and fights and picture the Indians as fierce fighters or intoxicated criminals (1871a). He acknowledged that many Indians had changed their ancient ways after having had contact with the White man and after having become acquainted with alcohol, but in his book Knortz focused on their myths, religious beliefs, and tales.

Knortz was certainly influenced by Catlin and Schoolcraft, since he mentioned both in his book *Amerikanische Skizzen* (1876a) when he introduced Indian legends in the chapter *Indianische Legenden* (1876a,139). In addition, one of Schoolcraft's works is *The Myth of Hiawatha and Other Oral legends, Mythologic and Allegoric, of the North American Indians* (1856). Hiawatha is also the subject of Longfellow's poem *The Song of Hiawatha*, which was written in 1855 and which very early had captured Knortz's interest. He translated it into German and edited it in 1872. A few years later he told many Indian legends, among them the story of Hiawatha, in *Amerikanische Skizzen* (139–68). To the end of that book he added two short chapters, on Indian mythology and on Father Baraga, who had died in 1868. Father Baraga, the Bishop of Marquette, had been a missionary among the Chippewa Indians on Lake Superior. For many years he had lived with them and studied their language and dialects. He had published a *Dictionary of the Otchipwe Language* (1853) and a *Theoretical and practical Grammar of the Otchipwe Language.*

Although Knortz admired Schoolcraft's knowledge of Indian myths and the Indian way of life, he was not impressed by the latter's knowledge of their languages. During one of his visits with Longfellow, Knortz inquired why Longfellow had used Indian words which he had taken from the works of Schoolcraft, who was no authority in this field. Then Knortz explained his own method: He had taken advantage of Father Baraga's *Dictionary of the Otchipwe Language* and he had gone to the Chippewa Indians themselves to learn their language, to listen to their myths, and to study their customs. During his stay there, Knortz had asked the Indians to pronounce different words for him, until he could write them down, complete with their exact pronunciation and accent (1882a, 25–6).

In *Amerikanische Skizzen*, Knortz spoke about this visit to the Chippewa Indians, undertaken some time before. In Sault Ste. Marie, on Lake Superior near the Sault River, he went to Chief Akiwesi Shawano and gave him a letter of recommendation from the chief's son-in-law, a lawyer, whom he had known in Detroit (56). He stayed with the Chippewa Indians for many weeks, traveled among them, and listened to and wrote down the legends which the chief and an old Indian woman on the Canadian shore of the lake would tell him (90–6). He also visited a famous medicine man, but he became very skeptical when the latter wanted money and whiskey, before he sang his sacred songs, danced, beat his drums, and gave an example of his power in a hut built for the ceremony (112–35).

Knortz's linguistic interest and his effort to collect data as accurately as possible led him to study not only the words but also the structure and grammar of Indian languages. In addition, those languages intrigued him, for example, when they lacked a word for a simple action like "to go," but abounded in expressions for the different ways of movements on land or in the water. He also commented on the absence of many abstract words. To demonstrate differences in world view, he quoted multiple Indian names for the same animals (1900b, 9) or remarked on the lack of a word for eye, hand, or foot (8).

From the beginning of his folklore studies Knortz had been an avid field-worker. After his first publications in folklore, he kept collecting Indian tales, legends, and myths. In the 1880s he published them in *Aus dem Wigwam* (1880), in a chapter about American flood legends in his book *Aus der transatlantischen Gesellschaft* (1882a, 240–67), and in *Nokomis* (1887). In 1882 he also gave two papers on Indian mythology and civilization, published as *Mythologie und Zivilisation der nordamerikanischen Indianer* (1882b).

Knortz was not only interested in Indian legends and tales but also in the legal, educational, and social problems of Indians. True to his plea for freedom and justice for all, he decried the way their rights and treaties were annulled and neglected, and in many of his publications he deplored the way the confrontation with the culture and civilization of the White settlers had undermined the Indians' own culture and their traditional way of life.

But Knortz's interest was also captured by the folklore of the people around him, Americans and immigrants from different nations, and by the way those people interacted with each other. He was fascinated by the process of acculturation undergone by the newcomers. In many books and lectures he addressed this problem, mainly with regard to his German fellow immigrants (e.g., 1889a, 5–8). Since Knortz had been living in Pennsylvania for several years, it had been quite natural for him to listen to the German-speaking Pennsylvanians, to collect their lore and customs, and to note the changes in their daily lives. He was, however, not the first to write about the many traditions of the Pennsylvania Dutch. In America there had been some interest in the life and customs of German immigrants long before Knortz's time. Benjamin Rush, for instance, had published a book on the way of life and the traditions of Germans in his *An Account of the Manners of the German Inhabitants of Pennsylvania* (1789).

Knortz held the opinion that the lore and tradition of any one people could be of interest to all humans and that it could help them to better understand each other and their histories. He saw many similarities among different nationalities and groups of people in their lore, as well as in the psychological forces that influenced them.

Knortz did not restrict his interest to "backward" people in the countryside. He also collected data in cities and from different places in many

American states while traveling. He watched people doing their daily chores, enjoying themselves at festivals, and relaxing at play. He collected their folk speech, their slang, their secret languages, their riddles, rhymes, songs, and legends. He often pointed out how people from different nations behaved in similar ways. And he showed their national idiosyncrasies, too.

While collecting data in the field, Knortz also turned his interest to written sources, be they newspapers, reports from agencies, or literature. In his own writings he often mentioned books that included some kind of folklore, above all American folklore, and recommended them to his readers. One example was Irving's story *Rip van Winkle* (1903, 15).

Since Knortz had left Germany in 1863, he might well have been acquainted with the beginning studies of folklore in his native country. In 1858, in a lecture in Germany, Wilhelm Heinrich Riehl had declared folklore (Volkskunde) an academic discipline and had shown its interdependence with other fields of scholarship. He had stressed that collecting material and studying the life of people, although important, ought to be only an auxiliary means within the scientific research of the natural laws of folklife (1935, reprint). Knortz followed Riehl rather closely. Although he collected vast amounts of material, he also tried to put those data into perspective and to explain their influences and origins. Like Riehl (1935, 21–2), he promoted the study of customs, language, and settlements, and also of religious, historical, social, political, scientific, and cultural developments. In addition, however, he took into account external influences on a people, as well as material culture. Riehl had rejected the idea that folklore should only study sources from old, bygone times. He saw sources of folklore in modern daily life (17), and so did Knortz. Differing from Riehl, however, who determined folklore to be an academic discipline only if it had found its focal point of studies in the idea of a nation (15), Knortz looked for data everywhere. He once defined folklore as "the quintessence of the thoughts and reflections of a whole people not yet touched by culture, who, in this case [national civilization, myths, religion] consist not only of aborigines and old-fashioned people but of all children of this world" (1896a, 5).

At that time, the concept of folklore as a discipline of its own was alien to American folklorists, who saw it as part of anthropology. William Wells Newell even stated much later that "many American students of folklore will not approve a definition which favors the establishment of a separate science of folklore; they will prefer to confine the name to a body of material and to consider the comparative examination of this material as a part of anthropological science . . . [T]he word 'folk-lore' itself is not of that abstract character which can properly be used as the title of a science" (1892a, 240). "In its broader meaning therefore, folk-lore is a part of anthropology and ethnography"(1890b, 134).

In America, folklore scholars were interested in native people and their way of life, including their myths and customs and superstitions. In Europe, on the other hand, folklore was understood as dealing with the peasant population of Europe. American Indians and other non-European peoples were regarded as 'savages,' and ethnologists, not folklorists would study them.

Knortz's idea of folklore, however, was comprehensive and inclusive. He collected data from Americans of different ethnic origins, from recent European immigrants as well as from Blacks and even from 'savages' like the Indians. His studies comprise traditional culture and oral tradition, as well as developments in the ever-changing present. Knortz's works therefore reflected not only European but also American ideas of folklore.

Since Knortz spent much of his time collecting folklore data, he eagerly joined the American Folklore Society when it was founded in 1888,[9] obviously hoping to learn more about this field of study and to exchange ideas. He often quoted articles or data he had found in the *Journal of American Folklore (JAF)*, but he seems not to have contributed any articles or regularly sent his books to *JAF* for review. Three of his books are mentioned in *JAF*. One was acknowledged as 'received' (*JAF* 4, 1891, 361: *Geschichte der nordamerikanischen Literatur*), and only two were reviewed: "Das deutsche Volkslied" (*JAF* 2 1889, 159) and "Folkloristische Streifzüge" (*JAF* 13 1900, 78).[10]

One reason for Knortz's scarce involvement in the *Journal*, despite his prolific work and his often innovative studies, may have been the trend among the leadership of the American Folklore Society to exclude non-professional scholars from their ranks. Franz Boas saw a problem with societies that were very successful in popularizing the subject matter of their science "because the lay members largely outnumber the scientific contributors"(Boas 1902, 805). His editorial policies eliminated practically all amateur contributions, at least those sent to the anthropological segment of the *Journal.* Newell held the same opinion. For some time he intended to restrict membership to an even more select group; however, he soon realized that local amateurs would no doubt continue to participate (see: Zumwalt, 29). Otis T. Mason also urged the American Folklore Society "to part company" with people outside the learned society (Mason 1891, 103). He wanted to move away from amateurism and intended to shift the membership of the Folklore Society to professionalism. This was quite in tune with scholarly developments at that time, which valued science and facts as a means to achieve progress and which established scientific methods of study for many disciplines.

Perhaps Knortz was not regarded as a serious scholar, since he had no academic connections, and he maintained that everybody should collect folklore data in order to preserve as much of the common heritage as possible (1900b, 6), an idea many members of the Folklore Society did not share. On the other hand, it might well be that Knortz was not eager to take an active part in the Folklore Society and that he was content gathering information and going on with his own studies. By just reading *JAF* he could gain new insights and learn about the most recent methods of research and trends in folklore.

Being a member from the very beginning, he was aware of and accepted the goals of the *Journal of American Folklore* as well as those of the Folklore Society, which Newell had defined. Knortz expressed his ideas about orally transmitted data with this definition: "Folklore is the spoken or sung literature of the common man, which contains his philosophy, religion, and poetry, and which answers the many questions of daily life in a way that conforms to his knowledge"(1896a, 5–6). Thus he concurred with Newell, who said folklore was "oral tradition, information and belief handed down from generation to generation without the use of writing . . . . [I]t must belong . . . to the folk rather than to individuals" (Newell 1890b, 134), and "Lore must be understood as the complement of literature, as embracing all human knowledge handed down by word of mouth and preserved without the use of writing" (Newell 1888b, 162–3). While Knortz agreed with the main objective, he did, however, not completely exclude written sources. In this respect he also differed from Lee Vance, who once stated: "But it should be remembered that folk-lore includes what is unwritten. It is limited to such human ideas and opinions as are orally transmitted from generation to generation, from age to age. This knowledge ceases to be the lore of the folk when it is put down in writing" (Vance, 1896–97, 250).

As I have pointed out, Knortz also agreed with Newell's opinion when the latter proclaimed: "That definition of 'folk-lore' which restricts the use of the word to the survival of prehistoric practices and beliefs is deficient, in that it leaves out of account the considerable mass of custom and opinion which is emphatically folk-lore, but by no means of archaic origin or character" (Newell 1891b, 356). This concept of folklore study was broader than the definition of folklore study given by the English Folklore Society, which greatly influenced American folklore: "the comparison and identification of the survivals of archaic beliefs, customs, and traditions in modern ages" (Gomme 1890, 5).

Newell also suggested that folklore had to cover not only the lore of mainly European immigrants but also of "savages." He stated: "Customs and superstitions found in the United States, for example, not only among recent immigrants, but also in families of purest English stock, have evident connection with practices and beliefs widely extended among savage tribes. It was therefore necessary to extend the term folk-lore so as to cover these" (Newell 1890b, 134–5). Newell actually advocated a new direction for American folklore, away from the European concept, and in this respect Knortz concurred with him fully.

Knortz had come to those same conclusions before and had already realized them in his studies of Indian lore. He also repeatedly praised the unique opportunity in the U.S. to compare all the data collected from one ethnic group to data from other ethnic groups (1900b, 4). Thus, he enumerated in his country of choice "the American Indians with their many tales, fables, and religious views; then the Blacks, Voodoo, and Creoles, whose tales show a surprising similarity to those in Africa and Europe; then the Chinese, Gypsies, Dutch, Irish, Italians, and German-Pennsylvanians, whose customs and songs give interesting testimony about their place of origin and their national idiosyncrasies" (1896a, 6). He embraced the opportunity for research, and was fascinated by the similarity of many of their myths, customs, and superstitions, and at the same time by the differences among them.

Knortz had observed and studied the ideas of folklore as they had been discussed everywhere. The Brothers Grimm and the Romanticists in Germany, G. L. Gomme in England, and many other folklorists in America had pleaded with people to collect the old traditions in order not to forget and consequently lose them. He found the same eager interest in tradition in Newell when the latter promoted the collection of folklore before it was forgotten, and proclaimed the collection of the fast-vanishing remains of folklore in America as one of the objectives of the *Journal of American Folklore*. Newell was interested in relics of Old English Folklore, in the lore of Blacks in the Southern states and of the Indian tribes of North America, as well as in the lore of French Canada and Mexico (Newell 1888a, 3). We have examples of data from all of these groups in Knortz's work. Knortz also had no problems with one of the goals of the American Folklore Society towards the end of the nineteenth century which Vance defined as "the collection of material to be collated and examined afterward according to scientific methods" (1893, 597).

At that time there was, however, one prominent theory in folklore which Knortz embraced for several years, mainly towards the end of the nineteenth century, and which many members of the Folklore Society were not endorsing: the solar myth theory. Edward Burnett Tylor had already cautioned against the full implementation of the solar myth: "Thus, in interpreting heroic legend as based on nature-myth, circumstantial analogy must be very cautiously appealed to, and at any rate there is need of evidence more cogent than vague likeness between human and cosmic life" (1874, 1:320). Newell, however, strongly decried the solar myth: "The result is that a mass of phrases, such as sun-myth, Aryan origins, and the like, are caught up by readers . . . . who seize upon such catch-words as if they really corresponded to any precise idea" (1890a, 23). He explained, "The phenomena of the external world, interpreted as the expression of divine purpose by regular descent, reflected themselves in mythology; actions of gods passed into narratives of heroes, those into the fireside tales of the modern world; folk-song and folk-tale were to be considered as the detritus of myth . . . . To the English public. F. Max Müller became the interpreter of such conceptions, and through his presentation the theory of the solar myth for a brief period reigned in current literature" (1906, 2).

Boas also argued against it: "Certainly, the phenomena of nature are at the bottom of numerous myths, else we should not find sun, moon, clouds, thunder-storm, the sea and the land play so important a part in all mythologies. What I maintain is only that the specific myth cannot be simply interpreted as the result of observation of natural phenomena" (1896, 7), and earlier: "It is particularly important to emphasize the fact that our comparison proves many creation myths to be of complex growth, in so far as their elements occur variously combined in various regions . . . . Therefore they cannot be explained as symbolizing or anthropomorphizing natural phenomena, neither can we assume that the etymologies of the names of the hero or deities give a clue to their actual meaning, because there never was such a meaning" (1891, 20).

However, Daniel Garrison Brinton, another prominent member of the Folklore Society, worked with this concept of the solar myth theory. When he studied creation myths of American Indians he saw their gods as gods of light: " . . . [T]he names Michabo and Manibozho . . . therefore mean the Great Light, the Spirit of Light, or the Dawn, or the East, and in the literal sense of the word the Great White One, as indeed he has sometimes been called" (1876, 179). Brinton stated: "As the dawn brings light, and with light is associated in every human mind the ideas of knowledge, safety, protection, majesty, divinity, as it dispels the specters of night, as it defines the cardinal points, and brings forth the sun and the day, it occupied the primitive mind to an extent that can hardly be magnified beyond the truth" (1876, 94). This sounds very much like Knortz's ideas in *Die ethische und mythische Bedeutung der deutschen Volksmärchen* (1889a, 65–9), which he applied to the stories of many different nations.

Although the solar myth theory has long since lost its significance, it was one of the most influential theories of the outgoing nineteenth century. In his lectures, Knortz explained that we could find a piece of old culture and of social life in "myths-tales" which show the battle between the gods of darkness and the gods of light in continuously changing forms (1889a, 65). He suggested that the old gods had been identified with heroes of legend and history and that they lived on (undetected by most) in children's rhymes, local and personal names, and above all in folk tales. (1889a, 65). When talking about German tales, he was convinced that the reader had to know the mythological universe of the Aryan peoples in order to understand the tales. Indra, Zeus, Wotan, Oedipus, Hercules, and Sigurt could, in his opinion, easily be explained as gods of light (1889a, 65–6). To illustrate his theory he interpreted many folk tales as solar myths, for example, "Red Riding Hood," "Cinderella" (1889a, 93), "The Table, the Ass and the Stick" (1889a, 93), "Frau Holle" (1889a, 84), and "Sleeping Beauty" (1889a, 67).

Knortz might have become acquainted with the solar myth theory while he was still in Europe. Max Müller had published books on this theory, and his sensational essay on the origins of mythology, *Comparative Mythology* (1856), was well known to interested scholars by the time Knortz left for America. Knortz may also have read some of Müller's later publications (1862, 1867, 1897). Müller had arrived at the solar myth theory through comparative philology, a field that fascinated Knortz greatly, since he was well versed in linguistics and fluent in many languages. Müller had traced the "barbarous elements" in Greek mythology to Sanscrit equivalents and finally to the Aryan stock.

In England, Andrew Lang ridiculed Müller's methods and theories on solarism, as well as those of the American, Brinton. Nevertheless, he wrote: "It seems to be commonly thought that the existence of solar myths is denied by anthropologists. This is a vulgar error. There is an enormous mass of solar myths, but they are not caused by a 'disease of language' and—all myths are not solar" (1968, 135).

During the years shortly after Knortz's departure from Germany, Müller's disciple, George William Cox, who like Knortz was interested in Greek history and mythology, also published works which relied on solarism. His *Mythology of the Aryan Nations* pushed the solar myth theory still further. In this book Cox wrote, "I have retained the word Aryan as a name for the tribes or races akin to Greeks and Teutons in Europe and in Asia" (1878, 1:viii). This definition of Aryan was the same that Knortz used, naming gods and heroes like Indra, Zeus, Wotan, Sigurt, etc. in connection with myths of the Aryan people (1889a, 65). In addition, Cox—like other folklorists of his time—promoted the idea that similar but not identical narratives point to a common source in India (1878, 1:145). He stated that if in the tradition of different Aryan tribes the same characters reappeared with no other difference than that of title and local coloring, it could be assumed that the Aryan tribes "must have started from a common center, and that from their ancient home they must have carried away, if not the developed myth, yet the quickened germ . . . " (1878, 1:99). Knortz concurred. He believed that many tales which seem to be true German folk tales had long existed in Asia (1889a, 65), and he proclaimed that "in their characteristic metamorphoses these tales point to our Asian original home" (1889a, 64).

In America, Brinton was a fellow supporter of the solar myth theory, but even apart from this, he and Knortz had many scholarly interests in common. Both were studying and collecting the creation myths of American Indians (e.g., Knortz 1871a; 1876a; 1880a; Brinton 1876). Both were very interested in linguistics and comparative philology, spoke several foreign languages, studied different American Indian languages (Brinton 1876, 7–8; Knortz 1882a, 25–6), and loved, produced, and even published literature.[11] Both were convinced that time was limited for the collection of old traditions and data about people's way of life. Knortz published folklore collected from people all over the world and through the centuries. Brinton suggested in *The Aims of Anthropology* (1895) that the "[c]ollecting and storing of facts about man from all quarters of the world and all epochs of his existence, is the first and indispensable aim of anthropologic science. It is pressing and urgent beyond all other aims at this period of its existence as a science; for here more than elsewhere we feel the force of the Hippocratic warning, that the time is short and the opportunity fleeting."

Like Knortz (1900b, 29), Brinton emphasized psychic unity (1895, 4;

1897, 6), rejected transmission across cultures, and was a strong proponent of the evolutionary doctrine and of the survival theory (1902, 51). But
differing from Brinton, who preferred to work in his library, Knortz was an
eager field worker.

Both scholars had studied in Heidelberg for a while. Heidelberg seems
to have attracted several American students with a general interest in folklore and in linguistics during the nineteenth century. Brinton spent some
time there, as, toward the end of the century, did Louise Pound, who
worked in the field of American literature, linguistics and folklore and who
regarded dialect studies as a branch of folklore.

Brinton could read German and knew some of the works of Knortz
(Brinton 1876, 43), although I doubt the two ever met. Like Knortz, Brinton had been a member of the Folklore Society from the early beginnings
and he became its president in 1890. At that time he was a professor of anthropology, and, unlike Knortz, had academic connections.

Knortz obviously had given tales a great deal of consideration. In
Knortz's opinion folk tales are as old as mankind. They are "talkative
myths [geschwätzige Mythen] and as such the core of an original religion
whose exterior has constantly changed with varying time and place; their
proper meaning even has sometimes completely faded and barely lives on
in incomprehensible sayings, proverbs, and customs" (1889a, 64).

In his interpretation of folk tales, which in general he did not understand as moralizing (1889a, 63), Knortz rejected the concept of prehistoric
borrowing. He regarded similarities in tales from different peoples separated by place and time as proof that "primitive situations with much in
common everywhere influence the imagination in the same way" (1900b,
29), thus adhering to the theory of polygenesis and stressing the psychic
unity of all people.

In this context, as in many other instances, Knortz arrived at conclusions similar to those of Brinton. However, Boas, also a scholar of German
descent, argued against psychic unity: "Instead of demanding a critical examination of the causes of similarities, we say now a priori, they are due to
psychical causes, and in this we err in method just as much as the old
school did" (1896, 10). He once said that Brinton belonged to those schol-

ars who "ascribe sameness of cultural traits wholly to the psychic unity of mankind and to the uniform reaction of the human mind upon the same stimulus," and that Brinton was "an extremist in this direction" (1904, 519). Brinton, on the other hand, stated: "Until the folklorist understands this [independent invention], he has not caught up with the progress of ethnologic science" (1895, 10).

But like Boas, Knortz also accepted diffusion: "Myths and the tales about giants, dwarfs, stepmothers, cannibals, simpletons, know-alls, enchanted and not enchanted maidens, which sprang from those myths, allow a highly interesting insight into the world of ideas of a people, especially, when we compare them to the variants of another people. For it is really astonishing which different forms the same tale can assume during its migrations through the world" (1896a, 11).

Boas was an avid proponent of diffusion and used this method in his studies of every aspect of American Indian life, above all in his collections of their folk tales, which often were accompanied by linguistic texts. He noticed that the "diffusion of tales was just as frequent and just as widespread in America as it has been in the Old World" (1891, 13). His understanding was that "[w]henever we find a tale spread over a continuous area, we must assume that it spread over this territory from a single center" (1891, 14–15). In Boas's approach, each culture develops from a common core in a different way, and one culture is not necessarily moving from a lesser to a more advanced stage. In this regard his approach is not evolutionary.

Newell, on the other hand, saw diffusion differently: "For the process of such dissemination I propose a rule, namely, that in folk-lore as in civilization diffusion takes place from the higher culture to the lower, whenever two races are in culture-contact, the more civilized, itself comparatively unaffected, bestows on its neighbor the entirety of its ideas and traditions" (1906, 4).

When Knortz looked at folk tales in *Was ist Volkskunde und wie studiert man dieselbe?* (1900b, 29), he was also very interested in their motifs. He mentioned J. G. v. Hahn's suggestions for types which appears in the first volume of Hahn's *Griechische und albanesische Märchen* (1864) and Baring Gould's *Story Radicals* (1866), which had been published in Henderson's *Folklore of the Northern Counties* (1866) and later in Gomme's *Handbook of Folklore* (1890). Knortz might also have become acquainted with Aarne Antti's *Verzeichnis der Märchentypen* (1910), but at that time Knortz was no longer concentrating on tales. He did not live long enough to read Thompson's *The Types of the Folk tale* (1928) and his *Motif-Index of Folk-Literature* (1932–36).

The age and the inherent wisdom and cultural tradition that Knortz claimed for the folk tale, seemed a part of the folk song as well. In his lectures on German folk songs and folk tales which he published in 1889, Knortz expressed his belief that "folk poetry is as old as the people itself and therefore a reliable mirror of its intellectual strife. A historical presentation of the folk song thus is an important component of cultural history" (1889a, 13). Knortz might well have been influenced in his opinion by the ideas of Herder and the German Romanticists, in particular the Grimm Brothers. But in a folk song not only the words and their message are important; Knortz also stressed the significance of the unity of melody and text (1884a, 47).

Contrary to many other folklorists, Knortz rejected the traditional difference between folk songs whose authors are unknown, songs "which originated from the people itself," and those songs "written by a gifted poet in the style of a folk song, composed into the people." In the broadest sense, he considered as "Volkslied" (folk song) "all poetic achievements which characterize a certain period of culture" (1889a, 14–15).

Since he did not insist that a folk song had to start among the anonymous "people," Knortz was in accord with Newell, who determined that in the beginning all songs, poetry, games, etc. originated with individuals. In a ballad, "each separate stanza also must originally have come from one mind in one place" (Newell 1906, 12), and "[t]here never was a time, since mankind emerged from the brute condition, in which literary invention and expression was not individual as it is to-day" (14). "The whole matter seems to amount to this, that the habit of writing has permitted the writer to fix permanently his own ideas and peculiarities. Before writing was used, a similar result was attained by groups of literati, who could trust to the memory of friends and pupils" (14). Newell stressed the fact that as a source an original remains unchanged when written down, whereas in oral transmission the original text is changed again and again (5).

Toward the end of the nineteenth century, Knortz had slowly moved away from the study of Indian lore to that of folklore in general, but in his later publications he continued to use Indian legends, myths, and customs as examples or for comparison. He had already published translations of Scottish ballads (1875b), and Irish folk tales (1886c), had lectured on German folk songs and folk tales (1889a; 1891b), and in 1896 he offered the first book in America with the word "folklore" in its title (1896a).

Knortz had his own method of writing. He possessed a profound knowledge of folklore and international literature which enabled him to compile and compare many kinds and genres of folkloristic material. He usually did not write up data in a careful order or compose lists according to genres, but wrapped his data in little stories which develop from one into another and which explain the similarities as well as the differences of folkloristic items from many countries. Often he included and commented on philosophic ideas.

The reader certainly has to adjust to the manner in which Knortz presented his data. He wrote colloquially, squeezing as much information into his chapters as possible. Often he told one loosely woven story, into which customs, superstitions, songs, or rhymes were interwoven. Sometimes he jumped from one topic to another, only to return to the main idea later. The reader who can feel Knortz's enthusiasm and sincere interest will forgive one of the weak points in many of Knortz's publications: although starting out briskly, he often strayed into his vast material and wandered off, seemingly forgetting the main topic of his book. He then moved around, touching folkloristic data from different countries or different genres, delving into the literature of many centuries, comparing lore taken from oral sources, or from literature or other collections, even quoting newspapers— a source which only much later, well into this century, has become part of folklore studies—and finally returned to his subject. Thus, Knortz frequently embarked on tangents. He even went so far as to ask the reader of one of his books to "accept graciously" the added supplement, *Folk songs from Yorkshire*, since he could not find another place for it (1889a, 3).

Although Knortz often admonished his readers and fellow folklore collectors not to show disregard for the beliefs of their informants, he himself sometimes could not refrain from ridiculing some excesses. Thus, he mocked at spiritualism (1905b, 37–8), magical healers (1905b, 21), or so-called experts who tried to convince people of "facts" which would prove that the Indians were descendants from the Israelites (1882a, 248). Josiah Priest, for example, claimed that a parchment with verses from the Old Testament, in Hebrew, had been found in one of the old Indian burial mounds (68–70),[12] and H. H. Bancroft alleged that his father had been a witness when a similar find was made in Ohio (1883, 94). There, the Ten Commandments had been inscribed on a stone slab, again in Hebrew.

Mainly in the beginning of his folklore studies, Knortz seldom referred to his sources, a fact which may frustrate the modern folklorist who wants to know exactly where the data originated. This is true for the data he had taken from written sources as well as for those he had collected himself. In some publications, mostly in his later works, he provided footnotes, but he rarely provided an index. The only time he attempted a rather incomplete one was in *Was ist Volkskunde und wie studiert man dieselbe?* (1900b). He did, however, write down date and source whenever he quoted from newspapers. Another shortcoming of his works is the lack of bibliographic lists of his sources. He mentioned some of the works he had used within the text, some in footnotes, but mostly he just gave the information without quoting the source.

Knortz did not restrict his data to America. *Folklore* (1896), written in Knortz's typical style, deals with folklore on an international scale. He wrote on songs and superstitions, on rhymes and children's games, on customs, folk tales, and riddles, on proverbs and sayings. Many examples are taken from America—Black and White—but many are also taken from Germany, and often Knortz referred to stories or other data from European or Asian countries. To the end of the book Knortz added a collection of one hundred American children's rhymes which he himself had collected in New York (fifty-two rhymes) and in Indiana (forty-eight rhymes), the majority of which had never been published before.

Toward the end of the nineteenth century, interest in folklife and folklore had spread widely. Professional people in academe and science, but also more and more the middle-class hobby folklorists, collected data while traveling or working. Branches of folklore or anthropology societies were established in cities across the country. The year 1888 had seen the beginning of the American Folklore Society, initiated by Newell. F. S. Bassett founded what was then the Chicago Folk-Lore Society in 1891. Within a few years panels of folklorists dealt with all kinds of folkloristic problems and suggestions at the many folklore congresses. The two folklore societies soon became rivals.

Bassett stressed the literary side of folklore and proposed more independence for the field. In his view, folklore should not be merely auxiliary to other sciences but a science in its own right. This idea, of course, collided with Newell's opinion and that of other members of the American Folklore Society, who regarded folklore as part of anthropology. The competition between those two groups came into full view when two congresses were organized in the same year, 1893. One was the World's Fair Congress of Anthropology, supported by the American Folklore Society, the other its rival gathering, the International Folklore Congress, organized by Bassett.

Although Knortz did not take an active part in this controversy, he was caught up in the general enthusiasm for folklore. After publishing *Folklore* in 1896, he decided to help those who wanted to collect data but did not know how to go about it. He compiled materials for a practical guide on how and what to collect. He had read existing works like those of Gomme (1890), E. Monseur (1890), A. Gittée (1888), and Otto Jiriczek (1894) and recommended them as further reading (1900b, 33). In his own book, *Was ist Volkskunde und wie studiert man dieselbe?* [What is Folklore and How Do You Study It?] (1900b), he listed data which should be collected, but he also gave practical advice on collecting and on extracting hidden folklore from sources. The title, *Was ist Volkskunde*, of his book implies that Knortz wanted to establish a theory of folklore. But aside from a few theoretical definitions, what he actually provided was a good and very extensive guide for the collection of data. This work attests to his concept of folklore as a vast and inclusive field.

In the much longer second part of *Was ist Volkskunde*, Knortz added detailed examples for each of his collecting suggestions: legends, superstitions, and also social or political events or customs from many different nationalities. Often he cited recent newspaper articles which described crimes, lynchings, injustices, or customs and traditions. Frequently he referred to events or stories which he had collected from informants. Many of his examples came from his immediate neighborhood or places he had been, but numerous others were from all over the world.

Knortz wrote this guide some time before 1900, published several copies privately, and sent them to people he thought might be interested. According to the preface in the 1900 edition, the book had met with so much approval that he decided on a second edition.

The concept of Darwinism was very influential and readily accepted among many scholars at that time. Knortz, too, seems to have been interested in evolutionary theory and the overwhelming importance of natural sciences, as is reflected in the first statement of his book: "Like language, the life of a people, as a product of external influences, is a part of the natural history of mankind and can thus only be properly understood and evaluated in connection with those factors" (1900b, 3). Knortz certainly recognized the extremely wide field of this new concept of evolution, which tried to deduct generally valid laws from the physical and mental aspects of people's lives when applied to folklore. Of course Knortz was not the only folklorist of his time who looked at developments in people's life styles while taking evolution into account. Many other folklorists of that time studied and researched in a similar manner. The American Otis Mason expressed the idea in an article in *JAF* in 1891 which he titled *The Natural History of Folklore*.

In *Was ist Volkskunde* (1900b), Knortz proposed a concept of folklore which is different from the one prevalent in the works of many of his European contemporaries. In Germany at that time, folklore (Volkskunde) was engaged in the study of the European peasant population. The study of non-European peoples belonged to ethnology (Völkerkunde), since those peoples were regarded as savages or primitives. Knortz also differed from the German-born American anthropologist Franz Boas, who believed that "folklorists occupy themselves primarily with the folklore of Europe and thus supplement the material collected by anthropologists in foreign lands" (Boas 1904, 520).

Another European definition which varied from that of Knortz came from Gomme: "Anthropology is the science which deals with savage beliefs and customs in all their aspects; Folk-lore deals with them in one of their aspects only, namely, as factors in the mental life of man, which, having survived in the highest civilizations whether of ancient or modern times, are therefore capable of surrendering much of their history to the scientific observer" (Gomme 1890, 4). And, again in the USA, Brinton stated: "This branch of anthropology is known as folklore. It investigates the stories, the superstitions, the beliefs and customs which prevail among the unlettered, the isolated and the young. . . . A department of it [psychical anthropology], folklore, is taken up with such survivals" (Brinton 1902, 51). Knortz concurred in part with this definition of folklore: "The study of these survivals which consist of folk tales, legends, proverbs, sayings, songs, and customs, is the task of a folklorist" (1896a, 6).

In his book, Knortz used the term "Volkskunde" in a much broader sense than the English word folklore, although "Volkskunde" usually is translated as "folklore." He counted among the subgroups of "Volkskunde" anthropology and ethnology, with folklore as a subset of the latter. True to this definition, he did not separate ethnology and folklore when he began to collect data and to write about the American Indians and their lore. With this concept of the emerging discipline, he could compare the way of life and thought of different peoples in either primitive or civilized surroundings, without the constraints imposed on folklore in Germany. But because he published his works in Germany, he did not conform with the accepted definition of folklore there, a fact which made him an outsider.

In his guide (1900b), he subdivided "Volkskunde" into anthropology, archeology, and ethnology. When he used the internationally accepted expression "folklore" he regarded it as a subset of ethnology, of the study of people as social beings. Ethnology, he wrote, "deals with man as social being. It deals with his laws, arts, religious concepts, languages, and historic recollections. The branch of this division which is interested in songs, games, festivals, folk tales, legends, languages, and customs of a people, is usually called by the English name: folklore, which has become part of most European languages" (1900b, 4).

It was folklore, this sub-branch of "Volkskunde," which Knortz introduced in his book. Although in America folklore was usually regarded as part of anthropology, in Knortz's opinion, anthropology did not include cultural aspects or the way of life of a people. In its strictest sense it dealt only with the physical aspect of man as a representative of a certain class or race. The term "Volkskunde" as Knortz used it included many fields of study, and even seemed to correspond in large parts to Frederick Starr's definition of comprehensive anthropology: "Under the comprehensive word anthropology we comprise physical anthropology, ethnography, prehistoric archeology and culture history" (1892, 54). Without distinguishing between "peasants" or "savages" Knortz's concept of ethnology deals with men as social beings. He saw ethnology very much in the way in which Tylor defined culture: "Culture or Civilization, taken in its wide ethnographic sense, is that complex whole which includes knowledge, belief, art, morals, law, custom and any other capabilities and habits acquired by man as a member of society" (1874, 1:1).

In the course of time there evolved different opinions among folklorists concerning the direction folklore should take and where it should belong. Soon two groups emerged. There were those who had mainly scientific interests, who wanted to study the cultural history of a people, and who thought folklore should be part of anthropology. Boas, for instance, wanted the *Journal of American Folklore* to deal with oral tradition, while material and social culture were to be regarded as part of anthropology. And there were those who had literary and cultural connections, who were more interested in the texts of tales and their diffusion, and who felt folklore should be tied more closely to those fields of study. Yet both groups agreed that the collection of data was of greatest importance; both were concerned with the past, with origins, and with the change of text or culture in the course of time or when moved from place to place. In the American Folklore Society, the anthropological preference prevailed.

In general, literary folklorists saw folklore as part of the unlettered tradition within literate European and American societies. This included all aspects of people's way of life and verbal art. But their focus was also directed toward the study of genres, and they compiled anthologies and collections, and, of course, they took written literature into consideration. Francis James Child, when working on ballads, even preferred old manuscripts to materials he had collected in the field (c.f. Zumwalt 1988, 48). Some literary folklorists, however, understood the importance of fieldwork and used it in their studies.

The anthropological folklorists regarded folklore mainly as verbal art and as oral literature. Yet they had a broader understanding of "folk" and included groups that were excluded by the literary folklorists. They mainly were interested in members of non-Western tribal cultures, studied cultures without writing, stressed fieldwork, and looked at the life of the people, usually studying a single aspect of folklore in different cultures or focusing on one culture only.

Knortz did not clearly side with either of the two emerging groups of folklorists in America. On the one hand, he was interested in the traditional way of life of illiterate people, mainly of those of European descent, within their literate surroundings, as well as in the unlettered literary forms of folklore in peasant communities. He also compiled anthologies and collections. This places him close to the literary folklorists. Like them, he stressed collection, preservation, classification, and tale-type identification. On the other hand, he included American Indians and Blacks in folklore studies and collected their oral literature and material culture. He also stressed fieldwork and the collection of every aspect of the people's lives, a concept held valid by the anthropological folklorists.

Although Knortz belonged to the American Folklore Society, he had much in common with Bassett, who had formed its rival organization, the Chicago Folk-Lore Society. Bassett favored the literary interests of folklore and insisted that it was time for folklore to be recognized as an independent discipline. In the introduction to volume one of *The Folk-Lorist*, the journal of the Chicago Folk-Lore Society, Bassett stressed the purpose of "collecting, preserving, studying and publishing traditional literature."

He also said: "This Society encourages the collection of such material, important to the study of the history of mankind, and in its bearings upon the many problems of life" (1892a, 5). Knortz certainly collected and published traditional literature, and from the beginning of his publications, he had promoted the idea that the occupation with folklore was a way of preserving the past and its history and literature. To him, the study of customs and habits of the usually conservative uneducated folk, is "the key to the oldest history of a people; and thus folklore, which has to deal with them, forms an interesting part of cultural history. This part is especially important since it bespeaks events which date back farther than any written documents" (1896a, 6).

Bassett's opinion of nonprofessionals was inclusive and welcoming, in contrast to that of many important members of the American Folklore Society who soon turned more to professionals and academics and alienated those who saw folklore as their hobby or their field of special interest or even those who used survivals and customs in their literary works.

Knortz's concept of "Volkskunde" was close to that of Bassett, who wanted to set up folklore as an independent discipline, since it differed from all other sciences: "As literature itself is a science correlated to the others, Folk-Lore is at once a part of literature and of science, but ought to be preserved apart from any other study, and not merged into or made a portion of any other science" (Bassett 1898, 22). In Bassett's view, folklore was "the demonstrator of the possible and probable in history, the repository of historical truths otherwise lost, the preserver of the literature of the people and the touchstone of many of the sciences" (1898, 19). Like Knortz, Bassett realized that folklore can exist in oral or written form and that therefore folklorists can do research in libraries or at home, reading "in obscure works, books of travel little known, and . . . in rare brochures and periodicals" (Bassett 1892b:11). Often he seems to have worked very much like Knortz, finding data for his books in literature and written sources from various countries (Bassett 1885).

As Knortz saw folklore in every aspect of life, so did Bassett: "Among the Indians, on plantation and cattle range, in the factory and on the farm, in the crowded city and in the little village, among miners and sailors, professional men of attainments and uneducated laborers, in busy avocations of men and in the household life of women, among children and gray-hairs—everywhere, folklore is abundant, for it is the lore of the people, not of any class, and is to be sought everywhere" (1892b, 6–7).

After he had finished *Was ist Volkskunde und wie studiert man dieselbe?* Knortz went on collecting and publishing many more books on folklore. In most of his publications he dealt with his material in his accustomed manner, that is, he compiled hundreds of data, arranged them according to their themes, and wove a thread of thought or a tale through the whole book.

Two "folkloristic excursions," *Folkloristische Streifzüge* (1900c) and *Streifzüge auf dem Gebiete amerikanischer Volkskunde* (1902b), which appeared within the next few years, were written in very much the same manner and with very much the same wide range of subjects. On the 431 pages of his first "excursion" Knortz compiled folklore data from all over the world, dividing the book into chapters which each have one common theme. He followed this pattern in the second excursion as well. There he presented American material as promised in the title of his book, but again we also find data from Germany and many other countries and from the present time back to early history. Pure American folklore finally appears in the chapter on riddles, where he inserted one hundred fifty riddles which he himself had collected mostly in Indiana. If he knew similar riddles from European cultures, he added them for comparison.

Knortz also concentrated on American folklore in his next books *Nachklänge germanischen Glaubens und Brauchs in Amerika* (1903), *Zur amerikanischen Volkskunde* (1905b), and in *Amerikanische Redensarten und Volksgebräuche* (1907a). In all of them he moved from one genre and one folklore item to the other without any segmentation. He often provided parallels from other cultures, in particular when he wanted to explain data or to explore their origins. In *Nachklänge germanischen Glaubens und Brauchs in Amerika* Knortz followed any traces of old Germanic beliefs in America, especially of the god Wodan. In this context, he suggested a Germanic legend as the model for Irving's *Rip van Winkle* and even discovered allusions to Wodan in Irving's story *Sleepy Hollow*. (Sleepy Hollow is a valley near Tarrytown, New York, where Knortz spent the last years of his life).

In *Zur amerikanischen Volkskunde* (1905b), however, Knortz restricted most of his data to American folklore. He insisted that in this book he only reported data which he had collected himself, often with the help of questionnaires. The practice of sending out questionnaires was widely used in Germany at that time, but rarely in America. Among those who had used it was John Fanning Watson, who had distributed questionnaires during the 1830s, but had soon returned to informants whom he could interrogate in person (cf. Bronner 1986, 6). To his book *Amerikanische Redensarten und Volksgebräuche* (1907a), Knortz added a chapter on folkloristic items in Longfellow's *Evangeline,* usually quoting a verse from *Evangeline* and then addressing any folkloristic allusions he could find in it. In the course of the discussion, he mentioned numerous folklore data from all over the world. However, Knortz did not explain the function of folklore items within a given verse or in the entire work; the time for that kind of interpretation had not yet come.

During the remaining years of his life, Knortz published still more books on folklore, all of them dealing with international folklore, except his work on contemporary American superstition: *Amerikanischer Aberglaube der Gegenwart* (1913a), a book full of contemporary superstitions. Here he seems to have complimented his own collections with many data found by Fanny Bergen (1896; 1899), Clifton Johnson (1896), and Fletcher Bascom Dressler (1907), and in articles from *JAF*.

For his next books, he collected thousands of data—legends, sayings, proverbs, riddles, games, songs, customs, etc.—using oral and written sources from all over the world. He now focused on special groups of animals, people, or legendary beings which he studied in several different genres. Thus he wrote on the human body, *Der menschliche Körper in Sage, Brauch und Sprichwort* (1909d), on insects, *Die Insekten in Sage, Geschichte und Literatur* (1910a), on reptiles, *Reptilien und Amphibien in Sage, Sitte und Literatur* (1911b), on witches and the devil, *Hexen, Teufel und Blocksbergspuk in Geschichte, Sage und Literatur* (1913b), and on birds *Die Vögel in Geschichte, Sage Brauch und Literatur* (1913d). A book on nudes was published posthumously, *Die Nackten in Sage, Sitte, Kunst und Literatur* (1920).

In summary, Knortz collected and researched folklore data in much the same way as most American folklorists of his time did, even if his concept of folklore was broader. He did not restrict himself to the study of only certain genres or only certain groups of people or nations. Since he was not part of the group of prominent folklorists in the folklore society, he was also not hemmed in by the ideas of either the literary or the anthropological faction within folklore. In many respects, he was ahead of his time.

In his folklore studies, Knortz relied both on orally transmitted and written data, thus realizing and accepting the fact that folklore data are not automatically destroyed when they are printed.[13] In addition, Knortz wrote a guide for people who wanted to collect folklore in which he gave valuable advice and countless examples.

When compiling his numerous folklore collections, Knortz used questionnaires (1905b), stressed fieldwork, and worked with the Graphophone, since he placed importance on language and the exact transmission and transcription of data (1900b, 7). At the same time, he valued correct translations, which conveyed the emotional meaning of the text (e.g., 1882a, 25–7), a trait he shared with Boas, who also was very meticulous in this respect (c.f. Zumwalt 1988, 71). In addition, Knortz was interested in the gestures of his informants and in their age, profession and education (1900b, 7). He warned against relying completely on information from a single person and encouraged collectors to find several data on the same subject and to compare them (1900b, 10). Knortz also took world-view into consideration when he collected data, for example, when he explained that "to marry" was a synonym of "to buy" in some American Indian languages (1900b, 19).

Knortz did not restrict the collection of data to rural areas, but noted customs and collected folklore in urban regions as well. And he did not restrict his studies to European peasants, but also extended them to "savages." As did Newell (1883, 7), Knortz employed the concept of *gesunkenes Kulturgut*[14] when he explained children's games as imitations of religious or military events of the middle ages, or when he saw old ballads dramatized in many games which were sung (1896a, 26).

In addition, Knortz focused on certain items in literary works, and by uncovering those items as folklore and interpreting them he helped the reader understand the broader meaning of many passages (e.g., 1907a, 53). Like the Grimms or like Mannhardt (Mannhardt 1858, vi), he recognized remnants of Germanic or Indo-European myths, legends, and beliefs in many contemporary customs and tales (e.g., 1903). For many years he also adhered to the solar myth theory. He was convinced that the ability to create myths had not disappeared through the centuries and that the creation of folklore would go on.

NOTES

1. Knortz was mentioned in *Who's Who in America?* from vol. 1 to vol. 10.
2. Knortz was mentioned in *Wer ist's?* from vol. 1 to vol. 7.
3. *Who's Who in America?* (1899–1900, 408) gives 1879 as the date of his marriage.
4. Knortz was mentioned in *Deutscher Litteratur Kalender* for several years.
5. *Who's Who in America?* Not only does his name appear in this publication from vol. 1, 1899–1900 to vol. 10, 1918–1919, but also his address is given.
6. Peter Assion (1988, 12) seems to have misunderstood Knortz's phrase: "auch bin ich längst von der Ansicht zurückgekommen, daß unsere deutsche Sprache so fest gewurzelt sei, um ohne die stets eintreffenden Einwanderer bestehen zu können . . . " (1899a, 8). His translation of this sentence changes the meaning of Knortz's statement to its opposite (cf. also Knortz 1882a, 5).
7. Many of the little stories or essays in these books deal with folkloristic topics, for instance: 1876a ("Indian Legends," p. 137–67; "Indian mythology," p. 293–302; his own experiences with the Ojibway Indians, p. 56–135); 1882a ("American legends of the Flood"); 1884a ("Customs at a funeral in Pennsylvania"); 1893a ("Christmas, described by American poets"), 1898c ("Voodoo," "Adam's first wife," folktales).

8. In this connection Knortz mentions Daniel Pastorius, the founder of Germantown, Pa., who in April 1688 had published the first protest against slavery in America (1894a,120–21). In many instances Knortz pleads for equal opportunity for Blacks and insists that they are as able as their White counterparts and should be given the same educational possibilities as the rest of the population (1884a, 165–67; 1898c, 81–9).

9. He was listed as a member in all the volumes of *JAF* from 1888 until 1905. In volumes 4, 5, and 6, he was listed as Rev. Karl Knortz.

10. Outside of *JAF* there are only very few of his books quoted in folklore literature or mentioned as sources, either in America or in Germany. *Handwörterbuch des deutschen Aberglaubens* (1927, 1:xl) gives a few of Knortz's books as some of its sources: 1900c; 1909d; 1910a; 1911b; 1913a; 1913d. Archer Taylor (1951), took examples from 1902b. In vol. 6, p. lx, of *The Frank C. Brown Collection of North Carolina Folklore* (1952–1964), Knortz is listed, but only one of his books is quoted: 1913a. A. Bach referred to two of Knortz's books: 1900b (Bach 1960, 63), and 1909d (Bach 1960, 291). A. Dundes comments on Knortz and some of his books (1964, 27–8). More recently, William K. Mc Neil introduces Knortz in his dissertation (1980, 253–5) and enumerats several of his works (1980, 268–9). J. Bronner (1986, 57), mentioned Knortz and his book *Zur amerikanischen Volkskunde* (1905b), which he called the first general book on American folklife. P. Assion wrote more extensively on Knortz and his works (1988).

Other works on American folklore, such as Richard Dorson (1959), Jan Harold Brunvand (1986), and R. L. Zumwalt (1988), do not even mention Knortz. D. Brinton (1876, 43), noted the "very careful collection of Prof. Carl Knortz, *Sagen der Nord Amerikanischen Indianer.*" And there are also books which only refer to Knortz's literary works and not to his writings on folklore, such as R. Cronau (1909, 46). In *The New Schaff-Herzog Encyclopedia of Religious Knowledge* (1908-c 1914, 3:185), Knortz (1896d) is mentioned in connection with the Amana Society.

11. Knortz' s bibliography gives testimony to this. As for Brinton, cf. Mc Neil 1980 1: 217–8.

12. H. H. Bancroft quoted this event in *Native Races of the Pacific States* (1883, 5:93).
13. Knortz took folklore data from literature as well as from newspapers, e.g., in 1900b, 157; 1905b, 33; 1913a, 73.
14. "*Gesunkenes Kulturgut*" is the idea that folklore has sunk from a high origin to become tradition among the common people.

· T w o ·

OUTLINES OF KNORTZ'S
WORKS ON FOLKLORE

Many of Knortz's books on folklore are not widely accessible in the
United States, and all of them were written in German.
Märchen und Sagen der nordamerikanischen Indianer (Tales and Legends of the North-American Indians) (1871b) presented eighty-seven
American Indian tales and legends which Knortz had gathered from various English and French books and from oral reports by missionaries, travelers, and interpreters. In the introduction to this book he briefly
discusses American Indian religion, dance, and superstitions, and he accuses White civilization and Christianity of alienating the American Indians from their way of life. *Aus dem Wigwam* (From the Wigwam) (1880a)
and *Nokomis* (1887b) are two more collections of American Indian tales.

Mythologie und Zivilisation der nordamerikanischen Indianer (Mythology and Civilization of the North-American Indians) (1882b) are two articles on the mythology and civilization of American Indians. Knortz talked
about myths taken from various American Indian tribes that explain the
origin of mankind and of the world and everything in it. He then speaks
about the importance of the number four, about legends, about the role animals and nature play in the American Indians' lives, about their gods,
about their medicine men (whom he viewed with suspicion), and much
more. As for civilization, Knortz expresses the view that American Indians
were often more civilized than the White man who tried to kill them or to
drive them from their land. He deals with the question of alcohol and diseases among American Indians, refers to statistics and to all kinds of materials from the Indian Bureau in Washington, speaks about the American
Indians' attitude towards schools, the church, agriculture, settlements, and

Sequoya's alphabet. He accuses the White man of breaking his contracts with the American Indians and makes suggestions for giving the American Indians more rights and bringing them closer to modern civilization.

Indianische Legenden (American Indian Legends), an article in the book *Amerikanische Skizzen* (American Sketches) (1876a), reflects the same attitude towards the American Indians and Western culture. Here, Knortz discusses Longfellow's *Hiawatha*, praises the latter's description of the Indian myth, and at the same time criticizes the end of the poem where Hiawatha introduces Christian missionaries as messengers of the "Great Spirit" (1876a, 158). The rest of the book, except for two chapters on American Indian legends and on present-day events among American Indians and an article on spiritualism, consists of a collection of autobiographical material and other essays not related to folklore.

Amerikanische Lebensbilder (Pictures of American Life) (1884a), is a mixture of short narratives and sketches of all kinds. The volume also contains some essays on folkloristic topics like the German song in America and its importance to German immigrants. Knortz talks about several kinds of songs (children, soldiers, professional, etc.) and stresses the significance of the unity of melody and text. He also presents a collection of superstitions in Pennsylvania. The major merit of the book, however, lies in the description of the life of his fellow Germans in the United States.

Deutsches und Amerikanisches (Things German and American) (1894a), contains some chapters of folkloristic interests, for example on "Loreley," "Christmas as seen by American poets," "the Fridthjof-Saga," and "American spiritualism."

Plaudereien (Chats) (1898c), another collection of essays, includes a study on "Voodoo." When mentioning Mary Owen's *Voodoo Tales* (1893), Knortz criticizes the way she recorded them from memory in their original dialect, since English orthography is not adequate to reproduce sounds unequivocally (1898c, 32). The book also includes a lecture devoted to folk tales, stressing their moral value for everyday life.

Die deutschen Volkslieder und Märchen (The German Folk Songs and Folk Tales) (1889a) are two lectures in which Knortz employs certain theories discussed in folklore at that time. He presents numerous songs, interprets and categorizes them, and uses them as examples for different life experiences and professions. Knortz also deals with the ethical and myth-ical meaning of German folk tales. He considers folk tales a part of every people's heritage and writes that although they classify people as good or bad, he could not identify a moralizing intention (1889a, 63).

In *Das deutsche Volkslied* (The German Folk Song) (1891b) Knortz re-turned to the German folk song again. *Folklore* (1896a) lists songs, riddles, superstitions, and all kinds of other folklore data, and also children's rhymes, songs, and counting-out rhymes, which he himself had collected in New York and Indiana and which are published in this book for the first time as a supplement to the collections of W. Newell's *Games and Songs of American Children* (1883) and H. C. Bolton's *The Counting-Out Rhymes of Children* (1888).

Folkloristische Streifzüge (Folkloristic Excursions) (1900c) is a collec-tion of articles and essays on various folkloristic topics. Here Knortz com-piled whatever he found on a certain theme, be it in oral tradition or literature, in America or in other countries. He offers an enormous amount of information. In many of his articles in *Folkloristische Streifzüge*, he not only investigates customs, superstitions, and beliefs, but traces them through literature, tales and legends. In this way he deals with calendric customs around New Year, the first of April, and Halloween, and with the folklore of marriage. While interpreting Ludwig Uhland's song *Der weiße Hirsch*, he also researches the folkloristic vestiges connected with the white stag, which he regarded as a survival of a solar myth. The book contains dis-cursive essays on the bee, the raven, salt, saliva, the bean, the evil eye, Peter Schlehmihl (where he traces the motif of the shadow), Rübezahl (the mountain spirit of the Giant Mountains in whom he sees the resemblance of Wotan), Prometheus, omina, "Tage- und Wächterlieder" (the alba of min-strel song), games, American sayings and proverbs, names and nicknames, and customs connected with marriage and the first of April. He also pre-sents excerpts from an old book on magic, *Der wahre Geistliche Schild* (1647), and researches the image of the teacher in literature and folklore.

Was ist Volkskunde und wie studiert man dieselbe? (What is "Volks-kunde," and How Do You Study it?) (1900b) is a practical guide on what to collect in the field of folklore and how to go about collecting it. The first part of Knortz's book is translated in its entirety in the following chapter.

In the second part, the author offers samples of data taken from different countries whose collection he discusses in the theoretical first part. His sources are books, newspapers and oral reports. The volume has an index, but bibliographical notes are mainly presented in the text and therefore difficult to find.

Streifzüge auf dem Gebiete amerikanischer Volkskunde (Excursions in the Domain of American Folklore) (1902b) is another collection of essays on folkloristic topics. Here Knortz deals with the customs, rhymes, games, songs, and tales surrounding Easter in different countries and at various times. Other subjects are superstitions, the language and literature of Germans in Pennsylvania, proverbs and their importance in peoples' lives, stories about the devil and about Christmas and the customs surrounding it in various countries, and American riddles, to which he adds riddles from other countries as well. He presents one hundred fifty American riddles (quoted in English) which he himself had collected, predominantly in Indiana. Wherever possible, he offers the German equivalents or European variants. One of the studies in the book concerns songs and rhymes, focusing on those of Blacks in the South, who, in his opinion, are the only truly musical people in the United States. He discusses their spirituals and plantation songs, writes down songs he himself had collected, and compares them to the songs of American Indians, which are rather monotonous and need gestures to help convey their meaning. He tries to explain the difference in songs partly as a reflection of people's lives; a farm hand can sing while working, but a hunter would scare away his prey by doing so (1902b, 243, 258).

In *Nachklänge germanischen Glaubens und Brauchs in Amerika* (Aftereffects of Germanic Belief and Custom in America) (1903), Knortz began with modern German influences in the United states (kindergarten, sports, arts, and music in public schools). When talking about food, it is the pretzel—in his view the symbol of the twisted spokes of the sun wheel—that lead him to all sorts of survivals. He investigates the influence of many Germanic gods, like Wotan, and their attributes, and he mentions dogs as companions of Hel (in Evansville he saw many tombstones decorated with dogs). In his usual unsystematic way he presents an abundance of folkloristic data from many areas. Toward the end of the book he elaborates on customs which were imported by German immigrants, such as the Easter bunny and Easter eggs. From there he moves on to customs which have nothing to do with Germanic tradition, like Valentine's Day and St. Patrick's Day and then on to numerous superstitions and customs.

Zur amerikanischen Volkskunde (A Contribution to American Folklore) (1905b). The material of this book supposedly consists solely of original data which Knortz received as answers to a questionnaire he had sent out, but he also mentions data from other countries and data taken from newspapers or books, which he sometimes quotes. In a narrative manner he moves from one topic to another, covering en route customs and superstitions, dreams, astrology, folk medicine, water witches, and prophecies. He touches on Thanksgiving and the temperance movement, finally finishing with slang expressions (1905b, 66),[1] proverbs, and sayings.[2]

Amerikanische Redensarten (American Sayings) (1907a) also covers proverbs and sayings. Knortz understood slang as a characteristic part of the speech of common people which is precise in meaning and offers insights into past and present cultures. He believed that numerous slang expressions had originally belonged to the literary language. In this context, he mentions several groups of people who have their own slang, such as students, artists, criminals, and craftsmen. He does not elaborate on their specific idiom, but intends to deal only with words that had come into common use. Within the German text he presents those items in English and explains them to his German-speaking readers when necessary. Whenever he found a German equivalent, he puts it beside the English version, stressing that only the general meaning, not the terms used, correspond to each other. Many examples of tongue-twisters and words that can be read backwards.

The second part of the book scrutinizes Longfellow's *Evangeline* for traces of folklore. Here, Knortz typically quotes a verse and then gives its folklore background, taking his references and examples from tales or stories in literature or folklore. He also notes customs and superstitions from various countries and discusses mistletoe, bees, swallows, wolves, spiders, and dryads.

Der menschliche Körper in Sage, Brauch und Sprichwort (The Human Body in Legends, Customs, and Proverbs) (1909d), *Die Insekten in Sage, Geschichte und Literatur* (Insects in Legends, History and Literature) (1910a), *Reptilien und Amphibien in Sage, Sitte und Literatur* (Reptiles and Amphibians in Legends, Tradition and Literature) (1911b), and *Die Vögel in Geschichte, Sage, Brauch und Literatur* (Birds in History, Legends, Customs, and Literature) (1913d) are all compilations of an immense amount of material on the parts of the body, insects, reptiles, amphibians, and birds, found in literature, customs, folk tales, legends, myths, art, superstition, magic, folk medicine, proverbs, sayings, games, children's rhymes, and riddles, not restricted to America or to the present time.

In *Hexen, Teufel und Blocksbergspuk in Geschichte, Sage und Literatur* (Witches, Devils, and Spook on the Blocksberg [Mountains] in History, Legends, and Literature) (1913b) Knortz relates witches to natural forces like wind and weather and to wise women in various countries. He then treats the topic of the devil and the devil's pact extensively, before elaborating on the Blocksberg scene, in the Harz mountains in Germany, where witches, devils, and spirits are said to meet once a year.

In the introduction to *Amerikanischer Aberglaube der Gegenwart* (American Superstition of the Present) (1913a), Knortz points out that superstition is part of all religions and that it offers more insight into a person's mind than psychology and physiology. He then presents his rich collection of superstitions from the United States and compares his data with similar data from other countries. Much of this material was taken from Blacks in the South and from Germans in Pennsylvania.

NOTES

1. He quotes from a list of slang expressions used in criminal circles, which was given to him by a member of the New York secret police.
2. Simon J. Bronner, *American Folklore Studies An Intellectual History*, Kansas (Bronner,1986,57), mentions Knortz briefly in connection with this work.

Part 2

•

*Selections from Knortz's Works
in Translation:
Definitions and Approaches*

• T h r e e •

FROM "WAS IST VOLKSKUNDE UND WIE STUDIERT MAN DIESELBE?"

A translation of the first part of *Was ist Volkskunde und wie studiert man dieselbe?* (1900b)[1] and excerpts from some of his other books is the best way to introduce Knortz as a folklorist and to present Knortz's ideas and theories on this new science.

Was ist Volkskunde und wie studiert man dieselbe?

(What is Volkskunde and How Do You Study It?)

Like language, the life of a people as a product of external influences is a part of the natural history of mankind and can thus only be properly understood and evaluated in connection with those factors. The discipline that tackles this task, folklore, is rather new. It deals with the strange aspects of the physical and psychological lives of people and tries to reduce those to general laws, as far as possible under given conditions.

The subject which "Volkskunde" covers is extraordinarily wide and can be divided into the following three subdivisions:

1. Anthropology, sometimes also called somatology, deals with the natural characteristics—e.g., anatomy, physiology, and biology—of an individual as a representative of a certain class or race.

2. Archeology deals with prehistoric antiquities like weapons, tools, artifacts, etc. and, using those, tries to paint as true a picture of past cultural conditions as possible.

3. Ethnology deals with man as a social being, his laws, arts, religious concepts, languages, and historic recollections. The branch of this division which is interested in songs, games, festivals, folk tales, legends, languages, and customs of a people is usually called by the English name, "folklore," which has become part of most European languages.

This last-named branch of folklore shall now be discussed. The folklorist sees people at work, at happy festivals and at sad ones, in pubs, at church, and at home; he listens to their prayers and curses; he shares their pains, happiness, hopes, and most secret wishes; he preserves their phrases, sayings, riddles, songs, and tales. This means that he must collect diligently, and to that end he has the best opportunity here in America. In big cities he meets representatives of nearly all European, Asian, and African nationalities; on farms of the East and the West, he mainly meets representatives of the different Germanic peoples; in the South he sees Negroes, Voodoos, and Creoles; in the far North, Eskimos; and in the far West, nomadic and settled American Indians.

All these people can give interesting information about their way of life and their understanding of the law, and they are quite willing to do so, if the folklorist understands how to win their confidence so that they speak freely. Some of what they have to say may not sound very pretty, but all the more natural, and this gives him the key to understanding the real character of a people. Whoever suffers from prudery may deal with mathematics or national economy, as far as I am concerned, but not with folklore. Whoever, when hearing a blunt saying or an obscene story, becomes morally indignant and shows this unmistakably through words or gestures is not suited to be a collector in our field.

When dealing with the common man, you must act with greatest caution, for, as a rule, he is taciturn and suspicious of strangers; he sees a spy of the government or the church in everybody who tries to ask him questions, and he fears to be brought before the inquisition because of his antiquated customs or his pagan beliefs, or, at best, to make a fool of himself in public. If you want to ask questions, you must not start right away; you must judge by the person's face how to treat him in order to encourage him to talk.

True gold mines of folklore material are the different trades, especially the charcoal-burners, smiths, and barbers, and also musicians, hunters, watchmen, shepherds, and other herdsmen. American farmers usually are more accessible than their European counterparts, and the Negro in the United States speaks his mind freely. Lawyers, physicians, and the clergy are very well qualified to collect original folklore material, since their profession brings them constantly into contact with the common man; they thus have the opportunity to know their customs and ways. Of course, they must have the necessary interest in folklore and must not lose the peoples' trust by making offensive remarks. In addition, anyone who is not an unsociable hermit can help to expand folklore by making notes of occasional observations and experiences or of recollections from his childhood and by placing those at a folklorist's disposal—nowadays you can find one of them nearly everywhere.

I will try to give a short introduction for the person who wants to study one people systematically. He must, above all, familiarize himself with their history as extensively as possible; for example, he must know exactly whether they once had a different religion and how their present religion defeated the old one; he has to know with which other peoples they had been at war or which intellectual influences were brought to them from the outside in order to find an explanation for certain religious, linguistic, cultural, and social institutions and opinions; he also must familiarize himself with the lines of business, the housing conditions, and the foods of the people he wants to study in order to understand their concepts.

One of the most important prerogatives is to study the language of a foreign people, if you want to deal with them and get to know their characteristics. America abounds in extraordinarily rich sources which can bring new and surprising information to the psychology of language, for there are two hundred, according to Brinton, and even around five hundred, according to Powell, aboriginal languages, of which up to now only very few have been studied. Setting up a vocabulary or writing down proverbs, sayings, or tales requires the greatest of circumspection; in doing so, you may not rely exclusively on a single interpreter. You must also address natives of different ages, to note possible changes in the pronunciation of certain words, which often are important in connection with etymology.

If the alphabet does not suffice to write down all sounds, you have to describe the physiological process of producing them, or, better still, you may use a Graphophone, which repeats the sounds later, in your office, as often as you like. Further, carefully note the length and brevity of vowels as well as the stressed syllables, and do not forget to mention whether the natives use certain gestures or movements of their hands or their heads to make themselves better understood. There is not only color blindness but also sound deafness, which every schoolboy who starts to learn English or French can prove.

Arbitrary distortion of a word in order to make a foreign word comprehensible and easy to pronounce can be found in any language, and it is the researcher's task to explain the word and to present it in its original pure form. An example may suffice. Near Chattanooga, Tennessee, there is a cave which in old times was called by its Cherokee name: Nick-a-jack. Later, white settlers, who had neither time for nor interest in studying the Indian language, simply changed it to Nigger-Jack and invented a story of a fugitive slave to explain the change (Vining 1885, 587).

In many Indian languages there is no special word for eye, foot, hand, etc. The expressions for those are always connected with possessive pronouns, which form the most confusing part of those languages, since they are not only joined to nouns but also to verbs and since they are put at the beginning, in the middle, or at the end of a word, as the situation requires. Often adjectives are also used as intransitive verbs. There may be no Indian language which has a special word for "to go"; many, however, have words which express movement on sea or land from one place to another. For many of our concepts, above all for the abstract ones, the Indians have no easily understood name. When the missionary Eliot wanted to translate the words "to kneel" in a religious context, he had to do so with the help of a long sentence, since his audience would not have understood otherwise. The names of animals are interesting and extremely numerous in some of the Indian languages. One tribe of the Algonquins calls the beaver "tree feller"; another calls it "creature that sticks its head out of the water," that is, an animal which breathes air. The word for horse in Delaware means literally "an animal which carries on its back." The Chippewa usually call the beaver *Amik*; a young beaver is *Amikons*; a beaver under two years of age is *Awenishe*; one between two and three years, *Aboiawe*; one of three years, *Bakemik*; a male, *Nabemik*; and a female, *Nodshemik*. They call the bedbug "stinking insect." They have no special word for bird, but they have different expressions for a small or a big bird, as well as for birds of varying colors. For instance, *Segibawanishi* is a black bird; *Odshawane*, a blue one; *Okanisse*, a gray one, *Odamaweshi*, a white one, *Bineshi*, a big bird. In the Ute language, the word for bear means "one who snatches." The Pahvant Indians call the school house *Po-kunt-in-in-yi-kan*, which, literally translated means "a place where sorcery is counted." *Po-kunt* is "sorcery is practiced," and the Pahvant call all written exercises sorcery, since in their opinion they can only be undertaken for this reason; *in-in-yi* means "to count or to read"; *kan*, which is derived from the verb *kari* ("to stay"), means "wigwam."

If you want to set up a vocabulary of a foreign language, including sayings which refer to the weather, to games, eating, drinking, to weddings, death, or people's occupations, it is advisable to find out ahead of time the rank, education, and character of the person from whom you expect information; not everybody is able to answer reliably all questions concerning his people. If you want to be certain, never rely on the information from one single person, but ask several people and afterwards compare their contributions.

Never translate a sentence from your mother tongue into a foreign language and then base philosophical deliberations on it, as, for example, J.C. Adelung and J.S. Vater did in *Mithridates,* when they analyzed nearly five hundred languages by using "Our Father" as a common base. By doing this, you violate the language you want to study, since many of the translated words and phrases can only be expressed by lengthy paraphrases.

Further, to find out about their method of counting, you must write down the numerals used by a foreign people. Special consideration must also be given to geographical names and their original meaning. In this regard, Germany and Ireland with their Celtic, and America with her Indian names offer a wide field for research. There are more than six hundred local names of Indian origin in the state of Connecticut alone, and still more in Pennsylvania. However, the spelling of those names has been so distorted by English orthography that their origin can often be established only with the greatest difficulty.

The names of colors must also be taken into consideration. Here it is best to use a strip of paper, whose colors run into one another in a way that the scale starts with white and ends with black. Note if any names of colors have derived from well-known animals or flowers.

Further, you must collect nick-names of well-known personalities and of certain villages, towns or countries and epithets which people give to certain scholars and craftsmen such as cobblers, tailors, teachers, ministers, and lawyers. You should also collect war cries, proverbs, weather rules, sayings, and striking inscriptions on window panes, churches, barns, and entrances to cemeteries, as well as on pipe bowls, plates, cups, mugs, powder flasks, snuff bottles, tombstones, and bells. In addition, write down the customary names of plants, minerals, stars, foods, garments, parts of the body, tools, money, musical instruments, months, days, and seasons.

You should also collect children's rhymes, such as "Bastlöse" [a certain kind of rhyme in a game] and counting out rhymes. Take special interest in incantations and folk songs, along with their melodies. Study the secret languages of certain classes as well as those of the children. You have to find out whether there exists a commonly understood language of signs and gestures and whether people use mnemonic devices like the notched stick, strings, knots, or quippos.

When studying domestic arrangements and housing conditions of a people, you first should try to find out whether families have temporary or permanent dwellings and what those are like, whether they are made of wood, stones, sod, reed, or animal hides, whether they are above or under the ground, what kind of rooms they contain, and what special purposes they serve.

Which customs do they adhere to when building a house? Do all the people of a village help or only friends and neighbors of the owner, and does the "Bauheben" [house-raising] as it is called in the center of Germany, end with speeches and common festivities? Is the threshold of the entrance door sprinkled with blood, are animals buried underneath it, or are other offerings given? Are certain parts of the house—like basement, oven, chimney, the corner near the stove, attic, or lumber-room—inhabited by good or bad spirits and how do they communicate? Does the father rule at home, or does the mother wear the breeches?

By which popular names do people call father, grandfather, mother, grandmother, uncle, aunt, brother-in-law, sister-in-law? What are the names for spinsters, bachelors, widows, and old people, and what is commonly thought of them? What fond names do they give to children and young girls of marriageable age? What are the opinions about step parents and parents-in-law? What do they think about women? Which proverbs, sayings, folk tales, and songs deal with them? Which superstitions are connected with them? Is the origin of sin and thus of all misery attributed to them?

As for the social circumstances of the people you study, you must find out whether they know the custom of blood friendship [blood brotherhood] and how this is entered into and what duties are imposed on the participants. And there still are the following questions to be asked: Do they practice vendetta or can injustice inflicted upon a person be atoned for in any other way than by murder? Do the children bear the family name of the mother or the father? Is there an aristocracy, and is it based on birth, performance, or bodily strength? Is slavery legal? Do polygamy and polyandry exist? Has the father the right to kill or sell the newborn child? How are deaf-mute, blind, and imbecile people treated? Are there secret societies and what is their effectiveness? Is the position of chief or leader of a village inherited or up for election? What are the rights of a chief or a leader, and how does he enforce them? Does a military organization exist, who belongs to it, and which are each member's duties? What kind of weapons do the warriors bear?

It is also of interest to know how the boundaries of a village or a district are established. In this connection you must ask by whom and how the official survey is done. Are, perhaps, schoolboys witnesses, since the future belongs to them, and are their ears boxed vehemently to make them remember this important event? What is the punishment for a person who moves a boundary-stone in order to fraudulently enlarge his private lot? Further, has the community any common property like forests, orchards, coal mines, or mineral springs? How are these administered and how are the proceeds distributed? Has a village a communal baker's oven and what rules must the inhabitants obey when they want to use it?

How are severe criminals punished? Are they drowned, quartered, be-headed, hung, strangled, electrocuted, impaled, torn apart with red-hot tongs, entombed, mutilated, or burned alive, as happens nowadays with Blacks in the Southern states of America when they have raped White women? How is conjugal infidelity or unlawful impregnation punished? Is a duel regarded as divine judgment?

Which industries exist in a certain area and by what local conditions are they favored? Do the workers in question use special customs or sayings? Which songs do they sing, unless—as in America—they have forgotten how to sing at work. Do they trade, and what is it they exchange?

How are servants and maids hired and what presents do they get on New Year's Day and at Christmas? Are there any legends that deal with the punishment of lazy servants? What is the main occupation of women? Do they spin, weave, and knit, or do they also work in the fields or in factories?

Further, you should collect reliable information on the following characteristic abilities and occupations of the inhabitants of a certain area: Are they skilled in shooting, running, swimming, mountain climbing, hunting, fishing, bird catching, singing, playing an instrument? Which trades do they prefer to practice? Has the trade a special guardian spirit? Are there guilds or similar workmen's clubs, for example, American workers' unions? What are their rules and how are they enforced? What mottoes, coats of arms, and distinctive signs do the members of those organizations have? What kind of life do fishermen, hunters, lumberjacks, shepherds, bird catchers, moonshiners, and trappers lead? What omens promise them good or bad luck while they are doing their work? What legends do sailors tell about phantom ships and sea serpents? Are sailors tattooed and in what manner? What ceremonies do they observe when crossing the equator? Do they take a mascot on board at the beginning of the voyage?

You often can collect valuable folklore material from shepherds who spend the larger part of the year in the open. From long personal observations they know a lot of weather rules which usually are more correct than those of our official weather prophets; they know most of the medicinal herbs and how to prepare them for practical use; they explain bird calls in an ingenious way, and are often inexhaustible in telling legends about lost villages, sunken bells, and greedy peasants who measure their fields with a red hot iron rod at night, because they moved their boundary-stones.

Hunters, too, usually will tell many tales, mostly too many; however, write down their Munchhauseniads [exaggerated stories][2] and local tall tales, even if they often are of no folkloristic value. At least they serve to enrich the humorous popular literature. Grave diggers usually have many hair-raising ghost stories in store.

You also should observe the arts of a people. You must study their performance in wood carving, pottery, glass painting, weaving, sculpture, pictography, and so forth. Further, do they produce their weapons and tools themselves, what are those made of, and how are they decorated?

Special attention must be given to collecting antiquities. In this regard folklorists have taken great pains as far as Indian tribes in America are concerned. Thus you can find so many spear and arrow heads and other weapons in the museum of the Historical Society of Wisconsin, that you could fit out a whole tribe. Among them are several that consist of copper and were cast in a mold and not, as is mostly the case, hammered in shape when cold, according to a speech which Prof. J. D. Butler gave to this society in February 1876. Prehistoric buildings, burial grounds, aqueducts, and trade routes must be examined. In the valley of the Ohio river and its tributaries, artificial mounds abound, whose true purpose has not yet been explained. In Wisconsin they often represent animals, in Georgia, birds. If you excavate the smaller ones, which obviously are just burial places, you must note the positions of the skeletons, then you must thoroughly examine the skull to find out whether it had been artificially deformed, for example, flattened, and how far it differs from skulls of contemporary inhabitants of the area.

The music of a people also deserves the attention of a folklorist. You should find out which instruments are played, and whether they are of domestic or foreign manufacture; the range of each must be stated as closely as possible. Further, the melodies must be written down, whether they are played or sung—the latter, of course, with their underlying texts—in this connection a Graphophone could serve you well.

As for the clothing of a people, try to answer the following questions: Is it made of animal hides or of woven material? By whom and how are clothes made? Do people wear special clothes at festivities, when hunting, fishing, at war and at home?

To inquire about a people's jewelry, you must ask yourself: Does it consist of stone, clay, metals, wool, feathers, beaks, claws, and the skin of birds and animals? Do people paint their faces, and what material do they use? Do they wear rings on their fingers, in their ears, lips, or noses, and do they attribute magic powers to them?

Now let us regard the food of a people. Of what does it consist mainly? How is it produced? Are snakes, insects, roots, or frogs eaten? Are stimulating beverages consumed, and how are they made? Do people use tobacco and in what way? Is there a special favored dish and beverage? What kind of dishes and pastries are eaten at festivities? Is salt used and how is it obtained? Is bread or any other kind of food blessed before people eat? At what time is the main meal of the day eaten? What toasts are usually proposed when people drink? What influence on health is attributed to certain dishes, like beans or cucumbers? Who presides at the table? Does each family member have a designated seat? Do they practice hospitality, and what rights do they grant a guest?

Wherever in the world there are young and old people, they play. Children play with marbles, beans, stones, balls, eggs, and dolls; they dance, walk on stilts, and play instruments which they have made themselves; they shoot with blow pipes, bows and arrows, little guns made out of hollow keys, and so forth. Old people spend their extra time with dice, cards, and ninepins; and they not only want to amuse themselves, but also to win some money or something that is worth money, if possible. In this connection you must describe exactly the equipment for each game, as well as the rules a player has to obey. You must especially stress the so-called national games and the dramatic games which are performed at certain occasions, like the expulsion of death or winter, and dances.

Now let us look at family life and the different customs, ceremonies, and festivities connected with it. In several Indian languages the word "to marry" means the same as "to buy." From this you can deduce that the bride was bought from parents or other relatives—a custom that even to-day exists among numerous peoples outside of America. Now you must find out what the price is, whether a matchmaker is used as go-between, as was John Alden in Longfellow's *Miles Standish* and the pharmacist in Goethe's *Hermann und Dorothea*, and what rules govern the engagement, called "handfasting" in Scotland and "bundling" in Wales. Further, you must inquire who is invited to the wedding, whether they are invited through a special person who is employed for this purpose [Hochzeitsbitter] and how the invitation is worded.

What do nuptial rites consist of? What influence has the wedding-day weather on the happiness or misfortune of the couple? How do you discover whether the husband or the wife wears the breeches? What clothes and jewels and ornaments do the bride and bridegroom wear? Is the wedding party stopped on their way to church and how does the bridegroom pay ransom? Are games played after the marriage ceremony, which resemble remnants of the formerly customary kidnapping of women? Does the bride secretly leave the wedding banquet and then have to be found by the bridegroom? Which days and months are preferred for weddings? Do people make speeches [Strohkranzreden] the evening after the wedding, and do children throw old shoes and pots at the young couple's front door to receive gifts? How is adultery looked upon, and how is it punished? What reasons allow a dissolution of the marriage? In what way are wooden, porcelain, silver, golden, and diamond wedding anniversaries celebrated? Are there charms to bring fertility? What is said about women desirous of marrying? Does a woman bring good or bad luck?

The most important event after the wedding is the birth of a child. What do people tell their adolescent children of their origins? What influence does the hour and day of his birth have on the future fate of the baby? What rules must the new mother obey until the child is baptized? Does the father plant a tree after the child's birth, and is its thriving connected to the health of the child? What are the duties of godparents? On which days—for example, Good Friday or commemoration day—do they not like to baptize children? What does it mean when the child cries during baptism? Do they baptize two children with the same water? Do they pour baptismal water onto vines and trees to help them grow? Do they have a special celebration when the mother appears at a social gathering for the first time after the birth of her child?

As for folk festivals, you must look into their history as far back as possible to discover their actual origins and purposes and to notice changes which they have undergone in the course of time. In addition, you must ask the following questions: Do people take part in them regardless of age or sex? Do they take place in the open, in special buildings, on mountain tops, or in a forest? Who organizes and manages them? Do people consume special food and beverages on those occasions? What popular folk plays are performed? Are parades and masquerades connected with them? What games of chance do people play? Do old and young fortune tellers make their appearance and try to predict the future for anybody who will pay for it, as is the case at most English folk festivals?

With regard to New Year's Day, you must find out what kind of gifts children and servants receive and how congratulations are expressed. You also must pay close attention to superstitious customs which mainly foretell the future. In a similar way, you should look at other festivals like Easter, Pentecost, Christmas, and Shrovetide (Shrove Tuesday). The Haberfeldtreiben,[3] too, may be regarded as popular entertainment. Furthermore, you must inquire into the following events which concern folk life: Are there initiation rites at puberty? How is a young man given his full rights by his elders, so that he can go to a dance or a spinning party or smoke a pipe without being bothered? What are the customs at spinning parties or other gatherings on winter evenings which young people attend? Are May poles put up for young girls of marriageable age? Do people elect a Queen of May? Do they still light fires on mountain tops and send burning wheels rolling down into the valleys on midsummer night? Do they leave a few sheaves in the fields at the end of harvest, and what are those called?

The last social event of human life is the funeral. Are there omens which predict the imminent death of a family member? What are they? Are windows and doors opened after a death has occurred to let the soul escape? Are mirrors and pictures covered or turned to the wall? What objects are put into the coffin with the corpse? Is there a wake and a funeral repast?

Facing which direction is the corpse buried? Are there paid female mourn-
ers? Is the death of the master of the house announced to the cattle and the
bees? For how long do people wear mourning? Which persons are not allowed to come near the corpse? Where and how are people buried who
committed suicide or people who were members of a "dishonest" trade? Is
the corpse put onto a high wooden scaffolding, thrown into the water,
buried in a cave, or burned? What happens to the ashes in the latter case?
Do people pile stones onto the grave of a person who died from an accident
or who was murdered? Are the stones supposed to hinder the ghost of the
departed from leaving the grave and haunting? What is a ghost in the peoples' understanding, and what shapes does it take? Do ghosts appear as giants or dwarfs, as teasing, merry, and helpful creatures, or as mischievous,
crafty, and malicious fellows? Do they appear as brownies, women in
white, wild huntsmen, Will of the Wisps, or mermaids? Are they mainly
seen at springs, on mountain tops, in forests, caves, basements, attics, on
crossings, or in cemeteries? Do they shun people or do they approach
them? Are they able to speak? Are there legends about national heroes
who, for centuries, wait for a favorable sign to return? How does the soul
leave the body? What do people think about the world to come? How does
the soul reach that place, and is it rewarded or punished there?

The religion of a people offers the best key to understanding their
character. What do they think of their gods? Are there gods of the four
points of the compass, of the stars, the thunderstorm, of mountains,
lakes, and rivers, and what are they called? Do people offer sacrifices to
those gods? What tales are told about them? Is there a devil? What does
he look like, and where does he mostly dwell? Does he enter into
covenants with people?

When studying different Christian sects, you must pay close attention
to special customs and the influence they have on social life. In this context, America, the country of unrestricted religious freedom, offers an un-
commonly rich field for study, for here we find—besides the main
denominations—Mennonites, Free-will Baptists, Sabbatarians, Two-seed
Predestinarian Baptists, Tunkers, River Brethren, members of the Apos-
tolic Christian Church [Neutäufer or Frölichianer], Weinbrennerians,

Campbellites, Arminians, Herrnhuters, United Brethren in Christ [followers of Philip Otterbein], Albright Brethren, Jumpers, Schwenckfeldians, Quakers, Shakers, Inspireds, Separatists, Harmonists, Plymouth Brethren, members of the Church Triumphant [followers of Schweinfurth], New Israelites, Sandemanians, Irvingites, Mormons, Hoffmanniates, Adventists, Millenarians [Chiliasts], Swedenborgians, Socinians, Spiritualists, Christian Scientists, and Theosophs.

In connection with less-civilized peoples, you inquire about the following: Do they worship fire, animals, snakes? Do they have idols? What is the influence of their religious beliefs on their morals, form of government, and social circumstances? Do they mutilate or torture people for religious reasons? Are there priests, prophets, and messiahs? What are the activities of the priests? Can they heal diseases, resuscitate the dead, tell the future, secretly harm their enemies, and generally work wonders? Are there sympathetic doctors, and do they use incantations and charms? Do they know the medicinal values of certain herbs? What remedies do they use in treating warts, freckles, nose bleeds, coughs, hiccups, gout, toothaches, consumption? What do people think of the origin of diseases, above all of epidemics? Are there witches and what do they look like? Are they bleary-eyed, with black hair, a beard, wrinkles, a pointed nose, and no teeth? How did they come to be known as witches? Do they brew love potions and tell the future? Where do they gather? Can they make themselves invisible or take on the shape of an animal? How are they treated by the people? Are there sorcerers and alchemists? Are there haunted houses?

Which omens are commonly known? What do people expect when a woman's apron string comes undone by chance; when a knife, a fork, or a spoon falls on the floor; when the clock suddenly stops; when the call of a certain bird is heard at night; when the house cat cleans itself; when the left or the right hand or another limb itches; when you have to sneeze constantly; when it rains and the sun shines at the same time; when the furniture squeaks; when you fall up the stairs instead of down; when you spill salt; when you stumble; when you meet old women, humpbacks, blind people, or cripples first thing in the morning; when you see a herd of pigs or sheep upon entering a strange town; when you open an umbrella indoors; when you forget something while going out and you have to return? How are dreams and forebodings explained? What do people think about moles and spots on fingernails? Are there days and numbers which bring bad luck?

What do people say about persons with red hair, widows who want to marry again, misers, Jews, clergymen, etc.? How do they explain the echo, the rainbow, lightning, low and high tides, the origins of mountains, lakes, and people, in short, of any natural phenomenon? By which Biblical phrases are new inventions, catastrophic accidents which affect the whole country, or the emergence of powerful war heroes said to have been foretold? What legends are told about famous citizens? By what fibs do they dismiss inquisitive children who ask annoying questions? Are there objects which bring luck (lucky money, charmed bullets)? How do they discover a murderer or a perjurer?

As for plants, you must note down all their popular names as well as all legends and tales that are connected with them, above all those by which characteristics are explained. You also ought to study which trees and bushes are inhabited by spirits, and how they avenge disturbances.

Furthermore, you ought to collect all legends that refer to mountains, rivers, lakes, rapids, springs, castles, islands, heaps of stones, gorges, houses, and especially strange trees.

The popular names of wild and tame animals, as well as the legends by which their most prominent characteristics are explained, must be recorded also. At the same time, you have to discover which animals are venerated like gods, how they are treated, and whether people offer sacrifices to them. Especially important are the popular opinions on toads, snakes, bats, rats, mice, wolves, stags, bears, hares, cocks, lizards, cats, ravens, swallows, storks, swans, foxes, beavers, and dogs.

Are there charms to drive away dangerous animals? Are some animals spared because people think they are inhabited by the souls of deceased persons? Which animals forecast the weather? Which animals are eaten and which are not? Are migratory birds publicly greeted when they return in spring? Which animals represent cleverness, deceit, thievery, vigilance, laziness, and diligence? Which animal plays the main role in fables? What words does one use when leading beasts of burden? What does it mean when a spider alights on a person or when a cock crosses one's way? In the latter case the English and the Irish expect luck, but the Indians, Arabs, Lapps, and South Africans on the other hand expect misfortune.

Fairy tales, legends, fables, humorous tales [Schwank], songs, and proverbs form the main part of a people's oral literature. A people without such products of their imagination and their intelligence has not yet been found. They are necessities for children and joy and edification for adults; that is why Luther said he would not be without the miraculous tales, he knew from his childhood for anything.

Myths and heroic legends derive originally from one single source, for the national god was also the national hero, who created and preserved the world and mankind. The folk tale thus not only represents an inexhaustible source of entertainment but also of information, since it answers all questions about nature and life, and it does so in a simple language which can easily be understood by everybody. It tells us how the world, the animals, and people originated, where the wind comes from, what the meaning of the milky way is, why the sun moves around the earth every day, why the moon waxes and wanes; it explains the picture in the moon [the man in the moon] and what shooting stars are all about.

In addition, the folk tale arouses and satisfies people's ethical feelings by informing them about deceived devils, about robbers, giants, and cannibals, about innocent stepchildren who were pursued and rescued, about enchanted princesses who were saved, about slandered women who later were vindicated. Buffooneries like those of Eulenspiegel [a German in the 1300s who practiced the mischievous pranks of a vagabond peasant], Münchhausen, the Schildbuergers [foolish inhabitants of the fictitious village Schilda], and similar pranks, however, are solely for entertainment. For some time, more effort has been put into writing down and studying folk tales from all existing peoples than into any other field of ethnology. Comparing folk tales has already become a developed science providing interesting and surprising insights into the ideas and feelings of a people. Even if many tales of peoples that are far apart in time and place are strikingly similar in their main features, there is no reason to assume prehistoric borrowing and credit it as proof of an original oneness of the human race; primitive situations with much in common everywhere, influence the imagination in a similar way and bring about the same results.

In order to study folk tales systematically, several scholars reduced them to their main elements and divided them into groups. The first scholar who did this was, as far as I know, J. G. v. Hahn [*Griechische und albanesische Märchen*, 1864]; he was followed by the English Baring Gould, whose essay "Story Radicals" was added to the first edition of Henderson's *Folklore of the Northern Counties* [1866] and later was included, with a few changes, in Gomme's *Handbook of Folklore* [1890]. A short list of a few main types may suffice here.

"The Cupid and Psyche Type." A beautiful maiden is loved by a strange man; he comes to her at night and asks her not to look at him. She does so anyway, loses him, and has to overcome great difficulties to find him again.

"The Melusina Type" is related to it. Here the man violates his wife's order not to look at her on a certain day of the week and thus loses her.

"The Swan Maiden Type." A man steals the swan coat of a bathing maiden [a swan could turn into a maiden by removing its swan coat], hides it, and thus forces her to marry him. As soon as she finds her coat again, she escapes.

"The Penelope and Gudrun Type."[4] For years a woman waits for the return of her husband or bridegroom, rejects all wooers, and finally is reunited with her loved one.

"The Genoveva Type." A wife is falsely accused of infidelity and is banished. She suffers unspeakable misery, and is later taken into favor again after her innocence has been proven.

"The Elixir of Life Type."[5] The life of a person depends on a certain object; as soon as it is stolen or otherwise lost, he dies. "The Samson Type" belongs here, too.

"The Serpent Child Type." A woman wishes to have a child, even if it is only an animal or a snake. She has a son. He grows up, marries, and is robbed of his animal or snake skin; thus he henceforth can only appear in his human shape.

"The Devil's Contract Type."[6] Somebody promises his soul to the devil and is either taken away by him at a certain time or outwits him.

"The Lear Type." A man chases one of his daughters away, is badly treated by the others, and finally reconciles with the daughter he had expelled.

"The Rhea Sylvia Type." A mother loses her children; they are reared by wild animals and later win very high honors.

"The Cinderella Type." The youngest girl or the stepdaughter has to work hard, while her siblings amuse themselves, but finally they have to let the slighted sister marry the coveted prince. "The Berta Type" belongs here, too.

"The Transformation Type."[7] People are magically turned into animals and regain their original shape after many adventures.

"The Taming Type."[8] Obstinate women or girls are defeated by cleverness, brutality, or the correct solution of the riddles they had asked; they then patiently accept their fate.

"The Simpleton or Boor Type."[9] A seemingly clumsy peasant boy fearlessly undertakes the most dangerous tasks, defeats his opponents in battle and in play, marries a princess, and becomes a king.

"The Bluebeard Type."[10] The woman who enters a forbidden room is killed.

"The Dragon Type."[11] A dragon devastates the land, and after he has kidnapped a king's daughter, is killed by a knight.

Also, you must write down tales about animals that showed gratitude towards people who had helped them, and legends about the creation of the earth, as well as about its destruction by water and fire. In general, every original legend has to be carefully recorded.

I have already pointed out that songs should be collected: hikers', hunters', soldiers', students', craftsmen's, fishermen's, and children's songs as well as lullabies and riddling songs, together with their melodies.

Likewise, proverbs and sayings in the common dialect must be written down. They represent a practical, well-tried worldly wisdom; they show people as they really are and what they think of kings, magistrates, clergymen, women, children, lawyers, usurers, spendthrifts, and physicians.

You also ought to record congratulations, greetings, protestations, oaths, prayers, wishes, insults, puns, joking questions, tongue twisters—in short, everywhere in the world among all nations there are so many things to collect that everybody, regardless of his position, can easily contribute something to folklore.

NOTES

1. The second part gives examples, explanations, and more folkloristic data.
2. Baron Münchhausen told many tall tales.
3. The *Haberfeldtreiben* was a secret moral court in Bavaria made up of neighbors who confronted a perpetrator with his unethical behavior. They came at night, made a terrible noise, and read aloud the list of misdeeds.
4. Baring Gould in Henderson, *Folk Lore of the Northern Counties of England and the Borders* (1866), does not combine the two types, nor does G. L. Gomme in *Handbook of Folklore* (1890).
5. Baring Gould does not have the "Elixir of Life Type." "The Heartless Man" root comes close to it; Gomme calls this the "Punchkin or Life-Index Type."
6. Both Baring Gould and Gomme call this the "Devil Outwitted" root.
7. Baring Gould and Gomme call this the "The Seven Swans Type."
8. It is "The Taming of the Shrew Type" with Baring Gould and Gomme, who only take into consideration violence as means of taming.
9. This type is mentioned by neither Baring Gould nor Gomme.
10. Gomme calls this the "Forbidden Chamber Type"; Baring Gould does not include it.
11. Gomme names this the "The Andromeda Type"; Baring Gould does not mention it.

•Four•

CONCEPTS OF VARIOUS GENRES

Knortz often gave short introductions to aspects of folklore in his books and studies. The following are his definitions and explanations of a number of genres.

Folklore

. . . [F]olklore is the spoken or sung literature of the common man, which contains his philosophy, religion, and poetry and which answers the many questions of daily life in a way that conforms to his knowledge . . . . Thus folklore is the quintessence of the ideas of a whole people who have not yet been touched by culture . . . . The original customs of a people, however, undergo modifications as soon as they are suppressed by a stronger people or are joined with them; their customs do not completely disappear but live on for centuries or even millennia in some form or another, even if their original meanings are lost in the course of time, as experience shows. The study of these survivals, which consist of tales, legends, proverbs, sayings, songs, and customs, is the task of a folklorist . . . . Habits and customs which thus survived [in the uneducated people] form the key to the prehistory of such a people; thus, folklore which deals with them forms an interesting part of cultural history which is especially important since it mentions data which reach further back in time than all written documents" (1896a, 5–6).

PROVERBS

There are proverbs for all possible situations in human life. They punish, console, weep and laugh, praise and mock, and are always expressed in so precise a way that they are easily remembered. They form the actual philosophy of the common people, who clothe them in characteristic words according to their thinking and their way of life. They refer to the shape of parts of the body and their functions; to weather and its influence on agriculture and the hunt; to festivities and the customs which go with them; to numbers and days which bring good or bad luck; to food and beverages and their effect on the body (1896a, 55).

Proverbs represent, in the most concise form possible, a people's worldly wisdom which has sprung from experience. Although often opinions and situations have changed since the unknown times of a proverb's origin, those sayings have lost little of their original meaning . . . . A short proverb often prevents more evil than a long speech. It appears . . . always at the right moment, comforting and warning; it knows all of people's misery and joy; it sympathizes only with honesty and truth, and reprimands indiscriminately. It does not cloak a crime with Christian love; it always speaks clearly, too clearly for many. It does not fidget, but hits the nail on its head without delay. It never violates religious feelings but often severely criticizes the weaknesses of the clergy and every other profession (1900c, 210–1).

The proverb forms a counterpart or a supplement to the folk song, as it were. While the latter has its roots in the heart of the people, the former comes from its head and intellect; it is mainly of a practical nature. It was taken from real life, and is meant to provide guidance for it. It gives the true, unadulterated wisdom of the people in precise, commonly understandable, and mostly blunt language; it uses fewer words rather than one too many, for it instinctively knows that it will stick in memory all the more securely through this compactness of expression. Proverbs contain the ethical and social principles of a people; they convey a true picture of the prevalent feeling for justice, and they often pass sentence upon all questions of public or private life in a more certain and mature way than the most learned philosophers do. In all of life's situations, the proverb offers consolation, advice, admonition, and punishment. It laughs and weeps with us; it sometimes appears in the fool's cap, to tease and jest, but it never denies its moral sincerity or its honest good will. It can be understood by people high or low, young or old, learned or simple. It does not use kid gloves but expresses itself freely and without embarrassment and does not care whether its mode of expression is reputable or not. It always hits the nail on its head, and if it sometimes seems to have a double meaning, it is never on purpose. All proverbs arise from experience and observation over long years; therefore they represent the undisguised wisdom of the people. The proverb consists of rules which proved themselves in practice, and which therefore were handed down from father to son . . . . A collection of proverbs thus forms a kind of folk Bible. It shows the people not only what they are, think, and do, but also how they should be, think, and act, for the proverb wants mainly to teach and warn . . . . Proverbs are proven rules for the heart and the house (1902b, 81–2).

FOLK AND FAIRY TALES

The fairy tale not only is an inexhaustible well of entertainment but it is also educational, since it answers all questions that nature and life pose, in a simple language that people can easily understand . . . . If many of the tales of peoples who are separated by time and space agree conspicuously in their main features, you do not necessarily have to presume prehistoric borrowing and to turn this circumstance into proof for the unity of humankind; primitive situations with much in common everywhere influence the imagination in the same way and bring about the same results (1900b, 28–9).

MYTHS

In mythology we can see not only a well thought-out natural symbolism and the creations and games of people with minds rich in imagination, but also the beginnings and the basis of any system of religion. Here, comparative linguistics doubtlessly rendered the most essential services, and only by its guidance was it possible to reach the very beginning of human thought. Mythology points out man's original relationship with all the world surrounding him and the emotions it evoked in him. Mythology speaks of his ideals, desires, and hopes and it gives him easily comprehensible answers to all those questions which life and nature pose. His myths are the oracles whose influence on customs, culture, and private and public life was of the most far-reaching importance (1882b, 1).

Superstition

Superstition is older than the known history of mankind, but it does not belong solely to the past in spite of scientific progress and all the efforts of enlightenment in the present. It has its adherents not only among the uneducated people who are untouched by culture and whose knowledge of life and nature is exclusively taken from Bible, catechism, and hymnal, but it also finds believers among respected and meritorious scientists. From ancient times until now, superstition has formed the main part of all religions; take this away, and there is nothing left that satisfies the need for emotion or the wishes and hopes of the blindly believing and nothing that answers the questions put by daily life. There are more temples built for superstition than for reason. He who takes average people's superstition away robs them of religious peace and of the patience to bear their unenviable fate; it forms their only religion of salvation, without which they would, enraged by their slave-like life, take revenge on those better situated by robbing and burning . . . . Even if superstition no longer has the practical purpose in life that it had in the middle ages, it still accompanies people from cradle to grave, and even beyond. It appears in countless forms; if it disappears in one place, it flourishes all the better in an other; in truth, it is immortal. Harsh laws have suppressed it now and again, but it grew even stronger in secret. It allows us a more accurate glimpse into human hearts and heads than all of psychology and physiology. Every rank, every age and gender has its own special superstition, for the allure of the miraculous is irresistible, and the intellectual ignorance of the masses is bottomless. Thus even the most clumsy deceit, above all if it has religious overtones, will be successful (1913a, 3–4).

Folk songs

Let us not forget the true folk songs and popular songs; they are cheerful, sprightly, and lively and thoroughly healthy, like the people from which they came. They are full of feeling, sometimes a little frank and with a touch of sensuality, but at the same time full of natural truth and unaffected tenderness, so that they never fail to find their way back to the heart from whence they came. Their language is simple like that of the proverb. They show man's close contact with nature; stars, flowers, winds, sunshine and moonshine take a lively interest in human joys and sorrows, thus heightening the former and taking the bitterness out of the latter (1884a, 47).

Children's Games

Of course, children's games were not originally invented by children; they are simply imitations of real events in the lives of grown-ups. We find games which remind us of religious customs of the middle ages; others have their origins in medieval tournaments or in wars, for we discern in the movements of the children the attacking and defending armies, the siege and capitulation of fortresses, the removal of prisoners who as a sign of submission have to march off with their hands up. These games, therefore, did not originate in villages, as was falsely believed up to now, but at princely courts; from there they found their way to the countryside . . . . Some children's games which are sung are nothing but dramatized folk ballads (1896a, 26).

Riddles

The old folk riddles give us a true picture of the humor, the naïveté, the imagination, and the moral views of a nation. . . . Their subjects, taken from daily life, are often dealt with in a most original way (1902b, 209).

SLANG

We understand as slang the typical words and sayings of the common people, who, when they choose their words, do not care about the rules set up by pedantic philologists nor about the opinions of sensitive aesthetes or prudish ladies. Slang affords us an interesting insight into both the former and the present cultural situation. Thus, it should not be regarded as a despicable, illegal extension of the mother tongue, which, like dialect, can only be used humorously. This is especially true now, when realism in literature requires so many concessions; also, it is not good science, since slang forms a characteristic part of folk speech . . . . Popular words and sayings usually hit the nail on the head and easily impress themselves upon our memory, especially when they are alliterative . . . . The older and more settled a people is and the less contact with the surrounding world it has, the more it sticks to its traditional dialect and its inherited form of expression, which often have a long life and are still used by old and young alike, after their original history and meaning have long been forgotten. Thus you can often hear many sayings in the eastern United States which have long since disappeared in their countries of origin. Because of their new and unfamiliar circumstances and occupations, the undaunted, self-assured pioneers of the West, who fearlessly challenge their fate, have enriched their vocabulary by new, strong, and characteristic expressions, which leave nothing to be desired as far as bluntness and clarity are concerned (1907a, 3–4).

Part 3

•

Collections,
Grouped According to Genres

• F i v e •

INTRODUCTION TO THE COLLECTIONS

Knortz spent most of his life teaching, writing, and collecting and publishing folklore data. His works on folklore are a valuable source for the interested reader and scholar. What follows is just a small part of all the data he accumulated. Although he collected folklore from all over the world, only data from America are included in this book

Since there are thousands of American folklore items mentioned in his works and since in very many cases Knortz does not indicate whether he collected them himself, it seems appropriate to list mainly those which he specifically marked as collected personally, from oral sources, via questionnaires, and from newspapers.

In some cases, however, data which he might have known from his own experience, above all when they deal with children, school, and church functions or which were common knowledge in areas where he lived or among people he knew, have been included even if Knortz does not give a source. These items are marked "§." If he quoted a book as the source of his data, or if the data could be found in *JAF* volumes, in collections, or in other books of his time, particularly in books which he recommended as valuable reading material on the subject, the folklore item is usually not included here. Data gathered from questionnaires are marked "‡."

If no symbol is given it is uncertain whether Knortz collected the data himself, but the item seemed interesting enough to be included. This is particularly true for categories other than superstitions.

Knortz was a conscientious collector who admonished folklorists to write down data exactly the way they heard them. Since he asked them not to take offense if they heard blunt language and not to be morally indignant if they heard an obscene story, he did not censor or exclude from his collections those items; nor did he leave out racial slurs. In many of his actions and in many of his stories he spoke out for minorities and proved that he was not a racist, but he recorded what he heard. The slurs in some of the children's rhymes or in slang or sayings are documents of their time. Knortz did not condone them by writing them down.

Symbols:

† specially mentioned as collected by Knortz.

‡ collected mostly from questionnaires. Knortz emphasized in *Zur amerikanischen Volkskunde* (1905b, 3) that he only used data which he had received as original information in answer to questionnaires he had sent out. However, there is reason to believe that he did not always follow this rule. Therefore, data from 1905b are specially marked.

§ a widely known item, or one that was believed by people Knortz came in contact with or was customary in places where Knortz lived, or an event which, according to Knortz, had happened only recently. Sometimes, no source is given; however, Knortz might well have learned it firsthand. The data are often either very specific, or Knortz gave the names of people involved, or he took the information from a newspaper of his time.

* translated from German.

E verses or text are in English.

•Six•

SUPERSTITIONS

Usually Knortz unsystematically presented in the texts of his books folklore data which he had collected himself. Sometimes, however, he grouped data together, as he did with superstitions in 1900b, 158–65 and 1900c, 192–209, mainly collected in Indiana, if they are American.

In *Amerikanischer Aberglaube der Gegenwart* (1913a), Knortz wrote down hundreds of current American superstitions, usually arranged according to events in a person's life. He maintained that the volume contained the results of his collections over many years (1913a, 7–8n). Many of these certainly were common knowledge, and Knortz did not feel obligated to mention a certain time, place, or person when, where, or from whom he got the item. Because of his failure to indicate which of the superstitions he had collected orally, hundreds of them were excluded from the following list. Even though Knortz often did not mark an item as collected orally, in many cases, those same data had been mentioned in earlier books as orally collected.

In some instances superstitions are not translated literally here, since they are part of a story line in Knortz's texts. In those cases, they are paraphrased.

Love and Marriage

Omens and Predictions

You take twelve apple seeds, give each a name and say:
One I love,
Two I love,

Three I love, I say,
Four I love with all my heart
And five I cast away;
Six he loves,
Seven she loves,
Eight they both love,
Nine he comes,
Ten he tarries,
Eleven he courts,
Twelve he marries.
The name of the last seed is, of course, that of the future husband (1905b, 6).* E ‡

If a girl's apron falls off, it is a sign that her lover has been unfaithful (1900b, 158).* †

If a girl's apron falls off, it is a sign that her lover is thinking of her (1900c, 195).* †

If you take the last piece of bread or cake from a plate, you will never marry (1900b, 162),*†(1900c, 194).* †

A girl who can't divide a cake with one cut will die a spinster (1900b, 162).*†

If you accidentally knock over a chair, you will not marry within one year (1900c, 195).*†

A four-leaf clover in your shoe brings luck and early marriage (1900b, 158).*†

When an unmarried girl finds a four-leaf clover, she carefully puts it into her right shoe, puts the shoe on, and leaves the house expecting to meet the man she is destined to marry. Or, she may eat the clover and then make a wish (1905b, 6).* ‡

If a piece of coal falls from an open fire place and singes a lady's dress, she will soon have a suitor (1900c, 193).*†

A girl who falls up the stairs will remain single for at least another year (1900c, 195),*†(1903, 92),* (1905b, 7).*‡

If two lamps burn in a room, a bride is in the house (1900c, 197).*†

A marriage between a blond man and a black-haired woman always turns out happy (1900c, 197).*†

Lighting a match will tell a girl about her lover's regard for her. If it burns weakly, he only loves her moderately; if it burns down completely, he really loves her; if the match breaks, he only thinks of her now and then (1900c, 196).*†

On the first of May, walk around a grove of trees three times, saying each time: "Bird so far and beast so near!" If you hear the song of a bird first, you will marry a young person; if you hear the sound of another animal, you will marry someone old (1900b, 162).*†E.

If a girl is in love and makes a rhyme early in the morning, she will see her lover before nine o'clock in the evening:
Make a rhyme,
You will see your bean before nine [beau] (1900c, 197).*†E

A spider crawling on the wall brings luck. If it crawls up the wall, there will soon be a wedding (1900c, 201).*†

If two persons put their spoons into the sugar bowl at the same time, there will soon be a wedding (1900c, 193).*†

If by chance two spoons are laid beside the plate of a young girl, she can expect a proposal within one year (1905b, 7).*‡

In New Orleans, girls carry pictures of St. Josef in their pockets hoping that he will help them find a husband soon. For the same reason, they wear yellow stockings and never accept a thimble as a gift (1905b, 7).*‡

Wearing yellow stockings insures against becoming a spinster, especially if they are a present from a bride (1900b, 162).*†

If a girl sleeps with a piece of wedding cake under her head, she will see her future husband in her dream (1900c, 199–200).*†

Yarrow has prophetic powers, a fact that is well known to girls in love. Cut a sprig of it with a silver knife on an evening in May, put it under your pillow, and say:
Yarrow, yarrow, tell me
Who my true love is to be;
The color of his hair,
The clothes he will wear,
And the day he'll be wedded to me.
If you put a sprig of it into your shoes, you will be sure to meet your intended husband (1905b, 6.)*‡E

WEDDINGS AND MARRIAGE

Rain on the wedding day is a sign of luck; snow, on the other hand, is a sign of misfortune (1900c, 197).*†

On her wedding day the bride should wear:
Something old and something new,
Something borrowed and something blue. (1900c, 196)†E.

If the bridegroom sees the bride in her finest jewels before the wedding day, the marriage will be an unhappy one (1900c, 197)*†

If the bridegroom speaks first to a man on the morning of his wedding day, he will be happy; if he speaks first to a woman, especially an old one, his marriage will be a disappointment (1900c, 204),*†(1913a, 152).*

If the bride kneels on the bridegroom's coat during the wedding ceremony, she will wear the pants in the family (1900c, 197),*†(1903, 96).*

Throwing an old shoe at the bride and bridegroom as they depart for their honeymoon is thought to bring good luck (1900c, 197).*†

If a young wife wants to avoid bad luck, she must not wear out her wedding shoes within the first year of her marriage (1900c, 197).*†

Whoever gets in bed first on their wedding night will be first to die (1900c, 204).*†

Visitors

If a woman's apron accidentally falls off, unexpected guests will arrive (1900c, 195).*†

If a woman drops her dishcloth, she will have visitors (1900c, 195).*†

If a dog rolls on the floor three times, a visitor approaches (1900c, 195).*†

If a door opens suddenly, a visitor is near. (1900b, 163).*†

If you drop a fork, a female visitor will arrive; if you drop a knife, the visitor will be male (1900c, 195),*†(1913a, 38).*

If you drop a spoon, a fool will arrive (Pennsylvania) (1913a, 138).*

If you find a hairpin and pick it up, you will receive an invitation three days later (1900c, 194).*†

If a rooster stands in front of the door and crows into the room, American farmers' wives say that a stranger is coming today, and get ready to receive their guest (1900c, 195).*†

Whoever sneezes before breakfast will have guests (1900b, 159).*†

If a spoon falls to the ground, grandmother will soon arrive (1900c, 195).*†

If you are a guest in a family who likes you and you leave some bread on your plate, you will soon be invited again (1900c, 194).*†

American women don't entertain guests on the anniversary of a family member's death (1905b, 5).*‡

American women usually don't accept visitors on Saturday (1905b, 5).*‡

If you do not want a certain person to visit you frequently, sprinkle salt on the floor of the room and then sweep it out the door (1900b, 160).*†

If you go for a visit and you stumble on the way there, if it was the right foot, you are welcome, if it was the left one, you are not (1900c, 194).*†

Infants, Children, and Adolescents

A child who is born in the morning will be more intelligent than one who is born in the evening (1900c, 199).*†

If you wrap a newborn boy in his father's shirt, he will grow up to be a proud man (1900b, 161).*†

A child who is baptized by a drunk clergyman, will die within one year (1900c, 198).*†

A child who cries during baptism will live a long life (1900c, 198).*†

If three children are baptized together, one of them will soon die (1900c, 198).*†

Never rock an empty cradle, or the child who is later put in it, will die at an early age (Indiana) (1900c, 192).*†

The child who rocks his own cradle will have luck (1900b, 164).*†

Making a baby touch a plate on which you have placed money, salt, a piece of cake, and a boiled egg will bring him luck (1900b, 161).*†

When a child is one year old, place a glass, a coin, and a book near him. If he reaches for the glass, he will lead a ruthless life and die poor (1900c, 199).*†

If a child is dressed in fur before he is one year old, he will have curls (1900b, 161).*†

If you put the hat of an old person on a child, he or she will develop well mentally but stay behind physically (1900b, 163).*†

If a cat licks the face of a baby first, it forebodes bad luck; if a dog does it first, it brings good luck (1900b, 161).*†

If a child has two cowlicks, he will eat his bread in two countries (1900c, 199).*†

It is a bad sign when a child cuts his upper teeth first (1900c, 199).*†

If a teething child gnaws on a coin, he will become rich (1900b, 161).*†

A child who has one tooth must not look into the mirror lest she become vain and coquettish. Corals and little bells around her neck will protect her against misfortune (1913a, 12).* [in 1913a, (8–20) Knortz accumulated countless superstitions pertaining to children, but he did not give any sources. With the exception of the preceding, they are omitted here.]

A child who is allowed to look in the mirror before he is one year old will not live to see his second birthday (1900c, 199).*†

If you cut your children's fingernails during their first year, they learn to steal. (That is why people bite off their children's nails) (1884a, 84),*†(1900c, 192),*†(1913a, 15).*

If a child likes to cross his legs, he will enjoy good health (1900b, 164).*†

The child who constantly stretches his fingers in his sleep will be much talked about in later life (1900c, 199).*†

A child who insists on pressing the soles of his feet against each other will become unhappy (1900b, 162).*†

If a child plays with his toes, he will start squinting (1900b, 163).*†

If a child wants to know if he is loved by a certain playmate, he throws apple seeds into the fire and says:
If you love me, pop and fly;
If you hate me, lay and die (1900c, 198).*†E

You cannot expect much good from a girl who whistles:
A whistling girl and a flock of sheep
Are the very worst things a man can keep.
A whistling girl and a crowing hen
always come to a very bad end (1905b, 35).*E‡

Death, Omens, and Funerals

If three persons swing on a horizontal bar, the one in the middle will soon die (1900c, 204).*†

If a white bat flies into the room, your youngest child will die (1900c, 204).*†

If a black bird circles a house, a person inside will soon die (1900b, 161).*†

He who sees a woman with a black birthmark will meet a tragic death. (1905b, 5).*‡

If small children sing a lot, somebody in the neighborhood will die (1900c, 203).*†

A clock which is wound regularly by its owner will stop working properly when its owner dies (1900b, 159).*†

Railroad workers believe in close calls. An accident with fatalities gives them forewarning; the third accident will definitely be fatal to them (1905b, 14).*‡

If a dead person's coffin is seen in a mirror, someone else in the family of the dead person will soon die (1900c, 204).*†

You should not put anything on a corpse. If you do, the owner of the objects will soon die (1900c, 205).*†

When a corpse is in the house, the mirror and all pictures should be turned to the wall in order to prevent another death in the near future (1900c, 204).*†

A corpse on board a ship brings bad luck (1905b, 54).*‡

If you are afraid of the dead, you have only to put your hand on the forehead of a corpse, and your fear will disappear (1900b, 158).*†

The chirping of a cricket and the hooting of an owl indicate an imminent death (1900c, 203).*†

If you do not want to hear the ghostly moans of your dead friends, never enter any crossroads at midnight (1900c, 202).*†

When a death has occurred, many people open the windows to let the soul fly away:
Open lock, end strife,
Come death and pass life (1900c, 205).*ᴇ†

Never step over somebody who is lying on the floor, unless you want that person to die soon (1900b, 161).*†

If you do not want to die soon, never let your tear drop into a coffin (1900b, 160).*†

Whoever is sprinkled with the blood of a dove will die an unnatural death (1900b, 162).*†

If a strange dove comes into your garden three days in a row, a young person will die (1900c, 204).*†

If the eyes of a dead person will not close, people say that he is looking for the person who shall follow him (1900c, 203).*†

If you happen to meet a funeral procession, a member of your family will soon die (1900c, 204).*†

If it rains into the grave while the coffin is being lowered into it, another death is imminent (1900c, 204).*†

It rains into a pious person's grave (1900c, 205).*†

In New York, many women do not allow their husbands to put their hats on a bed for fear that one of their friends will die (1900b, 162).*†

Whoever loses his hat on his first voyage across the ocean will soon make a second one, but he will not arrive at his destination (1900c, 202).*†

If a hen lays an egg with a soft shell, somebody will soon die (1900b, 161).*†

If a horse shakes his ears so vehemently that you can hear it, there will soon be a death in its owner's family (1900b, 159).*†

If a horse stumbles near the cemetery, its owner will soon die (1900c, 204).*†

Many Americans do not take out a life insurance policy, because they think it is a passport to the other world (1900c, 205).*†

If old people who have become rich have a beautiful new house built, they will soon die (1900b, 163).*†

Secret knocking in a room indicates an imminent death (1900c, 204).*†

If a mouse gnaws at a woman's petticoat, she must soon die (1900c, 203).*†

If a photograph fades, the person pictured in it will soon die (1900c, 205).*†

If a picture falls from the wall, there will soon be a death in the house (1900c, 203).*†

If a flock of seabirds flies so close to the boat that you can catch them with your hands, somebody in the boat will die within twelve hours (Lighthouse keepers near New York) (1905b, 14).*‡

If you see a shooting star, a member of your family will soon die (1900c, 204),*†(1913a, 109).*

If you have to wait to cross a street, do not stand on a sidewalk made of wood; if you do so, you will die a sudden death (1900c, 202).*†

Many Americans postpone writing a will to the last moment, fearing that if they do they will die soon (1900c, 205).*†

New Year

On New Year's Day, American farmers of Scottish descent light a big bonfire and throw a key through it. If they want to protect their cattle against disease, they jump through the flames several times (1900c, 208).*†

If you find some money on New Year's Day, you'll always have some money during the whole year (1900c, 194).*†

ARTISTS, CYCLISTS, AND CARD PLAYERS

If an actor whistles while entering the dressing room with a colleague, he will soon lose his job. The actor who sleeps in a room where somebody committed suicide will be ridiculed on stage. An actor does not pass under a ladder or open an umbrella on stage. If he has to carry an umbrella on stage, he sees to it that the color matches his suit. If an actor has forgotten something in his dressing room, he does not return to fetch it but sends somebody for it; otherwise, he will forget his part on stage. If two actors fight behind the curtain before the beginning of the performance, there will be a full house. A cross-eyed wardrobe master brings bad luck to the whole company. If an opera singer puts on his costume inside out, he will miss his best notes (1905b, 12).*‡

If the first ticket dispensed after the ticket-office opens is given away—for instance to a journalist—business will be bad, but if it is sold, there will be a full house (1905b, 11).*‡

Performances on the thirteenth day of the month usually are unsuccessful, especially if it is a Friday. If actors travel in a railway carriage numbered thirteen, the train will wreck or another misfortune will happen. The same is true when thirteen actors travel together, or when the train leaves thirteen minutes after the hour. Hotel rooms numbered thirteen are shunned; that is the reason there is often no room thirteen in many hotels. (1905b, 11).*‡

American cyclists believe that whoever rides past a hearse will die after a year has passed. A cyclist who is pursued by a yellow dog will soon fall off his bike. If a cyclist sees a boy with a sling at the side of the road, his bike will soon break. A cyclist who passes a horse which is led by a red-haired lady will soon have a flat tire, unless he puts two fingers in the air and says:

"cajandrum." The cyclist who chews tobacco and spits the juice onto the road will soon lose a spoke. If a cyclist has his bicycle repaired, he will not soon buy a suit (1900b, 164).*†

Card players believe they will get many trumps if they turn their chairs around in a circle after each game (1900c, 200).*†

ANIMALS AND PLANTS

A cat that eats grass causes rain (1900c, 206).*†

If you want somebody to be your friend for life, give him a cat (1900b, 161).*†

Never cross a street along which a black cat just ran (1900b, 161).*†

The owner of a black cat always has money (1900c, 201).*†

Whoever meets a black cat after dark will have bad luck (1900c, 201).*†

Whoever kills a cat will have bad luck for seven years (1900c, 201).*†

A tricolor cat brings good luck (1900c, 201),*†(1913a, 63).*

When you move, you must not bring a cat to your new house (1900c, 201),*†(1913a, 130).*

The owner of a cow must not kill a frog, or the cow's milk will dry up. (1900c, 202).*†

If the owner of a cow kills a frog, the cow's milk will turn sour (1900b, 161).*†

If a dog howls while looking at the floor, somebody will die soon; if he looks up, a fire will start in the direction of his glance (1900c, 202).*†

To prevent being bitten by a strange dog, simply press your thumb into your hollow palm (1900c, 202).*†

If the roosters crow after an earthquake, there will be a second one within three days (1900b, 163).*†

If you catch a fish and then release it, you should stop fishing (1900b, 161).*†

If somebody steps over your fishing rod while you are fishing, you will not catch anything (1900b, 161).*†

A crowing hen brings misfortune (1905b, 34).*‡

If there is a thunderstorm while a hen is sitting on her eggs, the eggs will spoil (1900b, 161).*†

Ladies in New York do not like to travel behind a carriage drawn by white horses (1900c, 203).*†

In Indiana, you not only have to meet a white horse and spit into your hand to have your wish fulfilled, you also have to see a girl with red hair shortly afterwards; only then may you make your wish (1896a, 51).*†

In Massachusetts, you also have to count to one hundred (1896a, 50).*

Whoever meets a white horse will soon find something, especially if he just saw a red-haired girl:
White horse, ding-a-ling-a-ling—
Where ever I go I'll find something (1900c, 200).*†E

If a locust flies into a room, it brings good luck (1900c, 204).*†

If a Black man sees an owl, he quickly throws a shoe at it to make it fly around without rest for seven days (1900c, 203).*†

If Blacks in Georgia hear an owl hoot, they immediately turn their pockets inside out and put their shoes on the ground with the soles up in order to prevent misfortune. (A few Whites do this also) (1900c, 203),*†(1913a, 40).*

If rats gnaw on your clothes, nothing can save you from misfortune (1900b, 162).*†

Whoever steps over a snake without seeing it, will have bad luck (1900b, 163).*†

If by chance you are beneath a spider web that is hanging from the ceiling, you can expect a letter (1900c, 201).*†

Swallows that nest in the chimney bring luck, but they must not be disturbed (1900c, 202).*†

Killing a swallow brings bad luck (1900b, 161).*†

When sowing grain, American farmers sing this verse:
One for the blackbird,
And one for the crow,
One for the cutworm,
And one for to grow (1900c, 207).*†E

If you put a flower into a book, and somebody takes it out again, that person will become your enemy (1900b, 160).*†

Bury an onion. If it is not rotten after twenty days, make a wish, and it will be fulfilled (1900b, 164).*†

Never thank someone for plants he gave you, or they will not take root (1900c, 194).*†

Baptismal water has to be poured out on a vine (1884a, 85),*†(1905b, 35).*‡

In Pennsylvania, baptismal water poured onto a vine will make the vine grow (1900c, 199).*†

Days

If a sick person gets better on a Sunday, it is a bad omen (1900c, 204).*†

If you do not tarry on your way to school on Monday, you will be able to answer all the teacher's questions; if, on the other hand, you tarry or even stop to play, you will have bad luck all week (1900b, 165).*†

If you cut your fingernails on Monday morning before breakfast, you will get a present before the end of the week (1900b, 164).*†

Few people dare to begin important business or start out on a long journey on a Friday (1900c, 187),* (1913a, 110).*§

It is very rare that a wedding takes place on a Friday (1913a, 110).*§

On Fridays, trains have fewer passengers than on other days of the week, and fewer ships leave port (1913a, 111).*§

Although there are a great number of passenger ships leaving New York every week, there rarely is one that leaves on a Friday; with merchant ships, the day makes no difference (1913a, 153).*§

In America you usually do not engage new servants or move into another dwelling on a Friday (1900c, 187)*§

Lion tamers avoid very dangerous performances on a Friday or on the thirteenth day of the month (1900b, 163).*†

The best days for planting are March 17 and 30 (1900c, 207).*†

The first of April is usually regarded as an unlucky day. Whoever can, avoids starting out on a voyage or marrying on that day. A young girl who wants to marry but falls up the stairs on that day has to wait for another year before she can go to the altar (1900c, 57).*§

Unlucky days are: the first Monday in April (Cain's birthday), May 3 (Dismal Day in Scotland), and December 31 (the day Judas hanged himself) (1900c, 207).*†

If you look into a cistern between twelve and one o'clock on May 1st, and you see a baby in a coffin, you'll have bad luck (1900b, 160).*†

American barbers do not sharpen their razors on rainy days; if they do, their razors will be ruined, and they will cut their customers (1900b, 163).*†

Good and Bad Luck, Horseshoes, Rabbit Feet, and the Number thirteen

The Creoles in Louisiana cut crosswise the bananas they eat (1900c, 202).*†

If, when walking, you step on a brick with a letter or a number on it, you'll have good luck (1900c, 200).*†

A button with an uneven number of holes brings luck (1900b, 158).*†

A black button brings misfortune and should never be picked up; a white one, however, brings luck (1900b, 158).*†

If a man finds a four-leaf clover and puts it in the pocket of his vest, he may confidently expect good luck in business or love (1905b, 6).*‡

Whoever steps on a broken cobblestone will have bad luck (1900b, 164).*†

The coin that lay on the eyes of a dead person must be buried, or it will bring misfortune (1900c, 205).*†

Jewelry in the form of a cross brings bad luck to the wearer (1900b, 164).*†

Stumble with [the] right foot—disappointment;

Stumble with [the] left foot—you will meet a friend (1900c, 201).E†

Whoever gets out of bed on his left foot will be in a bad mood and have a disagreeable day (1900c, 201).*†

Selling old heirlooms will surely bring bad luck (1900b, 163).*†

If you find a horseshoe or a brass key, carry it with you always or hang it on your entrance door, and you will have good luck (1900c, 200).*†

A horseshoe brings good luck (1905b, 4),*‡ (1913a, 27),* (1913a, 33).*

In America, people believe that a horseshoe is lucky. Mainly in the West, you find them on the doors of farmhouses, stables, and offices of physicians, lawyers, businessmen, and officials.

Women like to wear jewelry in the form of a horseshoe, and you can find it on Christmas and New Year cards (1913a, 33).*§

Whoever finds half a horseshoe will meet misfortune (1900b, 160),*†(1900c, 200).*†

A horseshoe protects against witches, devils, contagious diseases, and other evil (1903, 29).*†

Always carry three hairs of a black horse in your pocket, and you will have good luck (1900c, 200).*†

Sculptures of horses' heads are fastened to the doors of stables and barns for luck. One farmer on the road between Wilkes-barre and Bear Creek has three of them mounted on his house in order to bar the former owner, who always was quarreling, from returning there after his death (Pennsylvania Germans) (1903, 29).*†

If a ladder is stood against a wall while a house is being built, Americans will rarely pass under it, but would rather go around it to avoid bad luck (1900b, 206).*†

A mascot is a person or animal that is supposed to bring luck. American warships routinely carry at least one mascot to ward off misfortune (1900b, 71) [examples are given on pages 71–4: from the American naval vessel "Vandalia," the sailing boat "Valkyrie," the transporter "Thomas," etc.].* §

The possession of an opal brings misfortune (1905b, 56),*‡, (1913a, 57).*

Never pick up an opal from the ground if you want to avoid misfortune (1900b, 163).*†

Whoever tears a string of pearls courts misfortune (1905b, 7).*‡

Whoever loses a precious stone will soon fall ill (1905b, 7).*‡

A priest on board a ship brings misfortune (1905b, 55).*‡

A rabbit foot brings luck, but the rabbit has to have been shot in a cemetery under a new moon. (Trade in rabbit feet is booming, since most aristocratic women cannot live without one anymore) (1905b, 10),*‡ (1900b, 74).*

A rabbit foot protects against misfortune (1902b, 28).* (It has become fashionable to wear one, set in gold, as a brooch or on a watch chain. During the MacKinley-Brian election campaign, thousands of rabbit feet were sold set in gold, silver, or tin, and dealers reaped a good profit selling these "left hind feet" of rabbits shot under special circumstances) (1902b, 28-31).*§

Senator Ingalls from Kansas always carries a rabbit foot in his pocket; he also believes in the lucky effect of the horseshoe (1905b, 11).*‡

Whoever sings in the street can expect misfortune (1900c, 203).*†

If you are struck by the spark of a wood burning fire, you will be lucky (1905b, 5).*‡

If you wear stockings that do not match, you'll have good luck (1900c, 201).*†

A cross-eyed person brings misfortune (1905c, 35).*‡

Whoever drinks holy water will meet with misfortune (1900b, 163).*†

Putting a hoe in the house brings in misfortune (1900b, 161).*†

If somebody spills wine on your clothes, you will be lucky (1900b, 162).*†

The number thirteen is unlucky. A salesman stayed in a hotel room number thirteen which was haunted by the ghost of a murder victim (1905b, 12);†locomotive 1313, which had been involved in several deadly accidents, was in all the newspapers (1905b, 13);‡ and a New York lawyer bought a house numbered thirteen in 1908 and had nothing but bad luck with it (1913a, 121–2).§

High-rise buildings often have no thirteenth floor (1905b, 13),*‡ (1913a, 118).

In many apartment houses and skyscrapers in New York, there is no room number thirteen, since it would just remain empty (1913a, 121).*§

Often houses have the number twelve and a half instead of thirteen (1913a, 118).*§

The number thirteen signifies misfortune; 1313, however, promises enormous luck (1900b, 160).*†

Recently the turkey foot became a lucky sign. It is decorated by a goldsmith and not carried in your pocket but hung in your room (1913a, 35).*§

OBJECTS AND ACTIONS THAT BRING

HAPPINESS AND SUCCESS OR CONFLICT AND ENEMIES

If you make the sign of the cross with your index finger on freshly baked bread, blessings will come to you and to everybody who eats the bread (1900c, 202).*†

If you meet a person with one blue eye and one brown one, quickly make a wish, and you will see it come true (1905b, 7).*‡

If two persons reach for a piece of bread at the same time, both will live for many more years (1900c, 194).*†

If you want to find something precious, just count a hundred Blacks in the street and then write the number on a piece of paper and bury it. In two weeks you'll be pleasantly surprised (1900c, 200).*†

In Chicago there are several merchants who never sign a contract before having drawn with ink a small cross in the corner of the document. They call it a lucky cross. To be successful in his business, a garment factory owner in the same town, following the advice of a Gipsy, had a cross sewn with red thread on the right sleeve of each coat (1913a, 45).*§

A rich grain merchant in Chicago never wears shoes that are a matching pair, since he once made a very profitable business transaction while wearing one boot and one slipper. Another merchant always wears red neckties, and still another keeps buying hats that are too big for him—he fills them with paper so that they fit. All this is done to attract luck. A millionaire in the same town never passes a white horse without spitting over the little finger of his left hand; this is supposed to protect him from bad luck. A colleague of his has been carrying a piece of brown sandstone in his pocket from childhood; another colleague never employs a fat stenographer in his business. Nearly every merchant has a rabbit foot. Some roll up the left leg of their trousers before finalizing an important transaction. A lawyer in the same town has the custom of tearing out one of his hairs, dipping it in ink, and making a spot on the paper with it while working on an important document. In the beginning of his career he once had made a stain on the paper in this manner while unsuccessfully reflecting on a difficult legal question. While he looked at the spot, a good idea occurred to him and he won the lawsuit (1913a, 45–6).*§

Wearing a diamond protects against lawsuits, fear, and witchcraft (1900b, 162).*†

If you heard something sad and fear you will dream of it, pull your ears vehemently before going to bed (1900b, 159).*†

If you want to learn during your sleep, put a book under your pillow (1900c, 199).*†

A piece of the rope by which a person was hanged brings success to the professional gambler (1900c, 201).*†

If you want to ward sickness away from your house, keep an Easter egg from one year to the next (1900c, 206).*†

If you experience some inconvenience, put some fat onto your head, and everything will be all right (1900b, 162).*†

Parting your hair in the middle keeps your brain in balance (1900b, 163).*†

If a young girl does not mind losing her beauty, she only has to cut the tips of her hair in May or when the moon is waning (1905b, 6).*‡

The woman who puts into a pin-cushion all the hair she loses while combing will never be bald (among Blacks) (1905b, 7).*‡

If your hand itches, rub it on a wooden object, and you will get either money, a letter, or a present (1900b, 158).*†

If your hand itches, rub it with a coin, and you will soon get more money (1905b, 5).*‡

If your right hand itches, you will soon shake hands with somebody; if your left one itches, you'll get money (1900c, 200).*†

Laugh, and grow fat (1900b, 159).†

The woman who sweeps her house after supper will quarrel with her husband before going to bed (1900c, 195).*†

Do not marry a girl who bites her nails. She is quarrelsome (1900c, 193).*†

Wear only jewels in the shape of a heart, and you will become happy (1900b, 160).*†

If you whistle before a meal, you whistle away your appetite (1900b, 162).*†

Whoever wears a topaz will soon have a rival (1905b, 5).*‡

Whoever spills vinegar becomes rich (1900b, 160).*†

If you weep before going to bed, you will get up happy (1900b, 163).*†

NEEDLES, PINS, KNIVES, AND SCISSORS

A knife that is accepted as a gift cuts a friendship (1900c, 195).*†

If you see a needle on the floor one morning while lying in bed, you must pick it up. Then you have to keep on your person all the needles you find that day, or your money will be stolen or lost before nightfall (1905b, 4).*†

You should not have anybody give you a pin. You must take it without asking (1900c, 194).*†

You should not pick up a pin whose point is directed towards you (1900c, 194).*†

See a pin and pick it up,
All the day you'll have good luck;
See a pin and let it lay,
Bad luck you'll have all day (1900c, 195).ᴇ†

Whoever picks up a pin whose point is directed toward him will experience disappointment; if it points into the other direction, he will have good luck (1900b, 164).*†

If you do not want to have bad dreams, put a pair of scissors under your pillow (1900b, 160).*†

If you do not want to have bad luck, never pick up a pair of scissors that does not belong to you (1900b, 161).*†

PHYSICAL CHARACTERISTICS

Birthmarks are either red, brown, or black. Those which are on the right side of the body bring good luck. A woman with a birthmark on her right forehead will receive a big inheritance. A birthmark on the left forehead condemns a man to a long imprisonment, while it gives a woman two husbands. A birthmark in the middle makes a man cruel and a woman stupid and lazy. One on the back of the neck foretells both a happy life and death through drowning, while one on the left side of the upper lip condemns a man to stay single and a woman to live a sorrowful life. One on the lower lip instructs a man to beware of women, and a birthmark in the hollow of the chin promotes quarrelsomeness and sickliness in a woman, whereas on the tip of the chin it promises a good marriage and a long life, but it must not be black. Whoever has a birthmark on the neck will be hanged, but if it looks like a wart, he will drown (1905b, 16–17).*‡

Cross-eyed people bring bad luck (1905b, 35).* [Knortz tells of an event that was written up in a newspaper in April 1899, where a judge did not want to marry a couple because it was a Friday and the bride was cross-eyed.]§

Generous people have long ears; stingy people short ones (1900b, 159),*†(1909c, 97).*

Whoever has big ears is very generous and will therefore never be rich (1900c, 202).*†

Blue-eyed girls are luckier than black-eyed ones (1905b, 5).*‡

Eyebrows which grow together promise riches (1900b, 160).*†

Spots on fingernails may be various omens. In Indiana, spots on the nail of the first finger bring presents; on the second one, gain; on the third, praise; on the fourth, loss; and on the fifth, shame (1900c, 208).*†

C L O T H I N G

If a girl puts her apron on inside out, she can expect unpleasant news (1900b, 158).*†

A girl who pricks her finger while sewing a dress will be kissed when wearing that dress (1900b, 159).*†

If a woman puts on a dress and it gathers a wrinkle, she must make a wish before she smoothes it. The wish will then be fulfilled (1900b, 158).*†

The lady who puts on her dress inside out will experience something pleasant after twelve hours (1905b, 5).*‡

American women give away mourning dresses; they do the same with gloves, stockings, and petticoats which they wore at the time of some misfortune (1905b, 5).*‡

If you lace your shoe wrong, do not change it or you will have bad luck (1900b, 160).*†

Before you go to bed, put your shoes on the floor pointed away from the bed, and you will not have any bad dreams (1900b, 162).*†

If you want to sleep quietly, point your shoes towards the door (1900c, 199).*†

American shoemakers infer their clients' characters and futures from the wear of their shoes:
Worn on the right side, soon a rich man's bride.
Worn on the toes, spend[s] as he goes,
Worn on the heel, thinks a good deal.
Worn on the vamp, he's surely a scamp (1905b, 20).*E‡

FRIENDS

When a lady accompanies her friend home part of the way, she must not turn back in the middle of the block but rather on the corner, or she will be painfully disappointed (1900c, 203).*†

Nowhere in America may you follow your departing friend with your eyes for too long, or you will never see him again (1913a, 143).*§

When two friends cross the street together and a stranger

passes between them, they soon will quarrel unless they say "bread and butter" (1900c, 199).*†

When two friends go out together for the first time and it starts raining, their friendship will be of a long duration (1900c, 199).*†

Whoever finds a hairpin or a button will soon make a new friend (1900c, 194).*†

If two people dry their hands on a towel at the same time, they will not stay friends for long (1900c, 193).*†

Weather, Objects in the Sky

A comet is a sign of impending war (1905b, 15).*‡

If all the food is eaten at a meal, there will be good weather the next day (1900c, 194),*†(1913a, 156 [omits "the next day"]).*

If the groundhog leaves his hole on February 2, that is, on Candlemas, and he sees his shadow, he will quickly turn back, for he knows from experience that he must expect forty more days of winter (1913a, 156).*§

If you want to protect your house from lightning, cut a palm leaf into pieces and hang the pieces in your bedroom (1900c, 202).*†

Many Germans in Pennsylvania extinguish their fire in the kitchen during a thunderstorm, believing that lightning will be attracted by it. They also believe that lightning helps stones to grow (1903, 50).*§

Do not point your finger at a rainbow, or the feet of the angels will bleed (1900c, 207).*†

If you see a shooting star and say, "Money before the week is over," and you will find money (1900b, 158).*†

If you see a shooting star, say "money" three times in a row and you will receive some money (1900b, 164),*†(1913a, 109).*

If your stocking keeps slipping, expect rain (1900b, 160).*†

If you dream of a burial, it will rain (1900c, 204).*†

If it rains while the sun is shining, the weather will be good (1900c, 206).*†

Saliva, Salt

To protect their departing sons from homesickness, the Germans in central Pennsylvania sew salt into the seams of their trousers and make their sons look at the chimney (1913a, 57).*§

You must not return borrowed salt (all over the U.S.) (1900c, 126).*§

If you want to win at a game of cards, you have to spit into your left shoe (1900b, 159).*†

Objects in the House, Mirrors, Umbrellas, Money, and Renting a Home

If you open a book upside down, don't turn it right side up, or people will speak badly about you (1905b, 5).*‡

If you want to have a good journey, hop around a chair three times before leaving (1900c, 200).*†

If furniture being moved to another house falls from the car, disease threatens (1900b, 163).*†

If you drop a table cloth, you soon will quarrel with somebody (1900c, 195).*†

If all the teaspoons fall off the table, there will soon be much laughter in the house (1900c, 195).*†

You should not look into a mirror at midnight (1900c, 205).*†

If you break a mirror you will have bad luck for seven years unless a child says a prayer for you (1900c, 205).*†

If you break a mirror, your face will get wrinkled (1905b, 5).*‡

If you find some money and instead of spending it carry it in your pocket, it will attract more money (1900c, 194),*†(1913a, 40).*

Whoever adopts an orphan brings money into the house (1900b, 164).*†

He who always carries a wishbone or the finger of a dead Negro in his pocket is safe from all dangers and always has enough money (1900b, 158).*†

Whoever puts an umbrella on a bed or a sofa brings misfortune on himself (1905b, 7).*‡

Whoever puts an umbrella on a bed experiences nothing but disappointment during the day (1900b, 162).*†

There is much superstition connected with renting a home. Young mothers often suddenly break a rental agreement because they happen to have heard that a woman gave birth to twins in the house and that, on top of it, children do not thrive in that area of town. If several people have died in a house, it is very difficult to find renters for it. Also, it is difficult to let houses with the number thirteen or those in which a cross-eyed errand boy is employed or where the sign for smallpox is displayed. An apartment is rarely rented on a Friday; however, the person who signs a lease on that day usually pays promptly. When Arthur Mc Quade, one of the rascally aldermen of New York, had a streak of bad luck, his friends said it happened because he had bought house number thirteen on Thirteenth Street for $13,000 (1900b, 169–70).*†

WISHES, TELLING THE FUTURE

If you make a wish upon seeing a cart full of hay, the wish will be granted. If, however, you see the same cart again before it is empty, the wish will have been in vain (1900c, 201).*†

If you want a wish fulfilled, repeat it over a friend's ring and then put the ring back on its owner's finger (1900c, 202).*†

Your wish will be fulfilled if you count seven stars in the sky on seven successive evenings (1900c, 201).*†

You can tell the future from tea leaves left in your cup by chance. Drink your tea, but do not look at the leaves left in the cup, since this will bring about misfortune, then turn the cup around three times towards you, make a wish, and put the cup on a plate. A soothsayer will point to the leaves with a knife or a pencil, never with the finger, and the position of the leaves will reveal the future (1905b, 20).*‡

People believe you can foretell the future from cards (1884a, 84).*†

FORGETTING THINGS AND RETURNING FOR THEM

"My wife went out the other day and forgot her parasol; she returned to get it, put her purse on the table, and left that. She came back a second time and sat down. 'Don't you want to go out?' I asked. 'Yes,' she answered, 'but first I have to sit down a while to break the spell'" (1913a, 44).*†

If you have to return to your home because you forgot something, you will have bad luck. To break that spell, you have to sit down for a minute without talking (1900c, 208).*†

If Black people in Arkansas have to return because they forgot something, they make a cross mark on the ground with their heels and spit onto it (1900c, 208).*†

Old Pennsylvania Germans are completely convinced that you will have bad luck if you must return to your house because you forgot something (1900c, 208).*†

If you leave an object in the house of another without that person's knowledge, you must return soon, whether you want to or not (1900c, 208).*†

THIEVES

The way to fix a thief to a certain place, so that he has to stay there and hand over the stolen goods, is only known in Cambria County, Pennsylvania, and it is only practiced among the Germans who immigrated to that area or were born there (1903, 66).*§

American thieves and robbers are superstitious. None would work on a Friday or on the thirteenth of the month. Knortz gives an example from New York in the 1870s, where the thieves who did not follow this traditional belief were caught. Knortz also talks about Dan Kelly from Kentucky, who was caught and killed on December 13 in Louisville while breaking into a bank (1913a, 123–4).*§

If an experienced thief meets a black cat and soon afterwards a blind dog, he turns back at once and postpones his break-in to another day. For example:

> In 1882, Frank Mc Cormack, James Leonard, Tom Freemont, and Mike Duffy agreed to break into the well-filled safe of the flour plant in Lockport. Everything was favorable. The passing night train would muffle the noise of the explosion. On the night they sneaked through the railway tunnel to the factory, a black cat appeared suddenly. Duffy said to Leonard, "Count me out; I am going home," and he left. The three others broke into the safe. At that moment, guards came and shot at them. Freemont and Leonard were mortally wounded, and Mc Cormack got the chance to experience the Auburn jail for six years (1913a, 124).*§

Ghosts, Witches, and the Devil

Dogs can see ghosts (1905b, 46).*‡

Two brooms placed crosswise in front of the door will keep witches away (1900c, 202).*†

If a housewife's dough does not rise, it is not the yeast's fault; a witch has secretly bewitched the dough. A big fire is lit in the house to undo the charm (Pennsylvania) (1884a, 84).*†

If somebody has a sore on his hand, he asks a wise woman to blow on it, and it disappears within a few hours (Pennsylvania) (1884a, 84).*†

Knortz often quoted newspaper reports about ghosts and haunted houses. The following is an example:

> "This morning, a nervous Oliver Harring hurried to his lawyer and told him that the house on Broadway where he had

moved six days before was haunted. During the first night his family had been prevented from sleeping, since there was loud shrieking underneath the house. This hair-raising disturbance had gone on every night. One night they all had got up and had seen how a woman dressed in white had constantly moved from one corner to another and finally had disappeared in the oak floor. Once the ghost even had pulled all the blankets from their beds and dragged their mattresses to the floor (From Fort Wayne, Indiana, January 17, 1895) (1900b, 157).*§

The belief in ghosts, spirits, and witches still abounds in America. Knortz tells of a few of these events, which he heard from the people affected by them, or which he took from newspapers or from hearsay:

The belief in witches recently erupted in a violent way in a district in the mountains of Raleigh County, West Virginia. It happened in a little settlement on the Clark River near the Lawson post office among people, who ordinarily are on a higher cultural level than most of the inhabitants of the mountains in the South. According to the report of a Presbyterian missionary, four children of a certain Griffith Jarell, a ten-year-old boy and three girls between eleven and fifteen, became sick, suffering from strange convulsions. Soon everybody in the neighborhood believed they were bewitched. The boy not only affirmed this, but even named as witches an old man, Blizzard, and an old woman, Likens, who lived in the mountains. At once the superstitious parents called a witch doctor. He declared, after having performed all kinds of hocus-pocus, that it was, indeed, an act of witchcraft and that he was able to undo the spell. Murmuring terrible incantations, he cast a silver bullet with which the neighbors were to shoot the witches in effigy. For this purpose two human figures were formed and put up against Jarell's barn, and the shooting started. The figure representing the old Blizzard was hit by every shot, but supposedly nobody was able to hit the effigy of Mrs. Likens. This was, of course, more proof that she had a pact with the devil, and they decided to kill her. The men surrounded her house, and the woman doubtless would have lost her life had she not noticed their coming and fled into the forest. Nobody has seen her since. When the men returned without success, the sorcerer decided to use another method to rid Jarell's children of the evil spell. He filled a bottle with water, pins, and needles, corked it tightly, and put it on the fire. "As soon as the water boils, someone will come and ask a favor. Whoever it is, has bewitched the children." As was to be expected, the bottle could not withstand the pressure of the steam and burst with a loud bang. The needles were thrown into the crowded room. At that moment Blizzard came in and asked for some shooting equipment. He was lucky that nearly all the people had been hit by needles and were busy taking them out of their wounds. The old man certainly would have been killed, but thus Blizzard could flee. These incidents fueled the emotions in the settlement, and Jarell's neighbors suggested calling on a sorcerer who lived high up in the mountains. Jarell did so, and the sorcerer promised to do what he could to lift the spell from the children, adding he would need nine days of preparation. Meanwhile, the news of this madness had reached the Raleigh Court House and the physician, Daniels. He came with Dr. Humble and cured the children. But the conviction that the children had been bewitched could not be eliminated among their peers, and soon other children suffered from similar convulsions; it probably was psychic contagion. Little Jarell made things worse by telling a boy named James Shepherd that he, too, had been bewitched and never would be healed. James was seized with convulsions, became mad, and had to be taken to the mental hospital (1913a, 67–9).*§

Knortz also speaks about a recent event in Philadelphia :

A few days ago when a Black woman, Marian Craig, cleaned the marble stairs in front of her house, an elderly Black man approached her and said he could see from the look of the stairs that great confusion and much misfortune would befall the inhabitants of this house. However, he could prevent this from happening if he went to Mount Olvet Cemetery during the night, gathered roots and herbs from there, and brewed a drink which could ban the evil ghosts. Marion got frightened and told him, when he asked five dollars for his trouble, that she did not have that much money at home. She said she could give him twenty-five cents, and she would give him the rest later. When the Black man, who called himself "Professor

Howard," was gone, the affair seemed suspicious to her and she notified the detectives Hamm and Eckstein. They advised her to take the magic, but to defer the payment to the next day. When Howard came to get the money, he was apprehended. Howard had given her an amulet, a little bag with a calf's hair and a chicken foot, to be worn over her heart, and a bottle with a mixture of carrots, cabbage, bones, and water, to be placed under her pillow (1913a, 69–70).*§

Knortz reports what he read in an American newspaper in 1904:

"Since Mrs. Mary Leib possesses a white cat and a black dog, she was accused by her neighbor, Mrs. Cora Hiney, of being a witch, whose evil eye had caused the death of her child. Mrs. Leib sued her for damages. During the process hair-raising accusations came to light. The neighbor insisted that the cat and the dog were bewitched children, that the animals talked in human voices at midnight, and that their fur sparkled" (1913a, 73).*§

Knortz gives an example from Pennsylvania:

In Empire, a suburb of Wilkensbarre, Pennsylvania, there once lived a certain George Evans, who looked very innocent although he was a dangerous sorcerer. Once he wanted to buy a cow from miner John Caffrey, and when the latter did not consent, the sorcerer said he should keep the old animal and he would see to it that nobody would give a cent for it. From that very hour, the cow did not give any more milk. Caffrey eventually went to Evans and asked him why he had bewitched the cow. Evans made a new offer which was decidedly rejected. Then the miner's wife and children got sick, but fortunately not seriously. Caffrey now told all his neighbors of his experiences, and Evans did not leave his house for a long time, for fear of being beaten to death (1913b, 22).*§

In 1898 the inhabitants of Richfield believed they were bewitched. A strange illness befell several families at the same time. The people could not sleep and lost weight. Some patients said they were continuously followed by black cats, which grimaced and meowed at the patients. While some rooms in their houses were inhabited by the evil spirit, others were free from them. Even horses, cattle, sheep, and pigs were supposedly hit by the illness. The horses became wild, running around as if mad, lay down, and died. The cows gave bloody milk, got weak, and expired. The feathers in the beds were bound into knots by invisible hands. People finally burned the beds to get rid of the spell, but they suffered from it for a long time (1913b, 24).*§

The owner of a sawmill in New England had to work late one evening. A black cat nestled against him and came so close to the saw that one of her claws was cut off. Later, when he came home, he noticed that one of his wife's fingers was missing. He knew then that she was a witch (1913b, 19).*§

Once when Daniel Smith from New England was churning butter but without success, he was convinced that a witch was in the chimney. He threw a few drops of milk into the fire. When he met Widow Brown the next morning, he saw that she was badly burned. He knew then that she was a witch and had tried to hamper his churning (1913b, 21).*§

Two miles north of Milan in Ripley county, southeastern Indiana, lives Red Hosia, a very wealthy cattle breeder. He is convinced of the destructive influences witches can have on people and suffers from an evil which could be called "witch mania." Every year he sends for a witch from Cincinnati, whom he hires for good money to spend a long time on his farm in order to drive away imagined ghosts and witches from all nooks and corners of the living rooms, the kitchen, and the basement, as well as the stables and the well . . . In 1898 some of his horses and cattle got sick. He wrote to Cincinnati. At once he got an answer to the effect that his animals had been bewitched and that the evil person had to be found. In the letter, a plan for finding the witch was spelled out. He was to cut out the heart of the first head of cattle that died, cook it, and to hang it near the road that led past his farm. According to the letter, the first person passing would be the one responsible for bewitching the cattle. Farmer Hosia did as he was told. The heart of a dead horse was so suspended, and the first person passing was Charles Arhenburg, a rich timber merchant from Milan (1913b, 36–7).*§

In New Mexico, a strange cat once appeared in the room of a bride and disappeared again. Soon after, an owl flew into the room and bit the young lady's face, and then it, too, disappeared. The wound did not heal until the bride had given a present to a witch with whom she had quarreled shortly before (1913b, 40).*§

Another witch turned a man into a woman and left him like that for months, until he gave her a present (1913b, 40).*§

A few years ago, Mary Duncan was imprisoned in Louisville for having attacked her neighbor, Regina Reisberg, with a big knife. She was convinced the latter had contact with the devil and was a witch. Mrs. Duncan once sneezed for a whole day; supposedly she found out that Mrs. Reisberg had hung thirteen pots full of red pepper under her window. She also maintained she saw the woman make mysterious signs while passing her door. She said she fell ill after that and was only healed by the prayers of her friend. Not enough that Mrs. Duncan found herself in the power of the woman with the mysterious abilities, but Mrs. Reisberg is said to have also tried her magic on the husband of the woman in custody, who, being a superstitious person, believed that a man will be bewitched if he has said "yes" to a witch three times. Since Mrs. Duncan feared that her husband would speak those fateful words, she took a carving knife, and while Mrs. Reisberg talked to Duncan, attacked her and injured her so badly that she had to be taken to the hospital (1903, 53).*§

A truthful woman in Washington, Ontario, told Knortz the following event:

One day a witch came to me and asked for some food, which I refused. Angrily, she left the house, went down the street, and, holding up three fingers, called my cows. Later, when I milked those cows, I realized that only one teat of their udders gave milk and that the other three were dry. Since this was repeated the next day, I asked the advice of a well-known sorcerer, who, happily, healed the cows with the help of sympathetic remedies. Another time, when my cows gave curdled milk, the sorcerer also helped. I had to pour the milk into a pan on a hot stove and beat it with a whip until it boiled; that cured the cow from the spell (1903, 54).*†

Mrs. Rhode Prince, who lived near Greenup in Kentucky and who died there at an old age in 1895, told Knortz that she had been bewitched some years before. Under the influence of a mysterious being, she had rushed into the garden, had eaten grass like a cow, and had calmly returned to her house as if nothing had occurred. Supposedly she often went to the barn, and, behaving like a hen, scraped the floor looking for grain. Once she believed she was a goose and wanted her feathers to be plucked. When her request was not granted, she dashed out of the house, took off her clothes, and hid them in a barrel. Then she waded into a creek and acted like a goose. Once, when she played the role of a cat climbing a tree, she fell down and broke a leg. Every night she put three Bibles and two pairs of scissors under her pillow. If somebody secretly took those things away, she woke up suddenly, flailed her arms wildly, as if she fought against an invisible enemy, and only calmed down when the objects were restored to their place. People regarded her as a witch, but in reality she was insane (1905b, 36).*†

In 1895, there lived a bewitched lady in Portsmouth, Ohio, who sometimes ran into a cornfield and ate fresh corn from the stalks. Then she ran home and fell into a deep sleep. When she woke up, she always said a strange woman had appeared, had led her into the field, and turned her into a horse (1905b, 36–7).*‡

Belief in the devil is still widespread. Knortz gives a few examples, some of which had happened only a short time before:

In 1896 there lived a man in the Italian district of New York, whom people anxiously tried to avoid and whose wishes they did not dare to ignore. The police knew this and suspected that the man was a prominent member of the secret criminal society, the Mafia. Thus, they watched his every step but they could not find a reason to arrest him. Finally they did, however, and the feared Italian went to prison. When they looked through his few belongings, they found, among other things, a contract between him and the devil. It was signed with blood, and the devil promised him impunity for every crime. Now the influence of the devil was broken, and, later, the Italians who met him no longer grasped their crucifixes (1902b, 130).*§

In 1898, in the house of the rich citizen George Coleman in Lancaster, Pennsylvania, the devil was driven out of a sick child with the help of a quack doctor and a group of noisy women. For weeks the child of Coleman's married daughter had been severely ill. He suffered from a kind of consumption. The physicians had not been able to explain the cause of his illness. A wise woman in the neighborhood whispered to the anxious mother that the child was bewitched and that he had the devil in his body. In superstitious fear, she called a sorcerer to drive the devil away. Murmuring mysterious incantations, the sorcerer began his work. In the sick room he released a black cat from a sack, explaining that the devil had now moved out of the child and into the cat. The people listened to him, believing and fearful. He then took the poor animal and called a few courageous men to quickly kill it and thus send the devil back to hell. While the women who stood around cried out loudly and the child began to weep, several shots hit the animal, but the cat could not be killed by the bullets. Finally, they had to cut off its head with an axe. After this miracle, the sorcerer declared the devil had returned to hell, but he cautioned people to be very careful or the devil would return and harm the child (1902b, 160).*§

In October of 1897, a sect of religious fanatics with approximately twenty members, called the "Holy Ghost Gang," was indicted in Lynn, Connecticut. They had kicked and nearly killed an old widow who suffered from rheumatism. They believed she was possessed by the devil and they wanted to free her from the evil spirit (1902b, 160).*§

SUPERSTITIONS FROM THE AREA AROUND TORONTO

The following items were collected from oral sources (1913a, 97–102).*†

A child will be born within a year in the first house into which a baby under the age of one is carried.

When you visit a baby for the first time, you must bring him a gift.

A baby should not be baptized with the name of a deceased relative.

If a bird flies into a room in the evening and circles the bed of an ill person, the person will soon die.

In Canada, if you wash your eyes with the blood of a bat, you will be able to see in the dark.

Schoolgirls count their buttons:
A doctor, a lawyer, a merchant, a chief,
A rich man, a poor man, a beggar-man, a thief
and many of them have sewn on an extra button or taken one off, not to become the wife of a chief or a thief. E

The girl who loves cats will become a spinster.

Those who shake hands across a coffin, will soon die.

If a couple on their way to the marriage ceremony meets a funeral procession, the bridegroom will die first [before the bride].

If you want a bountiful cucumber crop, you must put old shoes on your bed.

If you mend a dress without taking it off, every stitch means a new enemy. Further, if a knot appears in the thread while you do so, you will live until the dress is worn out.

If you hear ringing in your ear and you suspect that somebody is talking about you, wet one finger with your lips, move it crosswise over the ear, and say:
If you are good, God bless you;
If you are bad, the devil shoot you!E

Epilepsy is cured in the following way:

On a Friday you hang up a mouse in a church, burn it completely, put the ashes in boiling water, and drink the potion.

If the hens of an Irish woman in Canada don't lay enough eggs or if the fruit on the farm does not grow properly, she obtains an object belonging to a person with the evil eye and punctures it with needles; the evildoer then falls ill.

Whoever keeps peacock feathers in the house will have to call the doctor frequently.

Fingernails must not be cut on a Sunday:
Cut them on Sunday, your safety seek,
The devil will chase you the whole of the week. E

If the firewood does not burn, say:
If the wood defies the fire
You'll get something you don't desire.
It also means that the spouse or the lover of the person lighting the fire is in a bad mood.E

You may make yourself invisible in the following way: Steal a black cat and cook it in a tightly closed vessel filled with water. When the cat is tender, take its bones and one after another put them between your teeth while looking into a mirror. If suddenly you do not see yourself in the mirror anymore, then the bone you have just put in your mouth is the one that can make you invisible on any occasion.

You never should let a piece of iron lie on the road.

You must not leave a knife on the table overnight.

If you forget what you wanted to say, it was a lie.

The house in which somebody works on Ascension Day will be struck by lightning. When a woman mended her apron on that day, lightning suddenly flashed. Her neighbor advised her to hang the apron on a tree in front of the house. Hardly had she done so, when the tree was struck by lightning.

Whoever washes his feet with the first snow will never have corns or frostbite.

When traveling, whoever meets a cross-eyed person, a red-haired woman, or a white horse will have some disagreeable experience.

If a star falls, a soul returns to God.

If a table cloth falls to the ground and leaves behind a damp spot, a man will come to visit.

You must swallow your first teeth in order to get beautiful, white, and healthy second teeth.

Schoolgirls say:

If you stab your toe,
You'll meet your beau.ᴇ

There is a simple cure for toothache in Canada: After you have washed yourself, you first dry your hands and then your face with a towel.

If you read the first verse of the 121st Psalm early in the morning on a Sunday and then look out of the window, you will see your sweetheart cross a hill.

•S e v e n•

DREAMS

If you dream that you are eating beans, you will soon quarrel with your friends (1900b, 159).*†

Whoever dreams of a bier will have many friends (1900b, 163).*†

Whoever dreams of birds three times in a row can expect a generous inheritance within a year (1905b, 5).*‡

A dream of Blacks means illness or death (1913a, 21).*

Dreams of a butcher bring bad luck (1900b, 159).*†

If you dream that you are tending cattle, you will acquire great riches through diligence and energy (1900b, 160).*†

A dream of cattle brings money (1913a, 21).*

Whoever dreams of iron chains can be sure that his friends are trying to ruin him (1900b, 160).*†

Whoever dreams of a cistern will soon be in danger of his life (1900b, 159).*†

If you dream that you are wearing a white dress, you will be lucky in your endeavors (1900b, 159).*†

Whoever dreams of an eagle will soon leave for a long journey and make his fortune (1900b, 160).*†

A dream of falling presages illness (1900b, 160).*†

Whoever dreams of ghosts should expect inconveniences (1900b, 159).*†

If you dream of a certain girl three times in a row, she will become your wife (1903, 94).*

Whoever dreams of a white horse can expect great riches (1903, 26).*

A dream of climbing a ladder predicts a high rank in society (1900b, 160).*†

A dream of mice brings bad news (1913a, 21).*

A dream of onions brings good luck (1913a, 43).*

Whoever dreams of pictures will marry rich (1900b, 159).*†

A dream of snakes brings bad news (1913a, 21).*

A dream of snakes brings luck (1913a, 125).*

Whoever dreams of sunshine will be lucky (1900b, 163).*†

If you dream of tombs, you will soon attend a wedding (1905b, 7).*‡

Whoever dreams of bad teeth will soon fall ill; whoever dreams his teeth were pulled will soon die (1900b, 159).*†

A dream of toads brings luck (1913a, 125).*

Whoever dreams of water will soon have to mourn a death (1905b, 7),*‡

If you dream of a wedding, it is a sign of a misfortune, mainly of death (1913a, 21).*

Whoever dreams of a wedding should be prepared for the death of a friend (1903, 96).*

· E i g h t ·

FOREBODINGS AND

PARAPSYCHOLOGICAL EXPERIENCES

Knortz gives two separate forebodings about the death of a person who had lived at a far away place. Each was seen by a relative who recorded the time and date of the appearance. The forebodings were related to Knortz by schoolchildren in Evansville, Indiana.

There were two sisters; one lived in Wabash, Indiana, the other in Brooklyn, N.I. [*sic*]. Once it appeared to the former that her sister, who lived miles away, was going through her room dressed in a German national costume. She took down the date and hour and sent them to my father. A week later he received a letter, telling him that the woman had died, and exactly at the time when she had appeared to her sister (1900b, 168–9).*†

Some years ago my great-grandmother died in Germany. The night when this happened, my grandmother, who lives here, felt that her mother came to her bed, touched her with ice-cold hands, and said, "I have died now." My grandmother wrote down the date, and some weeks later, when we got the news that my great-grandmother had died, we found out that it had happened the very day she had appeared here (1900b, 169).*†

In 1897, the actor Rummel stayed in the same town [Fort Madison, Iowa] overnight. He was given a room in which had lain the dead body of a man who had been killed in a train accident. Rummel hardly was asleep when it seemed to him that somebody was shaking his arm while calling his name. When he woke up, the dead man was standing before him and asked him to write to his relatives in Beaver Falls. He furnished their names and addresses and asked Rummel to notify them of his sudden death. Rummel did so and, as he himself related, thus found out that the information which the ghost had given him was correct (1905b, 40).*‡

• N i n e •

CURES

You must not cut a birthmark because it could become cancerous (1909d, 72).*§

J. W. Jacobs, of Jeffersonville, Indiana, in 1896, could stop bleeding even from afar (1905b, 29).*‡

In southern Indiana, certain doctors heal burns by blowing on the affected part of the body and uttering a charm. They also use a divining rod to find springs and are consequently called water witches (1905b, 30).*‡

If you have a burn, do not tell anybody, but spit onto one of your fingers and put it behind your ear to soothe the pain (Maine) (1900c, 140).*

To get rid of a painful corn, you rub your toe four times in a row in the evening (Boston) (1900c, 140).*

If you want to get rid of your cough, put your fingers in your ears, hold your nose, and stand on your head until you are black in your face (New Jersey) (1905b, 24).*‡

If you suffer from a cough, put a few keys underneath your shirt and against your skin (1913a, 54).*§

To make sure that your child never will suffer from whooping cough, give him three teaspoons full of baptismal water at his baptism (Pennsylvania) (1884a, 84).*†

The fat of a dog will protect you from consumption (Chicago) (1905b, 24).*‡

In Virginia, Pennsylvania, Maryland, and other states, people try to find out whether a sick or suffering child has consumption. Three days in a row, a wise woman murmuring magic formulas measures the child from head to toe and then from one middle finger of his extended hands to the other. Then the thread that was used in measuring is suspended somewhere. If it rots within a certain time, the child will get well; otherwise there is no hope for recovery (1903, 113).*§

To prevent cramps, the Amish wear a steel ring on one of their fingers (1902b, 70).*§

To keep diseases away from your house, save an Easter egg from one year to the next (1900c, 206).*†

A lady who has bad habits or who has a drinking problem can be healed if someone secretly puts an egg into the coffin of a dead person. As the egg rots, the vice disappears (1900c, 206).*†

A drunkard can get rid of his addiction, if he slips an egg into the coffin of a dead person without anybody noticing it. As soon as the egg is rotten, he is healed (1913a, 52).*§

If you touch the rope with which somebody was hanged, you will not get epilepsy (Pennsylvania) (1902b, 71).*§

In Massachusetts you use saliva to heal an inflamed eye. Sometimes people also use the green vegetation floating on quiet lakes, which they call frog spit (1900c, 140).*

Whoever has weak eyes should wear a few amber beads around his neck (North Carolina) (1909d, 79).*

If you roll a spider web into a little ball and swallow it with some brandy, you will get rid of your fever (Indiana) (1910a, 109).*§

In eastern Massachusetts and parts of New Hampshire, it is customary to wet a finger with saliva and make the sign of the cross over a foot that went to sleep. Sometimes the saliva is rubbed under the knee to bring relief (1900c, 139).*

In New England you heal a child that suffers from gout by taking one of his hairs and burying it at a crossroads under a full moon (1909d, 32).*

Whoever suffers from a headache on the right side should take a comb that was made of the right horn of a ram and comb through his hair; if the left side hurts, a comb made of the left horn helps (1913a, 127).*

When you want to get rid of a headache in Kansas, fasten the rattles of a rattlesnake to your hat; if there are no rattlers, the skin of any snake will do (1909d, 7).*

If you want a certain person to get a headache, take his picture and bury it with the head downward (1905b, 24).*‡

Carrying a walnut in your pocket cures hemorrhoids (Pennsylvania Dutch) (1902b, 70).*§

Rhymes which help cure hiccups, used by American children:
"Hickup, hickup, go away!
Come again another day;
Hickup, hickup, when I bake,
I'll give to you a butter-cake!"

"Hickup, snicup,
Rise up, right up!
Three drops in the cup
Are good for the hickup" (1902b ,72).ᴇ§

If you want to cure somebody of jaundice in Indiana, put a louse in his bread without his noticing it. This remedy is also effective against dizziness (1913a, 127).*§

In the states of New York and Massachusetts, shingles are cured by putting the skin of a black cat on the affected area. It must, however, not have the slightest white spot. If you want a sure and speedy cure, the cat's head must be cut off and the blood poured into a cup and then onto the skin (1913a, 128).*§

Everywhere in America, but mainly in Virginia, people believe that the so-called madstone will heal poisonings. There are only a few madstones in existence. If you attach the stone, which is about as big as half a lemon, to the wound caused by a poisonous snake or a rabid dog, it sucks away the poison. After a while it falls off and is put into water, where it gives off the poison. This procedure is repeated until the stone no longer sticks to the wound (1905b, 32).*‡

Knortz gives three examples showing the use of a madstone:
In the provinces of Essex and London in Virginia, people strongly believe in the healing power of the madstone. Edwin Tyler from Aldie, Virginia, tells the following (according to a report in the New York World, May 12, 1895): "My grandfather Capt. James Smith, a Scotsman, came to Virginia in 1785 when he was twenty years old and settled in Richmond. He made several voyages to Australia and East India. While spending a few days on an East Indian island in 1804, a friendly native came to him and offered him, among other things, a little blue stone for sale. To demonstrate the value of it, he took a scorpion out of a wicker basket and made it bite a cat. The animal trembled and died within a few minutes.

Then a man put his arm into the basket and let himself be bitten by the scorpion. They laid the madstone on the wound, it stuck firmly to it, and when it fell off after some time, the East Indian man was as healthy as he had been before. When Smith asked the people where they got such stones, they answered that they were not allowed to tell him, or they would lose their lives, according to the laws of their country." Smith bought twenty of these stones, gave some to his friends in Richmond, and kept the others for his own use. One of them later came into Tyler's possession. It was one and a half inches long and a half to three quarters of an inch thick, was of a dark blue color, and resembled a flint stone. The owner maintained that he had successfully healed several persons who had been bitten by mad dogs and poisonous snakes (1905b, 32–3).*‡

Some years ago Jacob Crossler of Columbus, Ohio, whose son had been bitten by a mad dog, had him quickly taken to a certain Tilberry Crabtree in Beaver, who owned a madstone. When he arrived, the latter was in church. Crossler rushed to the church and went right up to him. Since everybody seems to have guessed the reason for this surprise, his action caused such an excitement, that the church was soon empty. Everybody wanted to witness the success of the madstone. The stone was of a light brown color and about two inches long and one inch thick. Crabtree placed it on the wound on the child's arm. It stuck to it like a leech for eight hours and twenty-five minutes. Then it fell off. The boy's badly swollen arm had its normal size again. When Crabtree died, he bequeathed this miracle stone to the executor of his will, David Hayes (1905b, 33–4).*‡

According to a newspaper report, R. R. Spradley of St. Louis owns a miracle stone which he calls the "Chinese snake stone." It looks like a piece of coal and is light like a sponge and very porous. He claims that it has healed many people, who had been bitten by mad dogs. From 1874 to 1877, when he traveled through Texas to survey land for the Texas Pacific Railroad, he cured many workers who had been bitten by poisonous snakes (1905b, 34).*‡

Mosquito and other insect bites are cured by putting saliva on them (1900c, 142).*§

You stop nosebleed by putting a cold key under your shirt and letting it slide from your neck down along your back (Pennsylvania Dutch) (1902b, 70–1).*§

A Bible under the pillow makes pain disappear. Knortz gives an example which he took from a newspaper in Toledo, Ohio, July 30, 1904:

At this moment a case that might be unique in medical science interests physicians and priests here. Thirty-seven-year-old Ernest Case, who lives at 1209 Greenwood Avenue and who has been severely ill for quite some time, feels no pain as long as the Bible is under his pillow. As soon as the "good book" is removed without his knowledge, the man suffers from hysteric convulsions and cries out with bodily pain. His face turns deadly pale and a nervous tremor runs through his whole body. When his wife, in the presence of a newspaper reporter, took the Bible away from his bed and hid it in another room, the sick man got up with closed eyes and went directly to the place where the book was. As soon as it lay under his pillow again, he calmed down and all pain seemed to have left him (1913a, 50).*§

If the Germans in Pennsylvania want to protect their children from quinsy, they cut some of their hair shortly after birth, put it in a hole they have made in a tree, and close up the hole with a wooden wedge. Until the children have grown tall enough to reach the hole with their head, they are safe from quinsy (1909d, 34).*§

In Pennsylvania, rattlesnake oil is a remedy for everything. It helps against glaucoma and other diseases of the eye. If a wart has not disappeared, after being rubbed with a living toad, bathe it in rattlesnake oil and cover it with a piece of pork overnight. Next morning, bury the pork on the long side of the house where water from the roof can drip on it. The person who buries it must not look back, or everything was in vain. Eye diseases of all kinds, including blinking of the eyes and cataracts, are treated with rattlesnake oil. If a foal is growing too slowly, some rattlesnake oil is put under its tongue. If a sick sheep cannot chew its food, it is given a little ball of sour dough bread and the inner green bark of an elder bush which was barked downwards and smeared with rattlesnake oil. Rattlesnake oil will help a person who was bitten by a rabid dog, but it has to be applied within nine days. Small strips of rattlesnake leather around your arm or wrist will rid you of rheumatism. If there is a case of measles in the neighborhood, camphor and asafoetida is sewn in a little bag made of rattlesnake skin. It is put around a child's neck and fastened with a string of the same material (Pennsylvania Dutch) (1905b, 28–9).*‡

Brandy neutralizes the bite of a poisonous reptile (1902b, 67).*§

Brandy protects you from the bite of a rattlesnake (1907a, 40).*§

American hillbillies even today prepare a medicine for rheumatism by putting the flesh of a rattlesnake in brandy, letting it sit awhile, then pouring the "bitter" into bottles; they drink the brew during damp weather (1913a, 66).*

In Ohio people believe they are safe from rheumatism if they carry around a chestnut (1905b, 35).*‡

A good remedy for rheumatism is to carry a walnut in your pocket (Pennsylvania Dutch) (1902b, 70).*§

You can protect yourself against rheumatism by carrying a buckeye in your pocket (1900c, 206).*†

To cure rheumatism, carry a stolen potato or a horse chestnut in your pocket, or put one of your shoes into the other and place both under the bed before you go to sleep, or always wear a red flannel shirt (1913a, 48).*§

A pair of scissors under the pillow is an effective remedy against rheumatism (1900c, 352).*

If a boy in Pennsylvania, Ohio, or Maine has run so fast that he got a stitch in his side, he picks up a stone, spits on its underside, and puts it back in the same place (1900c, 138).*§

A sty will disappear if you rub it with your wedding ring (Pennsylvania Dutch) (1902b, 70),* (1913a, 24),* (1909d, 72).*§

You get rid of a sty by rubbing your lid with a golden ring (1900c, 206).*†

In the Alleghenies, people rub a sty with three pebbles, put the pebbles into an envelope, and say, while laying it down on a cross-road:
Sty, sty, go off my eye,
Go on the next one who comes by! (1909d, 72).*E

Italians in New York recommend intercourse with adolescent girls as a cure for syphilis (1913a, 52).*§

If you want to make to your baby's teething painless, boil an egg, put it in your pocket, "happen" to sit on it in another person's house, and then smear the crushed egg on your child's jaw (Pennsylvania) (1884a, 85).*†

Human oil will help if you have a toothache, even a very bad one (1905b, 24).*‡

For relief from toothache rub the painful tooth with a blade of grass that was taken from a grave at sunset (1913a, 51).*

You can drive away toothache by putting a worm in tobacco and smoking it in a pipe (1913a, 51).*

John Burkley of Jeffersonville, Indiana in 1896 makes warts disappear by moving his fingers over them (1905b, 30).*‡

Germans in Pennsylvania drip some blood from a wart onto a piece of paper and then put it in an envelope. They expect that whoever finds the envelope will get the warts (1909d, 71).*§

Sometimes people rub their warts with corn, then wrap the corn in paper and put it somewhere; whoever picks it up gets the warts (1909d, 71).*

Whoever carries a horse chestnut in his pocket will soon get rid of his warts (1909d, 71).*

Some Americans make a cross with chalk inside the chimney. As soon as it is covered with soot, their warts disappear (1909d, 71).*

Washing your face with water in which eggs were boiled, gets warts (Georgia) (1909c, 71).*

Black people in the Southern states rub their warts with peas and bury the peas secretly in the garden (1909c, 71).*

You can get rid of your warts by rubbing them with a copper coin, which you then throw away (1909d, 71)*

In Maine you get rid of warts by rubbing them with stolen beans (1909d, 72).*

Rubbing the warts with salt makes them disappear, but you later have to hide the salt in a hole that you cut in a tree (1909d, 72).*

• Ten •

LEGENDS ABOUT GHOSTS
AND THE DEVIL

When Knortz wrote down legends about ghosts and the devil, he often added a skeptic or ironic remark of his own. Several examples follow.

An experienced spiritualist once told [Knortz] that for some time now ghosts have been forbidden to communicate. [Knortz] answered that it would be wise for them to act accordingly (1905b, 38–9).

The existence of ghosts is a vital question for the many media in America, for without them they had to look for honest employment. All the evidence they produced, however, bear the stamp of ridiculousness and automatically provoke sarcasm (1905b, 46).

Knortz also sometimes tried to find a reasonable explanation for apparitions.

The following legends are taken from Knortz's article "American Folklore" (1905b).

The Capitol in Washington is said to be haunted by fifteen different spirits and ghosts. At certain times the so-called Devil's Cat is seen. At first sight it looks like an ordinary cat, but the longer you look at it, the bigger it seems to get (39).*‡

As guards and servants who work there will tell you, ghostlike footsteps are often heard in the Statuary Hall, where the statues of famous statesmen are displayed, without anybody who could cause them being seen. People think that the sound is made by the ghost of President John Quincy Adams, who died in that room (39).*‡

General Logan's ghost, recognizable by his long hair, appears every night in the room where the Committee on Military Affairs meets. Between midnight and one o'clock he silently goes through the room, sneaks down the stairs, and disappears (39).*‡

Fort Madison, Iowa, a city of twelve thousand inhabitants, has a haunted house where a ghost with heavy steps walks nightly through each room three times, while doors and windows are locked. Nobody has ever seen him, but everybody has heard his steps (39).*‡

A good-natured old spinster, who had lived near Fairford in Alabama and who had worn glasses all her life, was buried without them by her adopted son after her death in 1896. She appeared to him every night until he opened the grave and handed her the missing glasses (41).*‡

In an old house near Washington's Crossing in New Jersey, where General Washington spent the night before crossing the Delaware, the heroes of his army gather during the bewitching hour and have a parade. As eye-witnesses confirm, they wear breeches with buckles, three-cornered hats, and are armed with swords and muskets (41).*‡

A railroad foreman who worked near Pierre in South Dakota died suddenly and was buried by his men on the spot. The people planted two cotton plants on his grave and were happy to see that they thrived well, while all other plants died, partly from lack of moisture, partly from the tropical summer heat. Once, when a prairie fire destroyed all other plants, the two cotton plants remained unharmed. This was attributed to the ghost of the inspector, who appeared every night to water them, according to people who say they have seen him (41).*‡

In Lambertville, New Jersey, the ghost of Rufus Williams, who had been murdered on Christmas day, appeared every evening and sawed wood between nine and twelve o'clock (42).*‡

In Washington Heights, near New York City, everybody has heard of the Townsend ghost. When Townsend, a widower who lived with his children in an apartment building, went on a trip for a few days, his seventeen-year-old daughter looked at the image of her deceased mother and noticed that the head of her mother slowly disappeared and in its place the pale and haggard face of her father appeared. When this appearance was repeated the next evening, the girl became very frightened and fled to a neighbor, who informed her that her father had died (42).*‡

Fifteen years ago, a ghost appeared every evening at a river dam in Kansas City. This event had the following origin: One evening a man, armed with a shotgun, had hid behind the dam to ambush an enemy. As soon as the latter appeared, he shot him. When he looked at the corpse the next morning, he found out that he had shot his own brother. After his death, which occurred soon after the shooting, the murderer wandered along the dam in the evenings. Another ghost in the same town, who haunted the ruins of the Santa Fe Stage Company, was once hit on his head by a heavy stone, after which the haunting stopped (43).*‡

Approximately three English miles from New Haven, Michigan, there is an abandoned hut on the land of farmer Brandel. Here, three fishermen once stayed. During the night they heard a noise as if rats were running through the room. This noise finally became so loud that it sounded like the footsteps of heavy men. At the same time, the hut shook so violently that they feared it would collapse. One man tried to open the door, and when he couldn't, he jumped out of the window and opened it from the outside. Since the fishermen now had a way out, they took heart and lit a lamp, but they could not see anybody. They spent the rest of the night in the forest nearby. The next morning, when they told the farmer about their experience, he apologized for not having warned them that the hut was haunted. Seventeen years earlier, an old recluse had lived in the hut. He caught bullfrogs for a city hotel and was considered very rich. One day he was found dead, with a bullet in his head. Ever since then, the strange noise had been heard. The murderer was never found (43–4).*‡

In the lowlands of the Tombigbee River, there is a small lake known as "David's Lake." On its eastern shore, there is a sawmill which belongs to the Seabord Lumber Company. Near it are a few huts, set apart for Blacks. Once, when the mill was closed for a long time, the owners left a Black man behind to protect it. One evening this man rowed his boat into the river to set out fishing lines. Unfortunately, he fell into the water and drowned. His successor left his post on the second day, and a third did not fare any better. Now, four courageous White men set out to protect the property of the company. At midnight they saw a ghost with a fishing rod sneak past the house. He untied a boat on the shore and rowed away. Two men followed him in a small boat, but could not catch up. Then they shot at him, but they might as well have shot at the moon. At last they heard a loud cry, and the apparition disappeared in the water. When the men later told friends about their adventure, it was suggested that they had had a few drinks too many that evening (44).*‡

Near Bardstown, Kentucky, there is an old hut made of roughly hewn tree trunks, in which a certain Holder lived during the Civil War. He was reputed to be a thief, a robber, and a forger, and capable of any crime. In the summer of 1859 a stranger, who evidently carried much money on him, passed the hut and asked Holder for the way to Cumberland Gap, where he wanted to meet his brother, who was interested in a few mines in the area. He called himself James Traverse. What information he got is unknown. A few weeks later his brother started looking for the missing man and found out that he had stopped at Holder's hut and then had disappeared without a trace. He hired a detective to investigate the case, but the policeman also disappeared suddenly and nobody knew what had happened to him either. Holder, too, disappeared and the hut stood empty for a long time. A certain Ross, a rough fellow, who later moved into the hut, used to hear someone call "hello" in front of his door around noon every day; but nobody could be seen. As soon as the call was heard, his dog would hide. John Ditzmann, a German who settled on the farm later, had still worse experiences. Every night a ghost came rattling into the room, sat in front of the fireplace, and poked the fire so vehemently that it looked as if he wanted to set the whole house on fire. Finally, a few citizens of Bardstown decided to investigate the whole matter thoroughly. Under the floor they found the skeleton of a man whose skull had been crushed. Certain characteristics suggested that they had found the remains of James Traverse. The ghost, by the way, appeared again later, several times (45-6).*‡

Knortz also speaks about Nell Hilton, who only appeared near Jonesboro, Maine, and who, among others, prophesied the most recent Spanish-American War. Nell lived in the eighteenth century. She was the daughter of a fisherman from the Puritan colony at Stockfish Cape. Later the family moved to a sparsely inhabited place where now the little town of

Jonesboro is located. Nell befriended the Passamaquoddy Indians in the area, and their chief proposed marriage to her. One day her father, who did not know anything about the chief, found the two in his hut and at once shot the Indian and took his scalp. When Nell told him that he had killed her bridegroom, he suggested she get her things and live with the Passamaquoddy Indians. Without saying a word, she left. She was honored as a queen among the Passamaquoddies, her advice was heeded, and she helped them as an English and French interpreter and the person in charge when they traded with the white man. In 1746 Nell prophesied a long and bloody war between the English and the French. Although she saw an English victory, she advised the Passamaquoddies to remain faithful to the French, since the French had treated them more humanely.

In 1759, after the war, Nell moved to Grand Falls, where she taught in a French school. On March 1, 1775 she returned and prophesied a new war. She even gave details, from the Battle of Bunker Hill to the surrender of General Cornwallis. In February 1777 she was captured by the English, accused as a spy for the Yankees, and sentenced to death. Before she was hanged, she promised to warn her countrymen whenever there was a threat of war in the future. On March 1 of the year in which war was to break out, she would appear on the rock that overlooks the sea near Jonesboro and is called "Hilton's Neck," after her family, and would sing the battle song of the Passamaquoddies. She was buried by the Indians on Dana's Heights.

In the early morning hours of March 1, 1812, two fishermen, Charles and Edgar Wass, heard her sing the battle song and, sure enough, three months later the war against England was in full swing. Nell also warned her people when the war against Mexico was about to be waged in 1846. James Burton and Abe Kilmody, two of the fishermen who watched the apparition, are still alive and ready to swear they saw and heard her.

On March 1, 1861, four days before President Lincoln's inauguration, she appeared again on Hilton's Neck at the appointed hour. Her long hair blew in the morning breeze and she moved her hands in rhythmic accompanyment to her battle song, which resounded loudly for more than half an hour. This time, all the people from Jonesboro were there to marvel at the apparition. Finally, some courageous men prepared to climb the rock and address the prophetess, when the figure slowly vanished like an image in the fog [condensed] (47–4).*‡

Knortz told several legends about the devil in *Streifzüge auf dem Gebiete amerikanischer Volkskunde* (Excursions in the Domain of American Folklore) (1902b). Many of them take place in countries other than the United States. Of the American ones, only a few examples are given here.

Many years ago, during a storm, the devil took possession of Eastport, a town on an island in Maine's Passamaquoddy and he left the impression of his cloven foot on a rock at the eastern edge of the town. This impression is still visible, and the inhabitants of Eastport, as well as the Penobscot Indians, who live nearby, avoid passing the place in the evening. The devil had come from the east and had first sat down on a high sandbank to survey his future property. The rock which his foot touched first and on which he imprinted the mark of his foot as clearly as if it had been chiseled, is close to the water. But even the highest flood does not reach it, and dew never moistens it. During the night, the outlines of the footprint are said to glow, and a pilot insists he saw the devil playing with lightning during the storm in which a Canadian ship was wrecked (137).*§

In the same town a young German by the name of Heinrich Schmidt is said to have been imprinted with a sign by the devil. He lived with his mother and siblings in a strange little house at the edge of town. His father spent most of his time at sea. One night the town was hit by such a storm that the hut was shaking all over. A heavy weight fell on his mother's breast. The children, who slept in the same room, seemed not to be injured. The next morning, when the mother examined Heinrich's breast, she found, however, a sign which looked like a cloven foot. According to most recent news, the young man still has the sign on him (137).*§

Eliza Lasky, a poor widowed washerwoman who lived in the same town, had an eleven-year-old daughter who was so malicious that she once loosened the door sill to make her mother fall over it. The mother called out angrily: "You are no longer my daughter; the devil shall get you." A short time later, the girl sat in front of the door and laughed and joked, as if she was playing with somebody. There was, however, nobody to be seen near her. "Who is with you?" asked the mother. "The little devil is sitting beside me, don't you see him?" The mother cried out so loud that the neighbors heard her and came running. When they looked at the child more closely, they realized that she was dead (138).*§

To my knowledge, Eastport is the American town which is richest in stories about the devil. The best known certainly is this one: About twenty years ago, a foreign schooner wrecked on the shore. On it were three persons who did not speak English: an earnest-looking sick old man; an old, deaf Gipsy woman; and a beautiful, Spanish-looking woman. When they were rescued, they had no food, but since the young woman made a good impression everywhere, nobody was sparing of support for the people in need. The three moved into a shabby hut about a mile from Eastport in an area known as Cove Beach. Close by lived the rich farmer, Macdonald. The two women began fishing and tried to feed themselves as well as possible. One day, when it became known in the town that the old man was severely ill, a doctor hurried to see him. The old woman was bending over the fire to get warm, and the young woman was standing in the middle of the room, trembling from fear. On one side of the wall there were three beds, and in the uppermost there lay the patient. From the ceiling hung a shining sword in a richly decorated sheath. Since none of the three took any notice of the doctor, he left again. In front of the door he met a young man who greeted him in a friendly manner and then entered the hut. He had a long brown beard and wore closely fitting trousers, a green jacket, and a strange hat with a long feather. The doctor waited near the hut for the stranger to leave, to hear some details about the well-being of the old man. He waited in vain for a long time, then went into the hut again. He saw the old woman sitting in a corner, murmuring senselessly. The young woman lay on the floor, unconscious. The sword had fallen down and slit the throat of the old man from one ear to the other. Later the old woman told him in broken Spanish that the old man had been a pirate in Spanish waters who had once bribed the maid of the wife of a Spaniard who had mistaken him for an Englishman. The pirate had asked the maid to bring the Spaniard's wife on board his ship, and then he sailed away. In the course of time, the woman gave birth to a child, whom the unfaithful maid cared for. The Spaniard had long looked for the kidnapper of his wife. Finally he found him and a fight to the death ensued. The deceived husband lost all his men and eventually was killed himself. When his rightful wife saw this, she jumped into the sea. Now the victorious pirate sailed on and finally landed here, where he was killed by the sword which he had taken from the Spaniard. The evil old man was buried in Cove Beach, where his grave can be seen to this day. The strange young man who sometimes visited him is assumed to have been the devil (138–40).*§

· E l e v e n ·

SONGS

Father and I went down to camp,
Along with Captain Gooding;
And there we saw the boys and gals
As thick as hasty pudding.

Cornstalks twist your hair,
Cart wheels roll around ye,
Fiery dragon carry you off
Mortar pestle pound ye.

Yankee Doodle be a man,
Yankee Doodle dandy,
Yankee Doodle kiss the girls
Sweet as 'lasses candy.'

There are also these additional verses:

Yankee Doodle came to town,
On a little pony,
He stuck a feather in his cap,
And called him Macaroni.

And there was Captain Washington,
And gentlefolks about him;
They say he's grown so 'farnal pound,
He will not ride without 'em.

(1907a, 36–7).§
"Farnal pound" may mean infernal[ly] proud.

NEGRO SONGS

Knortz collected the following sixteen Negro songs mostly from oral sources (1902b, 244–51).†

1

Gabriel, blow your trumpet!
Lord, how loud shall I blow it?
Loud as seven peals of thunder,
Wake the sleeping nations;
Den yo' see pore sinners risin',
See the dry bones a creepin',
Far' yo' well, far' yo' well!

Den yo' see de world on fire,
Yo' see de moon a bleedin',
See de stars a fallin',
See de elements meltin',
See de forked lightin',
Hear de rumblin' thunder,
Earth shall reel and totter,
Hell shall be uncapped,
De dragon shall be loosened,
Far' yo' well, pore sinner,
Far' yo' well, far' yo' well!

2

Oh Deat' he is a little man,
And he goes from do' to do',
He kill some souls and he wounded some,

And he lef' some souls to pray.
Oh, Lord, remember me!

To find out whether somebody has stolen something, two chairs are put back to back, and a sieve is placed on top of them; then this rhyme is chanted:

3

By the Lord who made us all,
If John Doe did thus and so,
Turn, sifter, turn and fall.

4

I had a sister who lately died,
She fell from 'bundant grace supplied;
But she would go to de balls and play,
In spite of all her fren's would say.

A few days' sickness tore her down,
And death prepared her for de groun';
She called her mudder to her side,
Said, "Mudder, mudder, pray for me."

"No use, no use, I tole you so!
I can't do no good now, I know;
Tho' hell may ring with vengeance spite,
Christ will save your soul to-night."

This is a song from the Mississippi River:

5

The Natchez is a bully boat,
Hi-oh-ho,
She walks high on de water,

Hi-oh-ho,
De Captin, he's a clever man,
Hi-oh-ho,
And de mate is here from Georgia,
Hi-oh-ho.

6

Wish I was in Tennessee,
A-settin' in my cheer,
Jug o' whiskey by my side,
An' arms around my dear.

7

Oh, whare did you come from?
—Knock a nigger down—
Oh, whare did you come from?
—Jerry Miah Brown.

8

'Tain't never gwine to rain no mo',
Sun shines down on rich and po'.

9

Ole mis' she acted a foolish part,
She married a man dat broke her heart.

This is a plantation song:

1 0

Old master's makin' money now,
Jang gam a lang go hay,

We does it with the hoe and plow,
    Jang gam a lang go hay,
Dars old Be's gone to h—ll,
    Jang gam a lang go hay,
De niggahs hes sold nobody can tell,
    Jang gam a lang go hay,
Little piece of lean and a little piece of fat,
    Jang gam a lang go hay,
And the white folks grumble if you eat much of dat,
    Jang gam a lang go hay,
Wid all this trouble we all like ham,
    Jang gam a lang go hay,
An' raddah be a niggah dan a poo white man,
    Jang gam a lang go hay.

11

Ebo, Edmun, Simon Joe,
Ding that niggah what stole my oh,
Dat putyest sheep that was in my flock,
And Taggy stole my turkey cock.
    Old jawbone do go home.
Dar's ole marster promise me
When he died he sot me free;
Now old marster's dead and gone,
Here's dis darkey still hillin' up corn.
Old jawbone do go home.
    Jay bird up de sugar tree,
Sparrow on de groun';
Jay bird shakes de sugar down,
Sparrow pass it er 'round.

12

De Lord made a colored man,

Made 'im in the night;
Made 'im in a hurry,
An' forget to paint 'im white.

This song is a lullaby from North Carolina:

13

Dar'll be no mo' sighing, no mo' sighing,
O, no mo' sighing ober me, ober me;
An' befo' I'll be a slave,
I'll be carried to my grave,
An' go home to my Lord an' be free.

Dar'll be no mo' crying, no mo' crying,
O, no mo' crying ober me, ober me;
An' befo' I'll be a slave, etc.

Dar'll be no mo' weeping, no mo' weeping,
O, no mo' weeping ober me, ober me,
An' befo' I'll be a slave , etc.

Dar'll be no mo' slavery, no mo' slavery,
O, no slavery ober dar, ober dar;
An' befo' I'll be a slave, etc.

The following song originated during the Civil War:

14

No more peck o' corn for me,
    No more, no more;
No more peck o' corn for me,
    many tonsand [?] go.
No more driver's lash for me,
    No more, etc.
No more pint o' salt for me,

No more, etc.
No more hundred lash for me,
   No more, etc.
No more mistress call for me,
   No more, etc.

This song was sung by the fire brigade in Savannah, which consisted of Blacks:

15

Heave away, heave away!
I'd rather court a yellow gal than work for Henry Clay.
Heave away, heave away!
Yellow gal, I want to go, I'd rather court a yellow gal,
Than work for Henry Clay.
Heave away! Yellow gal, I want to go!

This song is addressed to the girls of Charleston:

16

As I went down the new-cut road,
I met the tap and then the toad;
The toad commenced to whistle and sing,
And the possum cut the pigeon wing.
Along came an old man riding by;
Old man, if you don't mind, your horse will die;
If he dies I'll tan his skin,
And if he lives I'll ride him agin.
Hiho, for Charleston gals!
Charleston gals are the gals for me!

As I went a walking down the street,
Up steps Charleston gals to take a walk with me.
I ke' a walking and they kep a talking,
I danced with a gal with a hole in her stocking.

• T w e l v e •

CHILDREN'S RHYMES AND SONGS

Said Aaron to Moses:
"Let's cut off our noses!"
Said Moses to Aaron:
"It's fashion to wear 'em" (1909c, 124).

April fool
Wash your face and go to school (1900c, 56).

April fool is coming
And you are the biggest fool a-running (1900c, 52).

April fool is past
and you are the biggest fool at last (1900c, 52).

If you love me, pop and fly;
If you hate me, lay and die.
[Said as an apple seed is put in the fire, to find out whether
your friends like you] (1900c, 198).†

Then [there] were two blackbirds
Sitting on a hill,
The one named Jack,
The other named Jill;
Fly away Jack,
Fly away Jill;

Come back Jack,
Come back Jill.
[In this children's game, you alternately lift up and put down your index fingers] (1909c, 155).

One, two, three
The bumble bee.
The rooster crows
And out she goes (1910a, 44).

One, two, three, a bumble bee
Stung a man upon his knee,
Stung a pig upon his snout
I'll be blamed if you ain't out.
[The last line sometimes runs< "Gracious Peter, you are out"] (1910a, 44).

One, two three, four, five,
Twenty bees in a hive;
Eight flew out,
And twelve flew about (1910a, 45).

De little bee suck de blossom,
De big bee made de honey,
De nigger wo'k terbacky, an'
De white man spen' de money (Blacks) (1910a, 45).

Burnie bee, burnie bee,
Tell me when your wedding be?
If it be to-morrow day,
Take your wings and fly away (from England) (1910a, 45) (1900c, 94).

Buff says Buff to all his men,
And they say Buff to him again.
Buff neither laughs nor smiles,

But carries his face
With a very good grace
And passes his broom
To the very next place.
Ha! Ho! Ha! Ho!
To my very next neighbor
Go, Broomie, go.
[Playing at forfeits] (1900c, 265).

Ding! dong! passing bell;
Fare thee well my mother.
Put me in my chip-chip-chap
Beside my darling brother.
My coffin shall be black,
Six angels at my back.
Two to sing,
Two to pray,
And two to take my soul away.
When I am dead and gone,
And all my bones are rotten,
Then this little book will tell
That I am not forgotten (1900b, 198).

Black eye, pinky-pie,
Run around and tell a lie,
Grey eye, greedy gut,
Eat the whole world up.
Blue eye, beauty,
Do your mamma's duty
[Sometimes the last lines are "Blue eye, beauty spot/New
York, forget me not"] (1900c, 291).

A cat may look at a king,
And surely I may look at an ugly thing
[Said if a child complains of being stared at] (1900c, 290).

Jack and Jill went up a hill
To fetch a pail of water;
Jack fell down and broke his crown,
And Jill came tumbling after (1896a, 8).

Monday for health,
Tuesday for wealth,
Wednesday the best day of all,
Thursday for losses,
Friday for crosses
And Saturday no luck at all (1907a, 7).

Lady bug, lady bug, fly away home,
Your house is on fire, and your children will burn (1896a, 25).

Lesson, lesson, come to me,
Monday, Tuesday, Wednesday, three,
Thursday, Friday, then you may
Have a rest on Saturday.
[Said by girls from New York] (1900b, 165).†

The north wind doth blow,
And we shall have snow,
And what will poor robin do then? Poor thing!

He'll sit in a barn
And to keep himself warm,
Will hide his head under his wing. Poor thing!

When the snow is on the ground,
Little robin redbreast grieves,
For no berries can be found,
And on the trees there are no leaves.

The air is cold, the worms are hid;
For this poor bird what can be done?

We'll strew here some crumbs of bread,
And then he'll live till the snow is gone (1913d, 277).

Rock abye baby upon the tree top,
When the wind blows, the cradle will rock,
When the bough breaks, the cradle will fall,
Down comes the baby, cradle and all (1896a, 19).†

Sam, Sam, the soft soap man,
Washed his face with a frying pan,
Combed his hair with a wagon wheel,
And died with toothache in his heel (Pennsylvania) (1909d, 45).

Spit, spat, spo,
Where 'd that go?
[If children in Massachusetts lost something, they spit on their hand, hit it with the forefinger of their other hand, and go off in the direction in which the saliva flew, to look for their missing item] (1896a, 49).

"Whistle, daughter, whistle,
And I'll give you a sheep."
"Mother, I'm asleep".
"Whistle, daughter, whistle,
And I'll give you a cow."
"Mother, I don't know how."
"Whistle, daughter, whistle,
And I'll give you a man."
"Mother, now I can" (1896a, 28).

In the foreword to his book *Folklore* (1896a, 3), Knortz wrote that the folk and children's rhymes which he was adding at the end, had been collected by him in the states of New York and Indiana and that few, if any, had been in print up to that time.

Fifty-Two Folk and Children's Rhymes from New York

(1896a, 59-73)†E

1

Acker backer
Soda cracker,
I love you.
Acker backer
Sweet cracker
One—one—two.

2

Ain't you mean?
You stole my ring,
You made my heart do
Tingl - a - tingl - aling.

3

Kitty is mad,
And I am glad,
And I know what to please her.
A bottle of wine
To make her shine,
And a nice little nigger to squeeze her.

4

Johnny had a fiddle,
He cut it in the middle
And - a - one - two -anel ago.

5

A doctor is a gentleman
Whom we pay three dollars a visit,
For advising us to eat less
And exercise more.

6

One - two - three - four - five -
I caught a fish alive.
Why did you let i[t] go?
Because he hit my little toe.

7

'T is raining,
'T is dropping,
The old man is hopping.

8

Here comes a lighter to light you to bed,
Here comes a chopper to chop off your head.
Last—last—chop!

9

Look up there
look down here,
See a little monkey
Sitting on a chair.

10

My father has a horse to shoe,
How many nails were in the shoe?

11

My mother uses
Pepper, salt, mustaw, cider,
Vinegar—vinegar—vinegar.

12

Rain, rain go away,
Come one [on] another washing-day,
Little Annie wants to play.

13

Chou-chou-chou-
Ching-ching-ching-
Chinaman, Chinaman,
Wou-wou-wou!

14

I-o—
Gipsy's toes,
Give her a kick
And away she goes.

15

"Have you got a sister?"

"Yes."
"A Black man kissed her."

1 6

The queen was in the parlor,
Counting out her money;
Jack was in the kitchen,
Eating bread and honey;
The maid was in the garden,
Hanging up the clothes;
Down came a blackbird,
Picking off her nose.

1 7

Knock at the door,
Nobody comes,
Knocked at the window,
Broke a pane of glass,
Down came a watchman,
Sliding on his ——

1 8

Five little squirrels
Sitting in a tree;
This one said: "What do I see?"
This one said: "I see a gun."
This one said: "Come, let us run!"
This one said: "No, let us hide!"
This one said: "I am not afraid."
Popp goes the gun,
And away they all run.

19

A horse ran away
Down Broadway.
Who let it run?
Johnny, catch a gun.

20

I had a little doll,
I stuck it in the wall,
That's all.

21

What comes after fifty-nine?
"Sixty."
Your father drinks whisky.
What comes after twenty-nine?
"Thirty."
Your face is dirty.

22

Nigger, nigger never die,
Black face and Chinese's eye.

23

Gipsy lives in a tent,
Can't afford to pay her rent.

2 4

A little boy was so cross,
So cross and cross that he turned
into a vinegar bottle.

2 5

He asks for ——
Is —— in?
She is not in,
She is not out,
She is in her skin.

2 6

Water, water, wild flower
Growing up so high,
We are all young ladies,
and we are sure to die,
Excepting ——.

She is the finest flower,
Wive [waive?] your shame,
Turn your back,
And tell your beau's name.

——is a fine young man,
He comes in the door with his hat in his hand.

2 7

Little redbird in a tree,
In a tree,
In a tree,

Little redbird in a tree,
Sing a song to me.

28

Fish in the water,
Hear what I say,
Could I but swim like thee,
Could I but swim like thee,
Hey—hey—hey—
I haste away.

29

Old Jim Brown was a funny old man,
He washed his face with a frying pan,
He combed his hair with a wagon wheel,
And died from toothache in his heel.

30

Aina, maina, mina, mo,
Catch a nigger by the toe,
If he hollers let him go,
Aina, maina, mina, mo.

31

I am a huckleberry,
She is a pudding,
She asked me to marry her,
And I said I could 'ut.

32

Two, two, two,
Buckle my shoe;
Four, four, four,
Knock at the door;
Six, six, six,
Pick up sticks;
Eight, eight, eight,
Lay them straight;
Ten, ten, ten,
A big fat hen;
Twelve, twelve,twelve,
We shall delve;
Fourteen, fourteen, fourteen,
The maids are courting.

33

One, two, three,
Mother caught a flea.
Flea died,
Mother cried,
One, two, three,
Out goes she.

34

What's your name?
"Putten tame."
What's your number?
"Cucumber."
Where do you live?
"In a lane."

Where was you born?
"In the cow's horn."

35

I hit you in the ear
With a glass of beer;
I hit you in the eye
With a pumpkin pie.

36

I tisk it,
I task it,
A green and yellow basket,
I sent a letter to my lover,
And on the way I dropped it,
Dropped it, dropped it.

37

The farmer in the dell,
Hey-o-the cherry-o,
The farmer in the dell.

The farmer takes his wife,
Hey-o-the cherry-o,
The farmer takes his wife.

The wife takes the child,
Hey-o-the cherry-o,
The wife takes the child.

The child takes the dog,
Hey-o-the cherry-o,
The child takes the dog.

The dog stands alone,
Hey-o-the cherry-o,
The dog stands alone.

38

One little piggy went to market,
The other little piggy staid home,
The other little piggy had roast steak,
The other little piggy had none,
The other little piggy went whee-whee-whee.

39

Your mother,
My mother
Live across the way,
One step higher
In Broadway.

40

Pussy in the ban-box
Don't you hear him holler?
Take him to the station house,
And make him pay a dollar.

41

As I went up the Silver Lake,
I met a little rattlesnake,
It ate too much of jelly cake,
That made its little belly ache.

42

Hay is for horses,
Seed (?) is for cows,
Milk is for babies,
None for the sows.

43

I got ten little fingers,
And ten little toes,
A sweet little mouth,
And a red little nose.

44

I had a little doll,
Her name was "hat,"
She would'ut wash the dishes,
She would'ut sweep the floor,
And she would'ut keep out of the candy store.
I made her wash dishes,
I made her sweep the floor,
I made her keep out of the candy store.

45

One for good measure,
Two for good treasure,
Three for the old cat
To die down dead.

46

The butcher, the baker,
The candlestick maker,
The[y] all jumped over a rotten potato.
A high swing,
A low swing,
A swing to get off forever—
Forever—forever.

47

Here's three butchers, three by three,
Call your daughter Emily.
We can't have a lodger here-o-here.
Here's three sailors, three by three,
Call your daughter Emily.
We can't have a lodger here-o-here.

48

I had a little dog,
His name was Snuff,
I sent him to the store
For a penny's worth of snuff.
He spilled my snuff
And broke my box,
And he would'ut bite you—or you—or you.

49

Here comes a crowd of jolly sailor boys
Who lately came on shore;

They spent their time in drinking lager beer
As they have done before.
As we go 'round—and around—and around,
As we go round once more.
And this is the girl, and a very pretty girl
Who lately came on shore.

50

There was a little girl,
She had a little curl,
It grew further—further—further
To her nose.

51

I know something I won't tell.
Three little niggers in a peanut shell;
One can sing,
The other can dance,
The third can sew a pair of pants.

52

As I went up the silver steeple,
There I met some crazy people,
Some were White,
Some were Black,
Some were o' the color of a gingersnap.
O-U-T spells "out,"
With a dirty dish towel
Turned inside out.

FORTY-EIGHT FOLK AND CHILDREN'S RHYMES FROM INDIANA

(1896A, 74-87).†

1

Rain before seven
Will clear up at eleven.

2

One, two, three, four, five, six, seven,
All good children go to heaven.

3

As I went up the hickory steeple,
There I met some funny people,
Some were White and some were Black,
And some were the color of a ginger snap.

4

As I climbed up the apple tree,
All the apples fell on me;
Bake a pudding, bake a pie,
Did you ever tell a lie?
Yes, you did, you know you did,
You broke your mother's tea-pot lid.
L-I-E spells "lie".

5

See a pin and pick it up,
And all day you'll have good luck.

See a pin and let it lay,
Bad luck you'll have all day.

6

There comes an old lady from Germany,
Germany, Germany,
With all her daughters around her.
One can knit, the other can sew,
Another can make a pretty white rose;
Say, won't you have one of my daughters ?
I take the fairest one I can see,
I can see, I can see,
And ——may come with me.

7

Poor Robin was dead and lay in his grave,
Oh, oh, oh!
There grew a fine apple tree over his head,
Oh, oh, oh!
The apples were ripe and beginning to fall,
Oh, oh, oh!
There came an old lady and picked them up,
Picked them up.
There Robin got up and gave her a thump,
Gave her a thump,
Which made the old lady go hippoty-hop,
Oh, oh, oh!

8

Red, white, blue,
Your daddy is a Jew.

Red, white, black,
Your daddy is a Jack.
Red, blue, white,
Your daddy smokes a pipe.

9

Speak to my back,
My face is engaged;
I'm a young lady,
And you're an old maid.

1 0

Joe, Joe
Broke his toe,
On the way to Mexico.
When he came back
He broke his back
On the big railway track.

1 1

(Joking question)
When does a rabbit sit on a stump?
When the tree is cut down.

1 2

(Riddle)
Up it goes white,
And down it comes yellow (an egg).

13

Twinkle, twinkle, little star,
I took a ride on the cable car;
The cable ran off the track,
I wish I had my nickle back.

14

Evansville is out of sight,
It got a car and electric light,
Tara-boom-de-ay.

15

I had a little dog,
His name was Jack;
I put him in the stable,
He jumped through the crack.

16

I had a little dog,
His name was Rover,
And when he died,
He died all over.

17

Nigger, nigger, never die,
Black face and china eye,
Crooked nose,
Crooked toes,
That's the way the nigger goes.

18

I got the key,
You got the lock,
I can trade back
and you cannot.

19

Fritz, Fritz,
Kartoffelschnitz
Ei, ei,
Kartoffelbrei!

[Fritz, Fritz,
Potato wedge
Ei, ei
Mashed potatoes] (Pennsylvania Dutch)

20

Papa!
What?
Stick your head in a coffee-pot,
And drink it out red hot.

21

Papa!
Hm?
Pigs say "hm!"

2 2

Mrs. Martin went up town
With a load of hay.
Mr. Martin came in a cart
And blew them all away.

2 3

My mother and father
Have gone to bed,
And left me up
To make huckleberry-bread,
So up the hill,
And down the hill,
Sweet-sour.

2 4

My wife and I crossed the river
On a hickory log;
My wife fell in,
The dog got wet;
We held on a little brown jug,
You may bet.

2 5

Harrison came along and spit in the gutter;
Cleveland came along and licked it for apple-butter.

2 6

Harrison is in the White House,
Drinking wine and pop;

Cleveland is in the alley,
Drinking up the slop.

27

Harrison is in the White House,
Cleveland is in the black;
Harrison comes out the front door,
Cleveland comes out the back.

28

(Joking question)
Did you wash your eyes out in the morning?
Yes.
How did you get them in again?

29

Do you like jelly?
Yes.
A punch in your belly,
Do you like bread?
Yes.
A punch in your head.
Do you like toast?
Yes.
A punch in your nose.

30

April's done past,
And you are the biggest fool at last.

3 1

How to spell New York.
A knife and a fork,
And a bottle with a cork—
New York.

3 2

Listen, listen,
The cat is p——,
Where, where?
Under the chair.
Run, run,
Get the gun.
O pshaw!
She is done.

3 3

(Joking question)
You know who is dead?
Who?
A louse on your head.

3 4

Bucket of wheat,
Bucket of rye,
Who ain't ready
Holler "I"!

35

Harrison is dandy,
Stuffed with candy,
Cleveland is rotten
Stuffed with cotton.

36

Dead rats
And pickled cats
Are good for the Democrats.

37

Ice cream and sugar lumps
Are good for the Republicans.

38

I know something I won't tell,
Three little niggers in a peanut shell;
One can sing,
One can dance,
The other can sew a pair of pants.

39

Tell-tale-tit,
Your tongue shall be split,
And every dog in your town
Shall have a little bit.

4 0

Jack sold his gold egg
To a rogue of a Jew,
Who cheated him out
Of the half of his due.

4 1

Old Humpty is dead and laid in his grave,
Laid in his grave,
Laid in his grave,
Old Humpty is dead and laid in his grave,
Oh, oh, oh!

There grew an old apple-tree over his head,
Over his head,
Over his head,
There grew an old apple tree over his head,
Oh, oh, oh!

The apples were ripe and ready to fall,
Ready to fall,
Ready to fall,
The apples were ripe and ready to fall.
Oh, oh, oh!

There came an old woman hippity top,
Hippity top,
Hippity top,
There came an old lady hippity top,
Oh, oh, oh!

She gathered the apples up flippity top,
Flittity top,
Flittity top,

She gathered the apples up flippity top,
Oh, oh, oh!

Poor Humpty woke up and gave her a knock,
Gave her a knock,
Gave her a knock,
Poor Humpty woke up and gave her a knock,
Oh, oh, oh!

4 2

Whatever happens twice,
Will happen thrice.

4 3

Ana, mana, mona, mike,
Barcelona, bona, strike,
Hare, ware, frowre, frack,
Hallico, ballico, we, wo, wack.
You are out.

4 4

When I was a baby,
A baby,
'T was this way and that way.
(Here you rub your eyes with your hands)
When I was a school girl,
A school girl,
'T was this way and that way.
(Here you slap your cheeks with your hands)
When I was a maiden,
A maiden,
'T was this way and that way.

(Your hair gets curled)
When I did get married,
Get married,
'T was this way and that way.
(Your hair is combed)
When I was a grandma,
A grandma,
'T was this way and that way.
(Taking snuff is imitated)

4 5

(Charm to make a sty disappear)
Sty, sty in my eye,
Go to the next that passes by.

4 6

Bread and butter,
Come to supper.

4 7

Quarrel, quarrel, go away,
Come along some other day.

4 8

A rainbow in the morning,
Sailor, take warning;
A rainbow at night
Is the sailor's delight.

MORE RHYMES COLLECTED BY KNORTZ (1902B, 270-7).†

Bat, bat,
Fly in my hat,
I'll give you a piece of monkey fat.
(A boy who sees a bat says this while holding up his hat.)

Star, star, shining high,
First one I have seen to-night,
Hope with will and hope with might,
Hope my wish will come true to-night.
(A girl says this when she sees the first star in the evening.)

Anna danna de da
Golla ralla me ma
Sida dida boma nida
Anna danna dix tus.
(Playing hide and seek.)

One, two, three, four, five, six, seven,
All good children go to Heaven.
(Playing hide and seek.)

(The following little song is dedicated to the fingers.)
This pig (thumb) went to market,
This pig (index finger) stayed at home,
This pig had a piece of roastbeef,
This pig had none,
This little pig cried wee, wee all the way home.
(Said while playing with the fingers.)

(If somebody is sick, children say)
Uncle John is sick in bed,
What shall we send him?
Three good kisses,
Three good wishes,

And a slice of ginger bread.
Where shall we put it in?
Take a piece of paper.
Paper is not enough,
Take a little saucer.

Rain, rain go away,
Come some other washing day.
(Said if it rains on the day you do your laundry.)

MORE CHILDREN'S RHYMES FROM INDIANA, ESPECIALLY

EVANSVILLE (1902B, 270-6).†

Sallie o'er the water,
Sallie o'er the sea,
Sallie o'er the blackboard
Cannot catch me.

As I climbed the apple tree,
All the apples fell on me.
Bake a pudding, bake a pie,
Did you ever tell a lie?
Yes, you did, you know you did,
You broke your mother's tea pot lid.
L-I-D spells the word lid.

The dude in the pickle,
John wants a nickle,
Climbing up the golden chairs.

Little Annie Rooney
Sitting in the sun,
Down went Mac Ginty,
Johnny catch a gun.

———is no good,
Chop her up for firewood;
When she's chopped,
Put her in a pot,
And eat her up for mutton-chop.

My mother has a fan,
And this is the way she opens it.

There was a crooked man,
He walked a crooked mile,
He found a crooked six-pence
Against a crooked stile,
He bought a crooked cat,
Which caught a crooked mouse,
And they all lived together
In a crooked little house.

Upon my word and honor,
As I went to Stoner,
I met a pig without a wig,
Upon my word and honor.

Little Tommy Pucker
Sang for his supper;
What shall he have to eat?
White bread and butter.
How shall he eat it
Without e'er a knife?
How can he marry
Without e'er a wife?

Mary, Mary, quite contrary,
How does your garden grow?
With silver bells and cockled shells
And pretty maids all in a row.

Shoe the little horse,
Shoe the little mare,
Set [let?] the little colt
Go bare, bare, bare.
Little Polly Flinders
Sat among the cinders,
Warming her little toes;
Her mother came and caught her,
And scolded her little daughter
For spoiling her nice new shoes.

Curly locks, curly locks, will you be mine?
You shall not wash the dishes, nor yet feed the swine,
But sit on a cushion and sew a fine seam,
And feed upon strawberries, sugar and cream.

Diddle, Diddle, Dumpling, my son John
Went to bed with his stockings on,
One shoe off and one shoe on,
Diddle, Diddle, Dumpling, my son John.

Handy, Spandy, Jack-a-Dandy
Loves plum-cake and sugar candy.
He bought some at the baker's shop,
And away he went hop, hop, hop.

I had a little husband,
Not bigger than my thumb;
I put him in a pint pot,
And there I bid him drum.

Cheap John, cheap John,
How do you sell your socks?
Wholesale, retail,
Five cents a box.

One for good measure,
One for good treasure,
One for the old cat
To die [lie?] down dead.
(Said when children swing.)

The butcher, the baker,
The candlestick-maker,
A high swing,
A low swing,
A swing to get off forever-forever.
(Said when children swing.)

Mrs. Marten went up town
With a load of hay;
Mr. Marten came in a cart
And blew them all away.

Whatever happens twice,
Will happen thrice.

One for the money,
Two for the show,
Three to make ready,
And four to go.

Here I stand on two little chips,
Come and kiss my sweet little lips.

Up went Mattie's hand,
Up went Pattie's hand,
Up went Freddie's hand, too;
But little Willie,
He was silly,
He didn't know what to do.

There came an old woman from Germany,
With all her children around her.
One could knit, the other could sew,
The other could make the lily white grow.

A lady who lived by the Niger
Went out to ride with a Tiger.
They returned from the ride
With the lady inside,
And a smile on the face of the tiger.

Don't steal this book, little rat,
For fear the owner may be the cat.
(Inscription in a book.)

Peter, piper, pumpkin eater,
Had a wife and could not keep her;
He put her in a pumpkin shell,
And there he kept her very well.

· T h i r t e e n ·

RHYMES

Take twelve kernels from an apple, give each of them a name, and while eating them say:

One I love,
Two I love,
Three I love, I say,
Four I love with all my heart
And five I cast away;
Six he loves,
Seven she loves,
Eight they both love,
Nine he comes,
Ten he tarries,
Eleven he courts,
Twelve he marries (1905b, 6–7).‡

If American or English children want to know whether a certain friend likes them, they throw apple seeds into the fire and say:

If you love me, pop and fly;
If you hate me, lay and die (1900c, 198).†

Said during a New Year's Eve game of bobbing for apples after having written three friends' names on pieces of paper and put them inside the apples:

Oh, apples ripe, oh apples three,
Please, tell me who my lover will be (1900c, 46).

A swarm of bees in May
Is worth a load of hay;
A swarm of bees in June
Is worth a silver spoon;
A swarm of bees in July
Is not worth a fly (1900c, 93).

Dream o' honey—lots o' money,
Dream o' bee—lib [live] at yo' ease (1900c, 94).

The following rhymes explain the significance of birthdays:
Sunday's child ne'er lacks in place;
Monday's child is fair in the face;
Tuesday's child is full of grace;
Wednesday's child is sour and sad;
Thursday's child is loving and glad;
Friday's child is loving and giving;
And Saturday's child shall work for its living! (1900c, 185).

or

Monday's child is fair of face,
Tuesday's child is full of grace,
Wednesday's child is merry and glad.
Thursday's child is sour and sad,
Friday's child is Godly given.
Saturday's child shall work for a livin',
Sunday's child never shall want,
That's the week and the end on't (1900c, 185).

Coffee grows on the white oak tree,
The rivers run with brandy;
My little gal is a blue-eyed gal
As sweet as any candy

Fly around my blue-eyed gal,
So fly around my daisy;
Every time I see that gal
She always runs me crazy (Blacks in Georgia) (1909d, 95)

Before fishing, beat the ground crosswise with a stick and say:
Bite, fish, bite,
Your mama said you might,
Your daddy said you must'nt,
So bite, fish, bite!

If the fish escapes, say:
Drop luck, pink and yellow,
Wish I had another fellow! (Blacks) (1913a, 65)

Bryan rides the white horse,
Mc Kinley rides a mule,
Bryan is elected,
Mc Kinley is a fool (1913a, 35).

White Christmas, a good harvest,
Green Christmas, a full graveyard (1902b, 172).†

When sowing corn the farmer sings:
One for the blackbird,
And one for the crow,
One for the cutworm,
And one for to grow (1900c, 207).†

The darkey viewed his new born boy
With feelings mixed with pride and joy,
Like newborn babes it had no hair
Or wool, its head was almost bare.
The babe began to squall—he fled,
"Great cry and little wool," he said (1907a, 16).

After a death has occurred, the windows are opened to allow the soul to fly out and this rhyme is repeated:

Open lock, end strife,
Come death and pass life (1900c, 205).†

Said to a lady bird:
Fly away East and fly away West,
Show me where lives the one I love best (1910a, 145), (1913a, 22).

Friday night's dreams on Saturday told
Always come true, be they ever so old (1900c, 188).

This Friday night while going to bed,
I put my petticoat under my head,
To dream of the living and not of the dead,
To dream of the man I am to wed,
The color of his eyes, the color of his hair,
The color of the clothes he is to wear,
And the night the wedding is to be (1913a, 149–50).

On a Friday she was launched,
On a Friday she set sail,
On a Friday met a storm,
And was lost, too, in a gale (1900c, 188).

A whistling girl and a flock of sheep
are the very worst things a man can keep.
A whistling girl and a crowing hen
always come to a very bad end (1905b, 35).‡

Whistling girls and crowing hens
Always come to some bad ends (1907a, 29).

In God we trust,
In Dakota we bust (1902b, 276).†

White horse, ding-a-ling-a-ling-
Where ever I go I'll find something (1900c, 200).†

Well, neighbor dear, in Jingleville
We live by faith, but we eat our fill;
An' what w'u'd we do if it wa'n't fer prayer?
Fer we can't raise a thing but whiskers an' hair (1909d, 52).

Whenever I marry
It will not be for riches,
But I'll marry a girl
That is six feet tall
So she can wear
The breeches (1907a, 7).

A girl turns her shirt inside out, puts some ashes on it, and
places it under her bed, saying:
Whoever my true love may be,
Come write his name in these ashes for me (1913a, 150).

A mole on the neck,
Money to the peck (1900b, 158).†

Moles on the neck
Money by the peck (1913a, 126), (1909d, 72).

Cut your nails Monday, you cut them for news;
Cut them on Tuesday, a pair of new shoes;
Cut them on Wednesday, you cut them for health;
Cut them on Thursday, 't will add to your wealth;
Cut them on Friday, you cut them for woe;
Cut them on Saturday, a journey you'll go;
Cut them on Sunday, you cut them for evil,
For all the week long you'll be ruled by the devil (1900c, 186).

Cut them on Monday, cut them for health,
Cut them on Tuesday, cut them for wealth,
Cut them on Wednesday, cut them for news,
Cut them on Thursday for a pair of new shoes,
Cut them on Friday, cut them for sorrow,

Cut them on Saturday, see your lover to-morrow,
But better had he never been born
Who on Sunday cuts his horn (1900c, 186).

There sprung a leak in Noah's Ark
Which made the dog begin to bark;
Noah took his nose to stop the hole,
And hence his nose is always cold (1907a, 45).

Granddaddy longlegs
Can't say his prayers,
I'll take him by the hind leg
And throw him down the stairs (Blacks in Maryland) (1910a, 108).

Oklahoma for Starvation,
Kansas for Desolation,
Texas for Devastion [sic]
Nebraska for Damnation,
Going to Ohio to sponge on wife's relation,
To hell with Democratic Administration (Seen on a prairie
schooner) (1902b, 276).†

See a pin and pick it up,
All the day you'll have good luck;
See a pin and let it lay,
Bad luck you'll have all day (1900c, 195).†

A heavy frost and a shower of rain
Meet together at the end of the lane.
Rain all day, and sunshine at four,
'Tis at an end, 't will rain no more (1900c, 206).†

Make a rhyme,
You will see your bean [beau?] before nine (1900c, 197).†

The rose is red, the violet blue,
Where you see three balls, you will see a Jew (1907a, 22).

As many grains of salt you spill,
So many days of sorrow you'll fill (1913a, 59).

I would I were a schoolma'am,
And among the schoolma'ams band,
With a small boy stretched across my knee,
And a ruler in my hand (1900c, 34).

Scotland grows the thistle,
England grows the rose,
Ireland grows the shamrock
And the sheeney grows the nose (Boys in Arkansas) (1907a, 22).

I stand my shoes in the form of a T;
Please let me dream who my lover will be. (New Year's Eve) (1900c, 45).

Point your shoes towards the street,
Leave your garters on your feet,
Put your stockings on your head,
You'll draw [dream?]of the man you are going to wed (1913a, 149).

If you wish to live and thrive,
Let the spider run alive (Massachusetts) (1910a, 107).

The meaning of a spider's color:
Black—sad,
Brown—glad,
White—good luck (Massachusetts) (1910a, 107).

Stumble with right foot—disappointment;
Stumble with left foot—you will meet a friend (1900c, 201).†

Sneeze on Monday, you sneeze for danger;
Sneeze on Tuesday, you kiss a stranger;

Sneeze on Wednesday, you sneeze for a letter;
Sneeze on Thursday, for something better;
Sneeze on Friday, you'll sneeze for sorrow;
Sneeze on Saturday, your sweetheart to-morrow;
Sneeze on Sunday, your safety seek;
The devil will have you the rest of the week (1907a, 29).

A little wife well willed,
A little purse well filled,
A little farm well tilled (1902b, 106).

If so be a toad be laid
In a sheepskin newly flayed,
And that tied to man, 't will sever,
Him and his affections ever (1913a, 26).

The bride should wear on her wedding day:
Something old and something new,
Something borrowed and something blue (1900c, 196).†

Married in white,
You have chosen all right.
Married in gray,
You will go far away.
Married in black,
You will wish yourself back.
Married in red,
You'd better be dead.
Married in green,
Ashamed to be seen.
Married in blue,
You'll always be true.
Married in pearl,
You'll live in a whirl.
Married in yellow,

Ashamed of the fellow.
Married in brown,
You'll live out of town.
Married in pink,
Your spirits will sink (1900c, 196).†

Wednesday is sometimes referred to as Weddinsday.

The best day for wedding:
Monday for health,
Tuesday for wealth,
Wednesday the best of all;
Thursday for losses,
Friday for crosses,
And Saturday no luck at all (1913a, 23).

Yarrow, yarrow, tell to me
Who my true love is to be;
The color of his hair,
The clothes he will wear,
And the day he'll be wedded to me (1905b, 6).‡

Put some yarrow into your mouth and say:
Yarrow, yarrow, if he loves me and I loves he,
A drop of blood I'd wish to see (1913a, 128).

On a Saturday evening the girls circle a big yarrow plant three
times and say:
Good evening, good evening, Mr. Yarrow,
I hope to see you well to-night,
And trust I'll see you at meetin' to-morrow (Massachusetts)
(1913a, 128).

•Fourteen•

RIDDLES

Knortz collected the following one hundred fifty riddles and word games mainly in Indiana (1902b, 210–40).†To them he added many European variants, mostly written in German, which are not included here. The American riddles are usually in English; if not, a translation is given. With few exceptions, the correct answer was written in German by Knortz; the answers are in italics.

1

Up it goes white and down it comes yellow.
An egg. *

2

If he come, he no come; if he us [not?] come, he come!
(If the crow comes, the corn does not come; if the crow does not come, the corn comes) * (Blacks in South Carolina).

3

Two legs sat upon three legs with one leg upon his lap. In came four legs and carried off one leg. Up jumped two legs, threw three legs at four legs, and makes [made] him bring back one leg.
A man sat on a three-legged stool, gnawing on a bone; his dog came in

and stole the bone. Then the man threw the stool at the dog and made him return the bone. *

4

What is that with one leg and one eye?
A sewing needle. *

5

Little May Margery sat on a tree, a stone in her throat, and a cane in her hand, and a red dress.
A cherry. *

6

Wos get de Stehk nuf un ragt se net a?
[What goes up the stairs and does not touch them?]
Smoke * (Pennsylvania Dutch).

7

Something goes round and round the house, peeps in every crack, yet no one sees it. What is it?
The wind. *

8

Twenty-four horses on a red hill,
Now they go, now they go,
Now they stand still.
Teeth. *

9

Patch on patch and a square hole in the middle.
A chimney. *

1 0

Humpty Dumpty sat on a wall,
Humpty Dumpty had a great fall;
All the king's horses and all the king's men
Could 'ut put Humpty Dumpty together again.
An egg. *

1 1

Throw it up straight and come down cross.
A pair of scissors. *

1 2

A green and a white house,
Inside of that green and white house is a red house;
Inside of that red house are all little niggers.
A watermelon. *

13

Black and white and red (read) all over.
A newspaper. *

1 4

A man rode across the bridge, and yet—he walked. How was that?
Yet was the name of his dog. *

15

There is a rickety hill, on this rickety hill stands a rickety house, in the rickety house is a rickety room, in the rickety room is a rickety table, on the rickety table is a rickety cup, in the rickety cup is something every one's got; what is it?
Blood. *

16

Which is the heaviest, one sack of flour or two sacks?
One sack of flour is heavier than two empty sacks. *

17

Small at the top, large at the bottom, something in the middle goes flip-pity-flop.
A churn. *

18

Wer es macht, der sagt es nit,
Wer es nimmt, der kennt es nit,
Wer es kennt, der will es nit.
[Whoever makes it, does not say so,
Whoever takes it, does not know it,
Whoever knows it, will not have it.]
Counterfeit money * (Pennsylvania Dutch).

19

Round as a biscuit,
Busy as a bee,
Prettiest little thing

I ever did see.
A watch * (cf. also 1900c, 94).

2 0

There is a yard with a fence around it; inside there is a white horse. The gate to this yard is open; how will the horse come out?
White. *

2 1

A man entered a store and there met a young man whom
he greeted very pleasantly. The store keeper asked him
if he knew the young man and received this reply:
Sisters and brothers have I none,
Yet this man's father was my father's son.
What relation are we?
The young man was the son of the older man. *

2 2

Riddeldy, riddeldy ro-te-tot,
I met a man with a little red coat,
A stick in his hand, a stone in his throat,
Riddeldy, riddeldy ro-te-tot.
A cherry. *

2 3

Black within,
Red without,
Four corners round about.
A chimney. *

24

As I was going to St. Ives,
I met a man with seven wives,
Each wife had seven sacks,
Each sack had seven cats,
Each cat had seven kits;
Kits, cats, sacks, wives,
How many were going to St. Ives?
Only one. *

25

As I was going across the bridge
I met my sister Anne,
Cut off her head and sucked the blood,
And left the body stand.
A bottle of wine. *

26

Something goes through a keyhole
Where nothing else can go through.
A key. *

27

What travels fastest, heat or cold?
Heat, because you can easily catch cold.

28

This riddle is of Old English origin. A young girl has been persuaded by her
false lover, who wants to rob and murder her, to meet him in the forest at

night. She comes early and climbs a tree to be safe from animals. Her lover arrives with another man and digs a grave. When she doesn't come, they leave. Next morning, when her lover complains to her for not coming, she says:

Riddle me, riddle me right,
Guess where I was last Friday night?
The bough did bend, my heart did quake,
When I saw the hole the fox did make.

29

It can run and can't walk,
It has a tongue and can't talk.
A carriage. *

30

Hippy, tippy, up stairs,
Hippy, tippy, down stairs;
If you go near hippy tippy, he'll bite you.
A wasp. *

31

East and west and north and south,
Ten thousand feet and never a mouth.
A flax comb. *

32

Flour of Virginia, fruit of Spain,
Met together in a shower of rain;
Put in a bag tied round with a string,
If you tell me this riddle, I'll give you a pin.
Plum pudding. *

33

Thomas A'Tattamus took two *T*s,
To tie two tups to two tall trees;
To frighten the terrible Thomas A'Tattamus!
Tell me how many *T*s there are in all t h a t.
There are two T*s in* that. *

34

A riddle, a riddle, a [s?] I suppose,
A hundred eyes, and never a nose.
A sieve. *

35

In marble walls as white as milk,
Lined with a skin as soft as silk;
Within a fountain crystal clear,
A golden apple doth appear.
No doors there are to this stronghold—
Yet thieves break in and steal the gold.
An egg. *

36

My true love lives far from me,
Many a rich present he sends to me.
He sent me a goose without a bone,
He sent me a cherry without a stone.
He sent me a Bible no man could read;
He sent me a blanket without a thread.
How could there be a goose without a bone?
How could there be a cherry without a stone?

How could there be a Bible no man could read?
How could there be a blanket without a thread?
When the goose is in the egg-shell there is no bone;
When the cherry is in the blossom there is no stone.
When the Bible is in the press no man it can read;
When the wool is on the sheep's back there is no thread.

37

What shoemaker makes shoes without leather,
With all the four elements together?
Fire and water, earth and air;
Ev'ry customer has two pair.
A horseshoer.

38

Round as a hook
Deep as a cup,
All the king's oxen
Can't pull it up.
A well. *

39

Long legs, crooked thighs,
Little head, and no eyes.
A pair of scissors. *

40

Nanney, nanney, nanney goat,
With a little petticoat;
The longer she stood the shorter she grew,

And when she died she had a black nose.
A tallow candle. *

41

What is it: First as white as milk, then as red as blood,
and then as black as ink?
A blackberry. *

42

The beginning of every end,
The end of every place,
The beginning of eternity,
The end of time and space.
The letter E. *

43

Round as a marble, green as grass.
A green grape. *

44

I was walking through a field of wheat,
I fished up something good to eat;
It was neither fish, flesh, nor bone,
But I kept it till it ran alone.
An egg, hatched. *

45

Before Luke, behind Paul,
Girls have one and boys none at all.
The letter L. *

46

A house with no windows and no doors and with a good
strong wall, and yet thieves break in and steal the gold.
An egg. *

47

Old Mother Twichet had but one eye,
And a long tail which she let fly;
And every time she went over a gap,
She left a piece of her tail in a trap.
A needle and thread. *

48

I went to the wood and got it,
I sat me down and looked at it,
The more I looked at it the less I liked it,
And brought it home because I couldn't help it.
A thorn. *

49

I'm in every one's way,
but no one I stop;
My four horns every day
In every way play,
And my head is nailed on at the top.
A turnstile.

50

Hoddy-doddy,
With a round black body;

Three feet and a wooden hat:
What's that?
An iron cooking pot. *

51

There was a little green house,
And in the little green house
There was a little brown house,
And in the little brown house
There was a little yellow house,
And in the little yellow house
There was a little white house,
And in the little white house
There was a little heart.
A walnut. *

52

A flock of white sheep
On a red hill;
Here they go, there they go,
Now they stand still!
Teeth and palate. *

53

As I was going o'er London Bridge [in New York they say "Brooklyn
Bridge"],
I met a cart of fingers and thumbs.
Gloves. *

54

Lives in winter,
Dies in summer,'
And grows with its root upwards.
An icicle. *

55

I have a little sister, they call her peep, peep;
She wades the waters deep, deep, deep;
She climbs the mountains high, high, high;
Poor little creature! She has but one eye.
A star. *

56

Hick-a-more, Hack-a-more,
On the king's kitchen-door;
All the king's horses,
And all the king's men,
Couldn't drive Hick-a-more, Hack-a-more,
Off the king's kitchen-door!
Sunshine. *

57

Black we are, but much admired;
Men seek for us till they are tired,
We tire the horse, but comfort man,
Tell me this riddle if you can.
Coals. *

58

Higgeldy piggeldy
Here we lie,
Picked and plucked,
And put in a pie.
My first is snapping, snarling, growling,
My second's industrious, romping and prowling.
Higgeldy piggeldy
Here we lie,
Picked and plucked,
And put in a pie.
Currants: curr + ants = *dog and ants.* *

59

What God never sees,
What the king seldom sees,
What we see every day:
Read my riddle, I pray.
A peer. *

60

When I was taken from the fair body,
They then cut off my head,
And thus my shape was altered.
It's I that make peace between king and king,
And many a true lover glad.
All this I do and ten times more,
And more I could do still;
But nothing I can do
Without my guider's will.
A quill [pen]. *

6 1

The land was white,
The seed was black;
It'll take a good scholar
To riddle me.
Paper and letters. *

6 2

Arthur O'Bower has broken his band;
He comes roaring up the land.
The King of Scots, with all his power,
Cannot turn Arthur of the Bower.
A storm. *

6 3

As high as a castle,
As weak as a wastle (twig);
And all the king's horses
Cannot pull it down.
Smoke. *

6 4

The words I know to be true,
All which begin with a *W*.
I, too, know them,
And eke three which begin with *M*.
Woman Wants Wit. Man Much More.

65

Banks full, braes full,
Though you gather all day,
Ye'll not gather your hands full.
Fog. *

66

The calf, the goose, the bee,
The world is ruled by these three.
Vellum, quill, and wax. *

67

I've seen you where you never was,
And where you ne'er will be,
And yet you in that very same place
May still be seen by me.
*In the mirror.**

68

There was a King met a King
In a narrow lane.
Says this King to that King:
"Where have you been?"

"Oh! I've been a-hunting
With my dog and my doe."

"Pray, lend him to me,
That I may do so."

"There's the dog, take the dog."
"What is the dog's name?"
"I've told you already."
"Pray, tell me again."
"Take."

69

A house full, a yard full,
And ye can't catch a bowl full.
Smoke. *

70

As I was going o'er yon moor and moss,
I met a man on a grey horse;
He whipped and he wailed;
I asked him what he ailed;
He said he was going to his father's funeral,
Who died seven years before he was born.
His father was a dyer. *

71

Lillylow, lillylow, set up on an end,
See little baby go out at town [down?] end.
A tallow candle (lillylow is the flame of a tallow candle). *

72

Which weighs heavier—
A stone of lead
Or a stone of feather?
Both have the same weight [namely, a stone]. *

73

At the end of my yard there is a vat,
Four and twenty ladies dancing in that;
Some in green gowns, and some with blue hat,
He is a wise man who can tell me that.
A flax field. *

74

I am become of flesh and blood,
As other creatures be;
Yet there's neither flesh nor blood
Doth remain in me.
I make Kings that they fall out;
I make them agree;
And yet there's neither flesh nor blood
Doth remain in me.
A quill. *

75

Jackatawad ran over the moor,
Never behind, but always before.
A will-o'-the-wisp. *

76

Link lank on a bank,
Ten against four.
A milker. *

77

Two legs sat upon three legs,
With four legs standing by;
Four then were drawn by ten.
Read my riddle; you can't,
However much ye try.
A milker on a milking stool. *

7 8

Over the water,
And under the water,
And always with its head down.
A nail on a ship. *

7 9

Formed long ago, yet made to-day,
Employed while others sleep;
What few would like to give away,
Nor any wish to keep.
A bed. *

8 o

Higher than a house, higher than a tree;
Oh, whatever can that be?
A star. *

8 1

A water there I must pass,
A broader water never was;

And yet of all waters I ever did see,
To pass over with less jeopardy.
Dew. *

82

I saw a fight the other day,
A damsel did begin the fray.
She with her daily friend did meet,
Then standing in the open street;
She gave such hard and sturdy blows,
He bled ten gallons at the nose;
Yet neither seemed to faint nor fall,
Nor gave her any abuse at all.
A pump. *

83

There is a bird of great renown,
Useful in city and in town;
None work like unto him can do;
He's yellow, black, red, and green,
A very pretty bird I mean;
Yet he's both fierce and fell,
I count him wise that can this tell.
A bee. *

84

As white as milk,
And not milk;
As green as grass,
And not grass;
As red as blood,

And not blood;
As black as soot,
And not soot.
A blackberry blossom. *

85

As I went over London Bridge
I met a brave knight,
All saddled, all bridled,
All fit for a fight.
I've told his name three times,
And now you can't guess it.
"All." *

86

Crooked as a rainbow with teeth like a cat.
A blackberry bush. *

87

There is something with a heart in its head.
A peach. *

88

Two legs up and four legs down,
soft in the middle,
And hard all around.
A bed. *

8 9

If a cat and a half can catch a rat and a half in a minute
and a half, how long will it take a cat and a half to catch
a rat and a half?
A minute and a half. *

9 0

Riddle me, riddle me, what is that
Over the head and under the hat?
Hair. *

9 1

Black upon black,
Black upon brown,
Three legs up and six legs down.
A Black man on a brown horse with a black kettle on his head. *

9 2

What is that which increases the effect
by reducing the cause?
A pair of snuffers. *

9 3

Why is a policeman like a mill-horse?
He goes the rounds. *

9 4

When you go to a miser's dinner,

Why are you nearly blind?
Because you can see little. *

95

Why is the average sermon like asparagus?
The end is the best. *

96

What belongs to yourself,
yet is used by everybody more than yourself?
Your name. *

97

In spring, I am gray in attire,
In summer, I wear more clothing than in spring,
In winter, I am naked.
A tree. *

98

We are little airy creatures,
All of different voice and natures;
One of us in glass is set,
One of us you will find in yet [jet?];
The other you may see in tin,
And the fourth a box within;
If the fifth you should pursue,
It can never fly from you
A, E, I, O, U.

99

What is that which is too much for one,
Enough for two, but nothing at all for three?
A secret. *

100

What is that which goes up the hill,
And down the hill,
And spite of all yet standeth still?
The road. *

101

A duck before two ducks,
A duck behind two ducks,
And a duck between two ducks;
How many ducks were there in all?
Three. *

102

When can a man have something and nothing in his pocket
at the same time?
If he has a hole in it. *

103

Whose best works are most trampled upon?
Those of a shoemaker, for good shoes last long. *

104

What can pass before the sun without making a shadow?
The wind. *

105

Why did Adam bite the apple which Eve gave him?
Because he had no knife. *

106

My first is a useful animal,
My second is a root,
And my whole is a root
Horseradish.

107

When are you like the dying embers of a fire?
When you go out. *

108

Why is rumor like a kiss?
It goes from mouth to mouth. *

109

Why is the profession of a dentist always precarious?
He lives from hand to mouth. *

110

Why is a kiss like the world?
It is made of nothing and yet is something. *

111

Why should a stuttering man be discredited?
He always breaks his word. *

112

What burns to keep a secret?
Sealing wax. *

113

Round the house, and round the house,
And makes but one track
A wheelbarrow. *

114

I am rough, I am smooth, I am wet, I am dry,
My station low, my title high,
My king my lawful master is,
I am used by all, though only his
A highway.

115

I've seen you where you never were,
And where you never will be,
And yet within that very place,

You shall be seen by me
In a mirror. *

116

What is that which a gentleman has not,
And never can have, but may give to a lady?
A husband. *

117

Brown I am and much admired,
Many horses have I tired,
Tire a horse and worry a man,
Tell me this riddle if you can?
A saddle. *

118

Why is it dangerous to walk out in the early spring?
Because the trees shoot, the flowers have pistols, and the bullrush is out.

119

As I went down to the garden gate,
Whom should I meet but Dick Red-Cap.
A stick in his hand, a stone in his throat.
Guess this riddle and I'll give you a groat.
A cherry. *

120

Es steht uf e Bei,
Hot's Herz im Kopf.

(It stands on one leg,
Has its heart in its head.)
A head of cabbage. *

121

Er geit ums Hus rum,
Hat e Sichel im Schwanz.

(He goes around the house,
Has a sickle in his tail.)
A rooster. *

122

Ri, ra, rüzel,
Gelb ist der Rützel,
Schwarz ist das Loch,
Wo mer der
Ri, ra, rützel
Drin kocht.

(Ri, ra, ruetzel,
Yellow is the Ruetzel,
Black is the hole,
Where we cook
The ri, ra, ruetzel.)
A carrot. *

123

Two hookers,
Two lookers,

And a switch about.
A cow. *

1 2 4

As I went up my humble gumble (1),
I peeped through my hazle gazle (2),
And there I saw a nibble nabble (3)
Going into stribble strabble (4);
I called my elgum pelgum (5)
To get nibble nabble
Out of stribble, strabble.
1 is stairs, 2 is a window, 3 is a pig, 4 is a yard, 5 is a dog. *

1 2 5

There was an old woman named Ann,
She lived a woman and d-y-ed a man.
The woman did not die but splashed paint on a man. *

1 2 6

White told white to go in white and get white.
*A White man told a White boy to go in the white cotton field
and get the white dog.*

1 2 7

A little red garden, enclosed with a white fence.
A mouth. *

1 2 8

Goes up with four legs,

Comes down with eight.
A cat with a mouse. *

129

Why is a wife like a bad bill?
She is difficult to get changed.

130

Why are some women like facts?
They are stubborn things.

131

Why is a cigar loving man like a tallow candle?
He smokes when he goes out. *

132

When is a pretty girl like a ship?
When she is attached to a buoy—a boy.

133

There is a hill,
And on that hill there is a house,
And in that house there is a closet,
And in that closet there is a dress,
And in that dress there is a pocket,
And in that pocket there is an Indian head.
—What is this head?
A cent, a coin. *

134

A man dyed six years ago and he is not dead yet.
He dyed; *not* died. *Both are pronounced the same.* *

135

Father, mother, sister, and brother,
All run after each other,
Yet they never catch one another.
The four wheels of a carriage. *

136

What is the difference between an old maid, a rooster,
and Uncle Sam?
*The old maid says, "Any dude'll do," the rooster says, "Cock-a-doodle-do,"
and Uncle Sam says, "Yankee-doodle-do."*

137

Over the water, and under the water, and not touch the water.
A woman who goes over a bridge with a pail of water. *

138

Niddy, niddy, two heads and one body.
A barrel. *

139

Little Miss Netticoat
With a white pettycoat,
And a red nose;

The longer she stands
The shorter she grows.
A tallow candle. *

140

Pray, tell us, ladies, if you can,
Who is that highly favored man,
Who, though he's married many a wife,
May be a bachelor all his life?
A priest. *

141

I am taken from a mine and shut up in a wooden case, from which I
am never released, and yet I am used by almost everybody.
A pencil. *

142

Down in the meadows there was a red heifer,
Give her hay, she would eat it,
Give her water, she would die.
Fire. *

143

There is a thing that nothing is,
And yet it has a name;
'T is sometimes tall and sometimes short,
It joins our walks, it joins our sport,
And plays at every game.
A shadow. *

144

My first is a pronoun, my next is used at weddings,
My whole is an inhabitant of the deep.
A herring: her + ring.

145

What is the difference between an old maid of ninety,
and a young miss of sixteen?
One is hairless and cappy; the other is careless and happy.

146

Why do chimneys smoke?
Because they cannot chew.

147

No doors there are in this stronghold,
Yet thieves break in and steal the gold.
An egg. *

148

What makes a box lighter than it is when there is nothing in it?
Holes. *

149

Why is an oyster like a man of sense?
Because it keeps its mouth shut.

150

It has four legs, but cannot walk.*
A bed.

What has the man in his trousers
that a woman would not like to have in her face?
Wrinkles (1909d, 75).*

• F i f t e e n •

PROVERBS

Most of the proverbs, slang, metaphors, and tongue-twisters included here cannot be verified as collected orally. However, since Knortz usually did not mention where he had recorded them, there is a possibility that they were taken from oral sources. Nearly all the data were written in English within the German text and explained or translated by him, if necessary.

Birds of one feather flock together (1907a, 17–8).

He who offers bribes needs watching, for his intentions are not honest (1900c, 215).

Cart grease reduces the cost of feed (1905b, 73).*‡

Noisy coachmen are like rattling carts—empty (1905b, 73).*‡

There are more bad coachmen than stubborn horses (1905b, 73).*‡

Green Christmas, lean pocketbooks (New York) (1902b, 183).

Two is company, three is a crowd (1905b, 60).‡

The devil take the hindmost (1907a, 44).

The devil dances in an empty pocket (1900c, 194).

The devil kisses those he likes best (1900c, 213).

Better an old man's doll than a young man's slave (1905b, 60).‡

Fine feathers make fine birds (1907a, 42).

Five cents spent for feed, is better than a dollar spent for a whip (1905b, 73).*‡

From the frying pan into the fire (1907a, 40).

The cat has a gale of wind in her tail (1913a, 130).

She has a gale in her tail (said of a cat) (1896a, 17).

God reigns, and the government at Washington still lives (from a speech by A. Garfield given on April 15, 1865, the day after Lincoln's death [before Garfield became President]) (1900c, 216).

The grey mare is the better horse (1896a, 29).

Honesty is the best policy (1900c, 212).

No house is big enough for two families (1902b, 93).*

Give me liberty or give me death (Patrick Henry) (1900c, 216).

Liberty and union now and forever, one and inseparable (Webster) (1900c, 216).

Marry in haste and repent in leisure (1907a, 32).

It takes a mine to work a mine (1900c, 214).

Robbing Peter and [to] pay Paul (1905b, 61).‡

Everyone has his price (1900c, 215).

Sing before breakfast, cry before supper (1900b, 162).†

These are the times that try men's souls (Thomas Paine) (1900c, 216).

Union is strength (1900c, 216).

The bigger the whip, the worse the coachman (1905b, 73).*‡

With words we govern men (Lord Beaconsfield) (1900c, 215).

·Sixteen·

FOLK SPEECH AND SLANG

Knortz sometimes associated expressions with certain categories of people. In these cases I have used special symbols.

꙰ actors' slang

🍺 drinkers' slang

🏃 soldiers' slang

⚭ thieves' slang

Knortz always explained the meaning of an English expression in German and often tried to trace its origin by telling anecdotes or giving facts about the historic event when it first was used (e.g., 1900c, 425–31). The following slang expressions are accompanied by the explanations of their meaning, which Knortz gave in German and which are translated here.

abolitionists (1900c, 425) people who fought against slavery

angels (1907a, 47) ⚭ people who easily can be deceived

angel's food (1905b, 70)‡ 🏃 very hard bread

(in) apple pie order (1905b, 60) neat, perfect, orderly

awful nice (1907a, 4) very nice (awful actually means very unpleasant, ugly)

baffled (1907a, 42) derided, ridiculed; deceived

ball (1905b, 68)† ⚭ detective

bare-faced (1907a, 14) impudent, brazen

barges (1909d, 183) big shoes

to barn (1907a, 3) to put one's goods into the barn (Used in England in Shakespeare's time, but it is no longer in use there)

barnstormer (1905b, 66)‡ an actor who performs in small towns

bay-window (1907a, 48) ⚘ person's protuberant stomach

beak (1905b, 68)† ∞ presiding judge

beau-catcher (1909d, 36) curl, lovelock

bed-presser (1907a, 16) lazy person

blackleg (1905b, 66)† ∞ thief

blackleg (1907a, 19) worker who does not belong to a union

blatherskite (1905b, 72)‡ person who talks rubbish, nonsense

blind pig (1905b, 63)‡ 🍺 an innkeeper who sells liquor without a license (in Iowa)

blind pig (1907a, 24) unlicensed saloon (in Evanston near Chicago)

blind tiger (1905b, 63)‡ 🍺 an innkeeper who sells liquor without a license (in Missouri)

blockade-runners (1909d, 183) big shoes

blockhead (1909d, 2) stupid person

blubberhead (1909d, 2) stupid person

(to have the) blue devils (1902b, 159) to be in a bad mood

blue lights (1900d, 428) members of a political party in America who tried to avert the threatening war with England (founded 1812)

Bohemians (1900d, 422) reporters for newspapers who are traveling a lot to get their stories *booby* (1900c, 422) blockhead, stupid person

booby prize (1900c, 422) the prize for the worst player at nine pins, hence, a prize for the worst performance in sports

boodle (1905b, 69)‡ money stolen from public funds by politicians

boodle (1907a, 34) money which is given to dishonest, scheming (New York) aldermen

boodler (1907a, 18) corrupt politician

boodling combine (1905b, 68)‡ group of politicians who help each other secure well paid positions or to embezzle public money

bootlegger (1905b, 63)‡ 🍺 an innkeeper who sells liquor without a license (in Missouri)

bottled snakes (1905b, 63)‡ 🍺 bottle of liquor

bottled snakes (1907a, 40) alcoholic beverages

braggart (1907a, 16) swaggerer

brass (1907a, 14) impudence

brass-faced (1907a, 14) impudent, brazen

brow (1907a, 14) impudence

bughouse (1907a, 47) insane asylum

bucket shop (1905b, 63)‡ 🍺 inexpensive beer house where you can get beer to take home in a pitcher

bull (1905b, 70)‡ 🪖 high military officer

to bulldoze (1907a, 49) to intimidate, to cow

bum (1900c, 220) dawdler, loafer

Bum Bumers (1900c, 427) politicians intent on destroying dishonest banks; also, young Democrats

buncombe (1905b, 72)‡ boring, empty political speech

bunkie (1905b, 70)‡ 🏃 a soldier who is assigned to sleep in the same tent as another

cabbage head (1907a, 15) extremely stupid person

cabbage head (1909d, 2) stupid person

cage (1907a, 47) ⚭ cell in prison

cake walk knife (1900b, 107) razor

canal-boats (1909a, 183) big shoes

carpet-bagger (1900c, 430) politician from the northern states who was sent to organize the southern states after the Civil War; he went with a bag and returned with riches

chainlightning (1907a, 9) 🍺 liquor

to chap (1905b, 73)‡ to haggle

cheek (1907a, 14) impudence, audacity

cheese head (1909d, 28) stupid person

chewing air (1907a, 47) ⚭ (a criminal) without means

chestnut (1905b, 65)‡ an old, often repeated gag

chump (1905b, 68)† ⚭ detective who can easily be deluded

clapper (1909d, 126) mouth

clean (1907a, 47) ⚭ (a criminal) without means, broke

climber (1905b, 67)† ⚭ a burglar who enters a house through the window

clod-hoppers (1909d, 183) big shoes

coal oil (1907a, 47) 🍺 liquor

cocktail (1905b, 64)‡ 📖 a kind of liquor

combine (1907a, 34) some of the most stupid and unscrupulous aldermen in New York

contrabands (1900c, 422) Blacks from the southern states who escaped during the Civil War and sought refuge in the northern states

cop (1905b, 67)† ∞ policeman

cop (1907a, 20) policeman in New York (because he has copper buttons on his uniform)

to cop (1905b, 67)† ∞ to catch a thief

copperhead (1900c, 428) politician in the northern states who tried to avoid the war with the South

crank (1905b, 71)‡ crazy person

crazy bone (1909d, 240) funny bone

crook (1905b, 66)† ∞ thief

cuffee (1900c, 422) Black man

dago (1900d, 221) an Italian who lives in America (the term comes from Louisiana, where it was used exclusively for Spaniards and Portuguese)

dam, damn (1907a, 15) without value; used as a curse

dandy (1907a, 16) overdressed young man

dark horse (1907a, 48) an unknown candidate for public office who gets the nomination in an election

darkey (1900c, 422) 🔳 Black man

dead broke (1907a, 47) completely penniless

deadhead (1907a, 26) 🔳 person who lets somebody else pay his bill in the restaurant *dead men's shoes* (1909d, 184) durable shoes with which dead people were dressed before the funeral (New York)

dead wire (1907a, 46) 🐿️ boring book or theater play

dip (1905b, 67)† ∞ pickpocket

dip or dipper (1907a, 47) ∞ pickpocket

dirty (1907a, 47) ∞ rich

ditched (1907a, 46) completely ruined

dog face (1909d, 66) face

doll face (1909d, 66) face

dough face (1909d, 66) 🐿️ politician who has no strong opinion but joins the majority

dough face (1909d, 66) face

dough faces (1900c, 428) politicians in Missouri who supported the abolition of slavery in their state but were easily manipulated by their opponents

dude (1907a, 16) overdressed man

dude (1900c, 221) overdressed man

Dutchman (1900c, 416) German

eye-opener (1909d, 77) liquor

[his] face hurts him (1909d, 67) 🐿️ broad, blank face

faddy (1907a, 34) frivolous, illhumored; a person who is not easily pleased or satisfied

fall money (1905b, 67)† ∞ money set aside to bribe a jury or judge

fence (1905b, 67)† ∞ a place where stolen goods are sold

fire-eater (1900c, 423) swaggerer, boaster

fire-eater (1900c, 427) people favoring the South (after 1856)

fire shovel (1907a, 16) big mouth

flatty (1905b, 68)† ∞ policeman

fly (1907a, 9) ▮ whisky

fly (1907a, 47) ∞ alert, saucy, cunning (thief)

fly bull (1907a, 47) ∞ a good detective

fly cop (1905b, 68)† ∞ detective

fly stiff (1907a, 47) ∞ a very skillful pickpocket

fly trap (1907a, 16) big mouth

fly trap (1909d, 126) mouth

flunky (1900c, 423) toady, sycophant

frog-eaters (1900c, 416) the French

full moon face (1909d, 66) face

geese (1907a, 21) Jews

General Boreas (1900c, 424) winter

ginnis (1900c, 416) Italians in New York and surroundings (their names often end in ini)

to goff (1907a, 35) to strictly investigate the administration of public offices

good foundations (1909d, 183) big shoes

good luck (1907a, 25) a toast

good things (1907a, 47) ∞ people who easily can be deceived *goose* (1909d, 2) stupid person

grafter (1907a, 18) thief, dishonest politician

grafter (1905b, 66)† ∞ thief

greenhorn (1907a, 20) a naive or unsuspecting person who easily can be deceived

growler (1907a, 11) a pitcher used to carry beer home from the saloon

grub boss (1905b, 70) 🏃 commissary; caterer

I guess (1907a, 41) I presume

gun (1905b, 67)† ∞ pickpocket

guy (1907a, 47) ∞ a person who was robbed

hardtack (1905b, 70)‡ 🏃 very hard bread

hardware (1907a, 9) 🍺 whisky, hard liquor

hairgrabber (1905b, 66)‡ circus rider

Halifax (1907a, 12) hell

hard shells (1900c, 427) conservative Democrats

hatchway (1909d, 126) mouth

heap (1907a, 51) a large amount (West and South States of the Union)

heartbreakers (1909d, 36) curls, lovelocks

heartbreakers (1909d, 167) young men who break a girl's heart

Hessians (1900c, 416) Germans

Hessian boots (1909d, 183) heavy, durable boots

hobo (1905b, 66)† ∞ thief

hobo (1907a, 48) thief

on the hog train (1907a, 47) ⚭ (a criminal) without means

hoodlum (1905b, 69)‡ a youthful ruffian, thug (mainly in California)

hoodlum (1907a, 19) youthful ruffian,thug, gangster

hooligan (1907a, 19) hoodlum, tough guy

horse sense (1907a, 13) intelligence, common sense

horse sense (1903, 29)* intelligence, enterprising spirit

howday, or huddy (Blacks) (1907a, 41) how do you do? (Indiana)

Huns (1900c, 416) Hungarians and Slavs who worked in coal mines and iron foundries in Pennsylvania

Hunkers (1900c, 427) conservative Democrats

Indian giver (1907a, 20) a person who wants to take back a gift he has given

intoxicated (1907a, 27) drunk

Jack-an-apes (1900c, 424) silly person, gaper

Jack-a-leut (1900c, 424) simpleton

Jack Frost (1900c, 424) winter

Jack Ketch (1900c, 424) hangman

Jack o'lantern (1900c, 424) will-o' the wisp

Jack of all tides (1900c, 424) shuffler

Jack of all trades [and master of none] (1900c, 423) a person who can do many different things fairly well

Jack Pudding (1900c, 424) buffoon, clown

Jack-sance (1900c, 424) cheeky fellow

Jack-tar (1900c, 424) sailor

Jack-weight (1900c, 424) heavy person

jailbird (1907a, 47) ○○ convict, ex-convict

[the] jakes (1907, 48) toilet

to jew (1905b, 73)‡ to bargain with a seller

to jew (1907a, 21) to cheat, to deceive

to jew [him] down (1907a, 21) to bargain with a seller in an attempt to make the purchase at a lower price

Jingo (1900c, 222) a person who admires wars and conquests

Jingoism (1900c, 222) the attitude of a jingo

by Jingo (1900c, 222) a curse

Johnny on the spot (1900c, 212) a young man who is present when needed, alert to his opportunities, crafty and cunning

joint (1905b, 67)† ○○ penitentiary

key worker (1905b, 67)† ○○ a burglar who uses a key to enter a house

kick (1905b, 67)† ○○ wallet, purse

kissing the baby (1905b, 63)‡ 🍺 🍶 drinking alcoholic beverages

know-nothing (1900c, 429) conceited, ignorant person

Ku-Klux (1900c, 431) Ku Klux Klan

leather (1905b, 67)† ○○ wallet, purse

liar (1902b, 57) derisevely for lawyer

liar (1900c, 421) derisively for lawyers

lickspittle (1907a, 9) toady, sycophant

live wire (1907a, 46) an active, reliable person; liquor

loco-focos (1900c, 430) Democrats in New York who favored extreme measures in 1834

loco-focos (1900c, 430) cigars which were ignited by friction

loggerhead (1909d, 2) stupid person

main finger (1905b, 68)† ◌◌ the higest ranking police officer

main guy (1907a, 46) ⚘ stage-manager (theater)

main guy (1907a, 47) ◌◌ chief of police

make-up (1907a, 46) ⚘ cosmetic

masher (1905b, 59)‡ a male flirt

to mauser (1905b, 70)‡ to kill with a Mauser rifle (a soldier in the Cuban war)

Mickey (1907a, 47) ⚋ bottle of liquor, gin

miscenegationists (1900c, 425) people who favored the mixing of the White and Black races

moll buzzer (1907a, 47) ◌◌ pickpocket

moll buzzer (1905b, 67)† ◌◌ a pickpocket who mainly steals from women

Mr Fudge (1900c, 422) a journalist who writes exaggerated, untrue, and pompous reports

Muckamuck (1907a, 51) a meal (at the Pacific coast)

mug (1909d, 126) mouth

mugwump (1907a, 35) a Republican who favored free trade and voted for the Democratic candidate for president in 1884

night footer (1905b, 67)† burglar

noodlehead (1909d, 2) stupid person

nutty (1907a, 47) madman, stupid person

old boy (1898c, 34) devil

Old Harry (1907a, 40) devil

Old Harry (1900c, 223) devil (originally Harry Main, a smuggler and wrecker at Ipswich in New England)

the old man (1900c, 223) father

the old woman (1900c, 223) mother

Old Zero (1900c, 424) winter

[he is] out of sight (1900c, 212) a person who surpasses everyone

Paddy (1900c, 416) an Irish person

Pantata (1907a, 35) policeman (used by Czech innkeepers in New York)

parkhursting (1907a, 35) strict judicial investigation of the administration of public offices

peach (1905b, 60)‡ pretty, attractive girl

pen (1907a, 47) ∞ prison

Peter Funk (1900c, 423) a man who drives up the price at an auction

pie face (1909d, 66) face

to pinch (1905b, 67)† ∞ to catch a thief

pixilated or pixyled (1907a, 41) bewildered (Maine)

plantsville (1905b, 67)† ∞ a place where stolen goods are sold

poltroon (1907a, 16) swaggerer

pops (1900c, 425) members of the People's Party

potato hole (1909d, 126) mouth

pot head (1907a, 15) extremely stupid person

pothead (1909d, 2) stupid person

poverty suppers (1900c, 223) suppers in private homes as fundraisers for a charity

prince (1907a, 32) the firstborn son

puddings (1907a, 47) ∞ people who easily can be deceived

pumpkin pated fellow (1909d, 2) stupid person

punk (1905b, 70)‡ 👤 anything that can be eaten (soldiers and New York thiefs)

quick step (1907a, 48) diarrhea

quilts (1905b, 61)‡ names for quilts: world's wonder (Louisiana), fool's puzzle (North Carolina), old maid's whim (New York), Chinese puzzle or Peter pay Paul (Massachuessets)

ragamufin (1907a, 35) villanous, ragged fellow

rapid transit (1907a, 48) diarrhea (among railroad workers)

rats (1905b, 70) 👤 rations

[he was bitten by a] rattlesnake (1902b, 188)*†he is intoxicated

rebs (1900c, 425) confederate soldiers during the Civil War

right guy (1905b, 68)† ∞ a person who shelters thiefs

ring (1905b, 68)‡ a group of people in politics, combined for the purpose of getting a good position or stealing from public funds

rookie (1905b, 70)‡ 👤 army recruit

round-up (1907a, 46) to take an inventory of supply in stock

sambo (1900c, 422) Black man

sandlot orator (1907a, 19) socialist agitator

sawdusthopper (1905b, 66)‡ circus rider

scab (1907a, 20) a worker who does not belong to a union

scrape (1905b, 68)† inconvenience (he got into a scrape)

scratcher (1905b, 67)† ⚭ forger, coiner

seam squirrel (1907a, 47) ⚭ a prisoner affected with body lice

seven-footers (1909d, 183) big shoes

sheeny (1905b, 72)‡ Jew

sheeny (1900c, 416) Jew

sheeney (1907a, 21) Jew

sheep's eyes (1909d, 77) a married man who looks at another woman lovingly has 'sheep's eyes'

shot (1905b, 70)‡ 🕯 intoxicated

side-tracked (1907a, 46) having unsuccessfully speculated (in stocks etc.)

skating rink (1907a, 48) bald head

sleepy head (1909d, 28) dull, lazy fellow

slick (1907a, 42) dishonest, glib, smooth talking

to slough (1905b, 67)† ⚭ to catch a thief

smart aleck (1907a, 50) a person who thinks he knows everything

sockhead (1909d, 2) stupid person

soft shells (1900c, 427) young Democrats, Bum Bumers

Sokrates (1900c, 420) a married Black man

spielers (1905b, 68)† ⚭ lawyers

spigoty (1907a, 23) from Puerto Rico

spoon (1907a, 15) stupid person

spoony (1907a, 15) romantic, affectionate

squeeze (1905b, 68)† ⚭ the highest ranking police officer

stall (1905b, 67)† ⚭ a pickpocket's accomplice who distracts the intended victim's attention

steel pen (1907a, 51) a tool with a point to use in writing with ink, made of steel

stick (1907a, 9) 🍺 whisky

stir (1905b, 67)† ⚭ jail, prison

stone getter (1905b, 67)† a thief who specializes in diamonds

Stoughton bottle (1907a, 40) useless person

strapped (1907a, 47) ⚭ (a criminal) without means

strong arm guy (1907a, 47) ⚭ a thief who uses violence to rob a person

tender foot (1900c, 222) a nicely dressed man from New England (in the West)

thickskull (1909d, 2) stupid person

thimble (1905b, 67)† ⚭ golden watch

turpentine (1907a, 47) 🍺 liquor, gin

villain (1907a, 35) scoundrel

wallflower (1905b, 59)‡ a girl who is not popular

whetstone (1907a, 9) 🍺 liquor

white satin (1907d, 47) 🍶 liquor, gin

white water (1907a, 47) 🍶 liquor, gin

whitewasher (1907a, 18) a person who covers up a misdeed (often in politics)

wild-cat currency (1900c, 217) paper money issued by short-lived banks, which often lost its value overnight (before the Civil War)

wire-puller (1900c, 430) a sly and cunning politician who uses influence to obtain a desired result

wise acre (1907a, 51) prophet, fortune teller

woman widow (1907a, 4) widow

wooden milestone (1907a, 51) a wooden pillar to show the distance in miles to a certain place

woodpecker (1909d, 39) a boy with red hair

woolly heads (1900c, 425) 1850, members of the Whigs

word mill (1909d, 126) mouth

Yankee (1907a, 36) a citizen of the US (in Europe), a person who lives in New England (in the US)

yanks (1900c, 425) soldiers of the federation during the Civil War

yellow Jack (1900c, 424) yellow fever

Expressions which changed in the course of time, or which should be replaced by the words following:

Belly—stomach (1907a, 6)

Breeches—pants—pantaloons—trousers (inexpressibles would still be better) (1907a, 6)

Ladies walk—closet—toilet. Also heard: my aunt (1907a, 5)

Legs—limbs—larger limbs (1907a, 6)

Shirt—chemisette (1907a, 7)

Spittle—saliva (1907a, 9)

Differences : English—American

autumn—fall (1907a, 42)

ill—sick (1907a, 42)

plain—homely (1907a, 42)

I presume—I guess (1907a, 41)

· S e v e n t e e n ·

FOLK SIMILES, METAPHORS, CURSES, EXCLAMATIONS, AND SAYINGS

Knortz, as a rule, gives the expressions in the English original and then explains their meaning in German.

[he has an] arm a mile long (1909d, 141) he has a great influence

[not able to say] boo to a goose (1907a, 15) a very stupid person

[from] bad to worse (1907a, 40) getting worse

[his] bark is worse than his bite (1907a, 16) said of somebody who threatens but doesn't carry through

beats my wife's relations (1900c, 217) makes my blood boil

[that] beats the Dutch (1907a, 20) said if an American wants to compliment somebody on a great performance

[he has a] bee in his head (1909d, 4) he only thinks of one thing; he is slightly crazy

[eyes as] big as saucers (1909d, 77) to goggle; to gape

bit the dust (1909d, 183) died

blows himself like the wind (1907a, 47) said of a villain who squanders the money he stole

bored through the nose (1909d, 121) easily controlled and deceived

born on the wrong side of the blanket (1907d, 8) born illegitimate

[my] bunkie was baked by a bull for jumpin' a gump (1905b, 71)‡ a soldier's way of saying that his roommate was imprisoned for stealing a hen

carry water to the Mississippi (1907a, 16) do unnecessary work

catch a weasel asleep (1900c, 218) be especially alert

clear as mud (1907a, 18) clear as daylight

cold as a dog's nose (1907a, 44-5) very cold

cook your goose for you (1907a, 13) ruin your plan, chances

[he has a] cow on his tongue (1907a, 45) he was bribed not to testify

cuts no figure (1907a, 15) does not play a role

[not worth a] dam or curse (1907a, 15) worthless

dead as a door nail (1907a, 18), (1900c, 213) entirely dead

dead as a herring (1900c, 213) completely dead

die game (1907a, 12) fight to the last moment

die in the last ditch (1907a, 12) prefer dying to giving in

die in their boots (1896a, 55), (1905b, 69)*† die a violent death

[have a] dog in one's belly (1907a, 12) be very angry

dull as a meat axe (1907a, 15) very stupid

dust one's jacket (1907a, 12) beat somebody thoroughly

*eat crows (*1907a, 11)* be forced to do something very disagreeable and humiliating

eat one out of house and home (1907a, 14) make one poor

eat Uncle Sam's beef and bread (1900b, 39)* be in the military

everything is lovely, and the goose hangs high (1905b, 73)‡ all is well; the prospects are good (Delaware) *eyes are bigger than the stomach* (1909d, 77) taking or desiring more food than one can eat

[his] face hurts him (1909d, 67) he makes an unfavorable impression and gets very angry because of it

face the music (1907d, 43) bear the consequences

fat (is) in the fire (1907a, 15) everything is confused

feel like a stewed witch (1900c, 218) said of someone who didn't sleep well the previous night

feel one's oats (1905b, 68)† be lively or frisky

[his] fingers are all thumbs (1909d, 155) he is clumsy, awkward

[to have a] finger in the pie (1909d, 155) to take part in doing something

[give him a] flap with a fox tail (1907a, 15) make a fool of him

fly off the handle (1907a,12) be out of control

[the] German's wit is in his fingers (1909d, 155) the German has learned a craft and therefore can get along

get into a scrape (1905b, 68)† get into difficulty

getting the mitten (1907a, 7) a form of rejection if a girl retracts her hand, leaving her mitten in her lover's hand, when he asks her to marry him

give him the cold shoulder (1907a, 14), (1900c, 218) to treat him in an unfriendly manner

give a pap with a hatchet (1907a, 15) to be confused, to get things wrong

giv'm Watts, boys (1907a, 45) an instigation to fight

go to the dickens (1907a, 44) go to hell

go to loggerheads (1909d, 3) have a fight (said of stupid people) *go to the pot* (1907a, 15) be deceived by everyone

God Almighty's overcoat wouldn't make him a vest (1900c, 220) his ideas are too big

going to the pot (1900c, 213) doomed to moral or physical death

[the] grass is short (1907a, 46), (1905b, 73)‡ to have no money

grease the palm of the hand (1909d, 143) bribe

[by the] great horn's spoon (1900b, 201) truly

hand and glove (1909d, 143) intimate; in close relations

haul over hot coals (1900c, 213) scold; blame

[have one's] head chopped off (1909d, 28) be dismissed

head strong (1909d, 4) he is rashly determined to have his own way

heating up a town (1905b, 68)† said of thieves who come to a town to carry out their profession

hold one's nose to the grindstone (1909d, 121) work long and hard

[I] hope to die (1900b, 201) I am speaking truthfully

[by] hook and crook (1905b, 71)† in any way at all; by fair means or foul

[by the] holy poker (1900c, 217) used as a curse

[it will be enough for a] horse to leave its oats (1907a, 13) something very terrible is going to happen

hurry up the cakes (1907a, 43) hurry up

[as] Irish as Biddy Murphy's pig (1900c, 220) said of an Irish-American who always praises his old country

jew him down (1907a, 21) beat down the price

keep a stiff upper-lip (1909d, 127) show no fear or discouragement *keep the pot boiling* (1907a, 13) keep one's eyes upon one's own interests

kick the bucket (1909d, 183) die

knocks the spots out of everything (1905b, 70),†(1900c, 213) takes all hurdles to become successful

knock the shit out of one (1900b, 201), (1905b, 71)† beat one viciously

laugh in one's sleeves (1907a, 18) gloat

let her go, Gallagher (1900c, 221) let it be; let it alone

let us saw wood and say nothing (1905b, 71)‡ let us attend to our own affairs and not talk about this occurrence

[if you don't] like it, you may lump it (1907a, 44) put up with it; said to somebody you do not respect

look for a needle in a haystalk [haystack?] (1907a, 15) look for something extremely difficult to find

lost his grip (1907a, 46) lost control

make a cat's paw of him (1900c, 219) make somebody take the blame for another person

make a mountain of a mole hill (1907a, 16) make important something insignificant

make or break (1900c, 213) cause to succeed or fail

mind your p's and q's (1907a, 44) be careful about what you say

[he has] molasses on his fingers (1907a, 40)* said in America of a Black who steals

money by the eye (1909d, 77) a great amount of money

money to burn (1903, 122) more than enough money

much cry and little wool (1907a, 16) an expression often used by Blacks for a new baby

[doesn't] need it anymore than a cow needs two tails (1900c, 220) doesn't need it at all

neither head nor tail (1909d, 25) without rhyme or reason

[he has a] nut factory (1909d, 3) he is crazy

off one's cabase [base?] (1909d, 3) crazy

Old Harry is growling again (1900c, 223) the sea is getting rough again (Ipswich, New England)

[to be] on one's jacket (1907a, 12) to beat somebody thoroughly

over head and ears (1909d, 26) completely immersed

over head and shoulders (1909d, 26) completely immersed

paint a town red (1905b, 68)† go on a wild spree or party

Peter pay Paul (1900c, 96) take a piece from here and put it there (referring to quilts) (Massachusetts)

put one's nose out of joint (1909d, 107) displace someone

pick a bone (1907a, 13) have an argument

pick a quarrel (1907a, 13) start a quarrel

piss one's money against the wall (1900c, 220) cause another person to pay a drinking debt

play hooky (1907a, 34) play truant

*play Jack with someone (*1900c, 424) lead a person by the nose

play the lady (1907a, 5) behave like a lady who does not do any work

pop the question (1907a, 7) propose marriage

[a] preacher cannot marry a woman from his congregation and stay (1900c, 346)if you prefer someone among competing persons around you, you will make enemies of the others and will soon have to leave

[to have a] presidential bee (1900c, 97) an American politician who desperately tries to become President

principle with a string (1900c, 212) principle with a condition attached to it

pull the wool over one's eyes (1907a, 14) deceive someone

puncture my tire (1905b, 73)† take the wind out of my sails; take away my advantage

put a bone in one's head (1907a, 13) bash one's skull in

put a flea into one's ear (1907a, 43) put ideas in one's head

put a hole through him (1900b, 201) kill him

put a spoke in my wheel (1905b, 736)† trip me up

rains cats and dogs (1907a, 43) rains very heavily

[more luck than a] rabbit has hair (1903, 122) very much luck

rats in the garret (1909d, 3) crazy

robbing Peter to pay Paul (1900c, 96) take a piece from here and put it there (referring to quilts) (Louisiana)

[have a] rod in pickle for one (1907a, 13) have a cause for argument with one

[he has] room to rent in his upper story (1909d, 3) he is crazy

[he has a] rooster under his hat (1907a, 45) said of someone who does not take off his hat

run with the machine (1900c, 221) [politicians who] follow the party line blindly

scrape an acquaintance (1907a, 14) ignore an acquaintance

scarce as hens' teeth (1907a, 18) nonexistent

scratch my back and I shall scratch yours (1909d, 171) help me and I will help you

[as] sharp as a tag [tack?] (1907a, 42) a very bright student (America)

sight is good for sore eyes (1909d, 77) compliment for a lady

sit and suck his claws (1900c, 213) starve

skin one's own skunk (1900c, 219) do dishonorable or dirty work oneself

snakes in his boots (1907a, 40) drunk

sound on the goose (1907a, 13) trustworthy

[he is of no more use than the] spare pump in a corncrib (1900c, 218) he is useless

spell baker (1907a, 13) successfully complete a project

[one cannot] spoil a rotten egg (1900c, 220) one cannot corrupt someone who is already corrupt (as a politician)

[you could not] strike water if you fell out of a skiff (1907a, 15) you do everything wrong

struck it rich (1907a, 46) became rich

struck oil (1907a, 46) became rich (Pennsylvania)

[as] sure as I am living (1900b, 201) truly

sure as I stand on this spot (1900b, 201) truly

tacks in one's head (1909d, 3) crazy

take a horn (1907a, 26), (1896a, 55) drink, especially from a gin glass

take the cake (1907a, 22, 43) take the prize

[not worth a] tinker's dam (1907a, 15) worthless

took the cake (1905b, 71)† surpassed everyone, excelled

throw up the sponge (1905b, 71)† abandon the contest or struggle

[your] trolly's off (1907a, 46) you're on the wrong track

turn up the nose (1909d, 122) treat with contempt

turned up his toes (1909d, 183) died

under the rose (1900c, 219) observe secrecy

upon my honor (1900b, 201) a pledge to speak the truth and do what is right

wear the breeches (1907a, 7) have the authority in the family

wear one's heart upon one's sleeve (1909d, 167) show one's feeling too plainly

went up like a rocket and came down like a stick (1907a, 45) was widely praised and then discovered to be a fraud

wipe another's nose (1909d, 121) easily deceived

In *Was ist Volkskunde* (1900b, 202–3),§ Knortz gave a list of American curses, exclamations, and sayings taken from a German-American newspaper.

Great Scott!

He's all right!

I should smile!

Step lively!

Oh, I see!

Did you ever see?

Because!

Don't put on such airs!

That'll do!

Cheese it!

That's it!

Go and hire a hall!

Go it!

Of course!

Give it to him!

There's no use talking!

What are you giving us?

You bet your sweet life!

Not by a long shot!

What's the matter with me!

I'll see you later!

Do you take him for a sucker?

Pshaw!

Never you mind me!

Here goes!

None of your business!

I don't care!

Don't you tumble?

Smarty!

D'you see any flies on me?

Got stuck!

He got off easily!

That settles it!

Don't you make a mistake!

Shut up!

And don't you forget it!

Oh, stop!

Go to grass!

Little snoozer!

Come off!

You don't say!

· E i g h t e e n ·

TONGUE TWISTERS AND WORDS WHICH

CAN BE READ BACKWARDS

The data in *Amerikanische Redensarten* (American Sayings) (1907a, 33) are taken from a list Knortz put together for his own use. His sources are not mentioned.

I went into the garden to gather some blades, and there I saw two sweet, pretty babes. "Ah, babes, is that you, babes, braiding of blades, babes? If you braid any blades at all, babes, braid broad blades, babes, or braid no blades at all, babes."

The bleak breeze blighted the bright broom blossoms.

A box of mixed biscuits, a mixed biscuit box.

Flesh of freshly fried flying fish.

A glowing gleam glowing green.

Hobbs meets Snobbs and Nobbs. Hobbs hobs to Snobbs and Nobbs. Hobbs nobs with Snobbs and robs Nobbs' fob. "That is," says Nobbs, "the worse for Hobb's jobs," and Snobbs sobs.

Oliver Oglethorp ogled an owl and oyster. Did Oliver Oglethorp ogle an owl and oyster? If Oliver Oglethorp ogled an owl and oyster, where are the owl and oyster Oliver Oglethorp ogled?

Robert Rowley rolled a round roll 'round. A round roll Robert Rowley rolled round. Where rolled the round roll Robert Rowley rolled 'round?

High roller, low roller, lower roller.

Sammy Shoesmith saw a shrieking songster. Did Sammy Shoesmith see a shrieking songster? If Sammy Shoesmith saw a shrieking songster, where's the shrieking songster Sammy Shoesmith saw?

It is a shame, Sam. These are the same, Sam. 'Tis all a sham, Sam, and a shame it is to sham so, Sam.

The sea ceaseth, and it sufficeth us.

Six thick thistle sticks.

Strict strong Stephen Stringer snared slickly six sickly silky snakes.

Susan shineth shoes and socks. Socks and shoes shines Susan. She ceaseth shining shoes and socks, for shoes and socks shock Susan.

Swan swam over the sea. Swim, swan, swim. Swan swam back again, well swum swan.

Words that can be read backwards:

Adda, Anna, bab, bib, bob, bub, civic, dad, deed, deified, devived, dewed, did, dood, ecce, eve, ewe, eye, gog, gig, gag, level, madam, Maram, noon, non, Otto, pap, peep, pip, pop, pup, redder, refer, repaper, reviver, rotator, sees, selles, semes sexes, shahs, sis, siris, stellets, tat, tenet, tit, toot, tot, tut, waw, welew (1907a, 34).

·Nineteen·

GAMES

"Blind Man's Buff" often involves the giving of a pawn. The players form a circle, facing outside. To redeem the pawn, one person takes a broom, holds it high, and says to his neighbor without laughing:

Buff says Buff to all his men,
And they say Buff to him again.
Buff neither laughs nor smiles,
But carries his face
With a very good grace
And passes his broom
To the very next place.
Ha! Ho! Ha! Ho!
To my very next neighbor
Go, Broomie, go.

If he laughs, he has to repeat the verse; otherwise he gives the broom to the next person and gets his pawn back (1900c, 265).*ᴇ§

"Rolling the Cheese" is played mainly by Italians in New York. Each player brings a wheel of hard, expensive Parmesan cheese, weighing between ten and forty pounds. The cheese is wrapped well to survive the rolling around. Each person throws his wheel as far as he can. After four attempts, whoever comes nearest to the goal gets all of the cheese. The game is played on the street, usually near a renowned restaurant. It starts and ends with a gala meal (1900c, 261–2).§*

At agricultural exhibitions, a big piece of cheese is often hung from the top of a high slippery climbing pole. Whoever manages to fetch it may take it home (1900c, 262).*§

At American picnics, players love a game in which a player is blind-folded and has to fasten a tail to the picture of a donkey drawn on a piece of cloth. He who fastens the tail closest to its proper place, wins (1900c, 262).*§

Eggs are carried on wooden spoons to a certain place. The person who arrives without dropping his egg, wins (New York) (1900c, 260).*§

"Gobbler." At Thanksgiving, a day no American celebrates without eating turkey, the guests are sometimes asked to imitate the voice of an animal when a certain signal is given. The person who does not know the game is secretly told he should gobble like a turkey. All the others know they have to remain silent. When the person gobbles, he is laughed at and called gobbler for the rest of the day (1900c, 266).*§

"Golf." Since 1891 this game has been popular, especially with the American aristocracy (1900c, 256).*

"Hare and Dog." Two boys are the hares. Each has in his pocket strips of paper which he throws away while fleeing. These represent the scent which the dogs have to follow faithfully as they try to catch the hares (1900c, 264).*§

"Hawk." The ball is regarded as a boar which everybody tries to drive into a ditch using a stick. American boys often use an empty oyster or sardine can or even a hard small piece of wood instead of the ball (1900c, 252).*§

"Hops Pickers' Dance." This wild, uninhibited dancing mostly takes place in rural areas on the Pacific coast. A rough platform is set up and supplied with a few wooden benches which are reserved for the ladies. The men usually dance without jackets, and everybody dances as wildly and regardless of rules as he likes. The master of ceremonies shouts:

Lady, 'round the gent, and the gent so-lo
Lady, 'round the lady, and the gent don't go!
but nobody listens (1900c, 265–6).*ᴇ

"Hunt the Slipper." The players sit in a circle. One person stands in the middle and holds up a slipper. He throws it up in the air and it is caught by someone who hands it to another player behind his back. The person who threw it must try to retrieve the slipper. The player from whom he snatches it must then take his place (1900c, 267).*§

"Hunt the Whistle." This game can only be played in a group where one person does not know the secret of the game. This person has to kneel down until the whistle is hidden, that is, until it is fastened to her dress. While she is looking for the whistle, a fellow player blows it without removing it from her dress. Thus, she is kept rushing around trying to find the whistle (1900c, 268).*

"Initiation into Polite Society." A needle is stuck into the wall and a young man who does not know the game, has to point at the needle and remember where it is. He then is blindfolded, led about the room for a while, and eventually has to try to touch the needle with his outstretched hand. While moving around blindly, touching everything that is in his way, he is a source of laughter for the others (1900c, 266).*

"London Bridge" (the most popular children's game in the eastern United States.) Two children hold up their hands to represent the bridge. The other children pass under the bridge and each time they do so, the last child who passes is caught and has to line up behind one of the children representing the bridge, until all the children are lined up on either side. All the while they sing: "London Bridge is falling down—falling down—falling down." Then they form a chain and tug until the chain breaks, and the game starts anew. In Pennsylvania the game is called "Die holländische Brücke" [Dutch Bridge] (1896a, 36).*§

"Peanut game." American farmers' wives hide peanuts in the living room and in the kitchen during long winter evenings. Whoever finds the most within a given time wins. Instead of peanuts, potatoes are often used (1900c, 263).*

"Peanut." Each player gets a dozen peanuts and a knife. On a signal the players must carry the peanuts on the blades of their knives into another room and put them onto a plate. Whoever finishes first, wins (1900c, 267).*

"Potato game." This game is played by men and women. Twelve potatoes are put into two rows. Two players have to try to carry the potatoes in their respective rows to a certain place, using a spoon. The person who finishes first challenges another player and so on, until everybody has tried his luck (1900c, 267).*

"Puss in the corner." Four persons stand in the four corners of a room; a fifth stands in the middle. When he calls "Puss in the corner," the players rush to change corners. At the same time the person in the middle tries to reach one of the corners. Whoever loses his corner by the latter's success is called "puss" (1900c, 268).*§

"Quoit." A flat piece of iron in the shape of a horseshoe, a kind of disk, is thrown at a target. The player who comes closest to it, wins (1900c, 251).*§

· T w e n t y ·

CUSTOMS

APRIL FIRST

The first of April is the day when interest has to be paid. People drink a lot on that day, but drunkards are frowned upon and are the target of many practical jokes (Pennsylvania Dutch) (1902b, 66).*§

The first of April is called April Fool's Day. People can make a fool of others and play tricks at their expense (1900c, 49).*§

Knortz gives several examples of tricks and jokes that take place on the first of April: Jokes work best in the early morning, before people take note of the meaning of the day. American children are most happy to make April fools of their parents. Fathers have to be especially aware of surprises on the first of April. If they come home late in the evening and fall over a chair in the doorway, they can be sure that a promising son has played a trick on them. If they want to put on their jackets to go to work after breakfast, they might find out that the sleeves have been sewn together. Sometimes somebody wakes them up early because of an important affair, and when they jump into their slippers they burn their feet, because some scoundrels have put live coals into them. Children may ask their father to write something for them, and if he does so and dips the pen into the inkwell, he finds out that it is filled with water. He laughs heartily and secretly is happy that he has such smart kids.

The jokes that Americans play are sometimes very rude. If a boy has "money to burn," he puts a silver coin onto the stove, and when it has become very hot, he throws it on the sidewalk. He stands nearby and laughs heartily when the lucky finder burns his fingers. On this day girls go for a walk and "eat confection." If they meet a good friend who loves sweets, they offer her, most innocently, fake sweets made of soap. Sometimes people make gifts of a bunch of flowers filled with cayenne pepper. The sugar bowl often is filled with salt. Kids also think it is funny to heat the handle of a poker. Sometimes they fasten a thin string to a parcel and put it on the rails of the tram. When the conductor stops the tram to have the object removed from the tracks, the malicious boys pull it away, laughing wildly. A purse which is nailed onto the street is also regarded as funny. At parties, handkerchiefs and fans may be fastened to the floor, and the polite man who tries to pick them up can be sure of the guests' ridicule. At other times the seat of a chair is removed and the hole covered with a cloth or a rug. The unsuspecting guest who sits on it sinks down, to the greatest joy of those present (1900c, 53–4).*§

Once, when two American students who shared a room had gone out on a cold April evening, a few classmates secretly slipped into their apartment, put out the fire, poured icy water into their beds, and hid the clothes of the two students in the stove. Since the victims found the room cold after their return, they wanted to go to bed quickly, but their beds did not offer them the usual warmth, so they decided to make a fire. When the whole room was inexplicably filled with smoke, they could do nothing but stay awake all night and think of revenge (1900c, 54–5).*§

A soldier who had served in the Northern army during the American Civil War once told me the following April joke: His regiment was stationed on a much traveled road near the headquarters. Since a big Union flag flew over the building, a lady who did not hide her sympathy for the South, always detoured around that spot, because she did not want the flag to fly over her head. On April first, a soldier placed a counterfeit dollar note on the road underneath the flag. When the lady saw the note, thinking nobody would see her, she suddenly lost her Southern patriotism, hurried under the flag, and picked up the money. This action was greeted with scornful laughter by the soldiers, who had hidden nearby. As long as the Northern army was stationed there, the southern lady did not venture onto that street again (1900c, 55–6).*†

If an American lady has a servant who is not very intelligent, she sends him to the tailor on April first to buy a pound of buttonholes, or to the pharmacist to buy a foot of dove's milk, or to the bookstore to get the autobiography of progenitor Eve. The maid usually presents him with a cigar filled with gun powder or a cake filled with cotton and sand (1900c, 56).*§

The Americans use to shout at boys:
April Fool
Wash your face and go to school (1900c, 56).*§

On the first of April, teachers must put up with students who attach strips of paper to their jackets or paint the seats of their chairs with chalk. For them, it is best to join in the joke and not spoil their charges' fun. On April first, it is not unusual to see American ladies with cat's tails, dishrags, and similar items sewn to their dresses. On this day, in several places in Pennsylvania, boys are allowed to beat girls (1900c, 56).*§

Americans take great pleasure in inviting a group of friends over on the first of April. When they arrive, they are surprised to find a slip of paper on the closed door saying "April Fool!" Even the clergy is made a fool of, and not in a gentle way, either. They are called by telephone to a seriously ill member of the church and asked to give the Eucharist, finding when they get there that the patient in the best of health. Sometimes they are called in for a christening, only to find out that the house in which their services were requested, is inhabited by an old spinster. Physicians are similarly fooled when they are called to help a woman in childbirth (1900c, 56–7).*§

APPLE BUTTER

In the fall, making apple butter brings young people together in the evenings. Along with corn husking, it takes up a place in their social life similar to the spinning room in Germany. First the apples are peeled, then they are thrown into a big pot that hangs over the fire. They have to be constantly stirred so that they do not burn. The person whose job this is cannot leave his post and becomes the target of jokes and teasing (Pennsylvania Dutch) (1902b, 61).*§

ARBOR DAY

Arbor Day started as a day when people planted trees to protect fields from harsh winds. Soon it became a yearly event which spread to other states. On Arbor Day, school children visit a public park and learn from their teachers the importance of the forest. Then they plant some trees while singing songs (1905b, 59),*‡ (1907a, 80–1).*

BEES

Knortz talks briefly about "bees": By the expression "bee," Americans define a meeting for a social cause. If a settler wants to build a house and has transported the logs to a certain place, he calls his neighbors together to help him. This is called a "building bee" or "raising bee." It is the duty of every settler to help; if he does not, he is called "Lawrence"(in Virginia) and he is outlawed. If a parcel of land has to be cleared of trees or stones, the pioneers get together in "chopping bees" or "stone bees." This happens especially if a public building is to be built on the land. Among the younger people "husking bees," where corn cobs are husked, have taken the place of the German spinning rooms. The young man who finds a red ear has the right to ask a kiss from every girl present. As Longfellow in Hiawatha attests, this was originally an American Indian custom. In "spelling bees" people try to find out, who is able to spell the best.

Only women take part in "quilting bees," when hundreds of pieces of fabric are sewn together to form a big blanket. Nearly each meeting ends with music and dancing. These quilts are sometimes real works of art. The many colorful pieces of cotton are often put together in such a way that they represent animals, trees, flowers, or furniture. In eastern parts of Massachusetts, the quilts are called "Peter pay Paul"; in Louisiana people say "Robbing Peter to Pay Paul," a name that stems from the practice of cutting out a piece of cloth again here or there and adding it to another part. These elaborate quilts take their names from the subjects depicted on them. Thus, especially in Ohio, the "Sugarbowl Quilts" and "Fly Quilts" are numerous. In Illinois there are "Bear Claws Quilts," and in Massachusetts, "Duck Feet Quilts." If they consist of very many colored pieces, they are called "Crazy Quilts"(1900c, 95–7).*§

In some little country towns in the Union, wives and young women gather during long winter evenings and pass the time sewing so-called quilts, bed covers made of countless pieces. These quilts sometimes have strange names. In Louisiana they are called "World's Wonder"; in North Carolina, "Fool's Puzzle"; in New York, "The Old Maid's Whim"; in Massachusetts, "Chinese Puzzle" or "Peter pay Paul," which is named "Robbing Peter and Pay Paul" in Louisiana (1905b, 61).*‡

BIRD DAY

A Bird Day has been recently introduced here and there. On this day, school children learn about the usefulness of birds and are admonished not to harm them with guns or slingshots (1905b, 59).*‡

BUNDLING

Since farmhouses were very small in former times, consisting of only a few rooms, young engaged people in most cases had to lie down in one bed, fully dressed [when the bridegroom staid overnight]. This custom, which is called "bundling," is still known in a few New England states and in the American West (1902b, 63).*

CAKE WALK

As the name implies, the "cake walk" [among Blacks] is an entertainment in the course of which guests walk for the prize of a big, good-looking cake. Cake walks are seldom organized by private citizens but rather by social clubs, especially formed for this purpose. Couples walk around, a man and a woman, the woman on the man's right side. Sometimes the test is to see which couple walks the most gracefully or who is the most sure-footed. In the latter case, the man must carry a flag and be careful that it does not move unnecessarily, or he must walk along a line which is drawn on the floor with white chalk, without swaying, while his girl walks beside him on his arm. The winning couple gets the cake (1900b, 106–7).*

The well known saying "take the cake" has its origin in Black people's "cake walk," with which a ball usually is ended. Couples chosen by lot walk past a huge cake. An arbitor awards the cake to the couple that is dressed the most elegantly and moves the most gracefully (1907a, 22).*

CHRISTMAS

On Christmas Eve, presents are most important, and children especially are sure to put out stockings for the Christ Child to fill quickly as he passes (1894a, 65).*§

On Christmas Eve, Santa Claus, with a long white beard and his voluminous body wrapped warmly in fur, goes from house to house with his sleigh, drawn by reindeer. He stops before the door and climbs up on the roof; with a loud noise, he squeezes down the chimney into the children's room and empties his basket (1903, 33).*§

It took a long time until Americans began to have a Christmas tree, decorated with lights. In New York whole shiploads of fir trees are unloaded and sold now, for Christmas has become something of a national holiday. Only the French people who live in New York do not like to decorate their rooms in this way, but they celebrate Christ's birth with all kinds of other amusements. No house where Poles or Germans live is without a tree (1902b, 166).*§

At Christmas, American soldiers and sailors get as much liberty as possible. For example, they place a young conscript on a blanket and throw him into the air, until he finally escapes. The more he screams and curses, the more his tormentors laugh. In former years a greased pig was sometimes let loose on the parade grounds for the soldiers to catch (1902b, 183).*§

CURFEW

According to a report from Tucson, Arizona, which appeared in the New York *Staatszeitung* this custom [the curfew] is still intact to this very day in several settlements in the West. In Tucson itself the curfew bell sounds at nine in summer and at eight in winter, at which time all children have to be off the streets (1907a, 23).*§

ELECTION DAY

At the end of political elections, people often light big bonfires (1896a, 54).*§

FUNERALS

If there is a death in a family, women from the neighborhood come together to cook, bake, and prepare the funeral repast for friends, acquaintances, and relatives who gather on the day of the funeral. At the meal, the liquor bottle makes its rounds, and the festivities often end in revelry (Pennsylvania Dutch) (1902b, 65).*§

Among the Pennsylvania Dutch, a death in the family can be financially ruinous since all the neighbors and friends arrive and have a kind of feast. After drinking and eating, only a few of the guests are sober enough and willing to accompany the family to the cemetery (1884a, 70-1).*†

The custom of feasting at a funeral comes from Europe and took root in America, especially in the countryside where farmers who come from afar to a funeral can expect hospitality. Unfortunately, as I can confirm from my own experience, these events sometimes turn into wild revelries (1903, 113-4).*†

EASTER

In America, at Easter the hare [bunny] jumps about in the sun and lays Easter eggs, just as in Germany (1913a, 113).*§

On Easter Monday, children gather in Washington [D.C.] in the garden of the White House to engage in egg rolling. Often four to five thousand children take part. There are both rich and poor children present and even children of foreign ambassadors, who otherwise would never dare to mingle with plebeian republicans. They roll the eggs down a slope. The child whose egg breaks has to give it to a rival, who usually eats it at once (1902b, 36).*§

In the districts of New York which are inhabited by Germans, the children do not go to public schools on Easter Monday, although it is not a holiday ... Children expect the swift Easter Bunny to rush up the countless stairs in apartment houses and to go into the many rooms and hide gifts for the children behind cupboards and under their beds. Americans began to like this custom, have adopted it, and for some time now have used it commercially. Before Easter, you can see in store windows artificial and live bunnies surrounded by colored eggs, chocolate eggs, or those made of porcelain. Most of the time, the Easter eggs in stores are an artificial product imported, perhaps, from Paris and destined to decorate the table of rich snobs (1903; 72–3).*§

In Pennsylvania, children present each other with colored eggs and Easter bunnies that their mothers made of cloth and stuffed with wool (1903, 73).*§

The Armenians in Boston believe that the sun dances on Easter morning. Young people gather in a cemetery on Easter Day. They try to win each other's eggs by hitting them on their tops. The eggs are colored red in remembrance of Jesus' blood. Whose egg breaks is the loser (1903, 72–3).*§

ENGAGEMENT

The American man who wears a ring on the index finger of his left hand shows that he would like to end his bachelor status (1900c, 352).*§

HALLOWEEN

On Halloween, American families often perform *tableaux vivants* as entertainment. They all have the purpose of revealing the future. Called "tableaux of fortune," they are often very expensive as far as costumes and scenes are concerned (1900c, 409).*§

Americans often have a "dumb supper" on Halloween. During its preparation no word may be spoken. The guests go backwards to the set table, sit down backwards, and read a book backwards, while nobody says a word (1900c, 409).*§

Halloween is a typical American holiday, and Knortz often describes Halloween customs. He took the details of the following scenes partly from newspapers, but mainly from *Good Housekeeping* magazine.

Invitations are written in Old English characters and language. When the guests arrive, they enter a room that is only dimly illuminated by candles inside pumpkins. A ghostlike figure, the hostess, greets them without saying a word. She is wrapped in a bed sheet, wears a white mask on her face, and has a pillow case draped around her head as a head dress. Its closed side hangs down her back, and the open side is fastened with pins to her masked head. The male guests are welcomed by the host, who is disguised in a similar way. Each of the two now guides their guests into a separate room and costumes them in the same manner. As decoration and as a sign of recognition, they pin onto the men a black snake and onto the women a bat. Now the whole group assembles in the parlor, which is lit by pumpkins. The light is just barely enough to see ghostlike figures moving about.

A number of live black cats huddle among the guests. When the piano starts playing, people begin to dance. This is an adventurous affair, since everybody is busily trying to handle his drapery, not to step on a cat, and to guess the identity of his partner. Suddenly a red light flares up in a neighboring room, and a soothsayer in a tent can be seen. Now, one after the other is told his future and receives a miniature pumpkin of papier-mâché, which contains a written motto and a souvenir. This is the end of the spooky part. Everybody enters another room and takes off the drapery and masks. Bright lights are turned on, and people go to dinner. They have fruit, nuts, cider, lemonade, the traditional pies and cakes. In the latter several items are hidden: a ring, a thimble, a dime, a key. Whoever finds the ring will marry before next Halloween; whoever gets the thimble will remain single; the coin stands for riches; the key for travels. The more surprises there are, the better it is. You can, for example, mix among the nuts a few which you cut in half and filled with a motto or a jumping snake instead of the kernel and glued together again. There can also be fortune telling from the cards, from molten lead, from coffee grounds; above all, everything must be loud and lively. Teasing is in order, too. You might secretly give everybody a container with a slip of paper in it saying: "Don't tell anybody! Look under the piano at midnight exactly!" The guest can hardly wait till the clock strikes twelve. He sneaks out of the room, trying to reach the piano in the next room by a roundabout way. And there he finds all the others who, like him, are looking for something. They, too, secretly got the same message, and all find something hidden there.

In another case, people were invited to a "ghost story party." Everybody had to tell a ghost story, the spookier the better. There was only candlelight in pumpkins or a green light to create an eerie feeling. A prize is offered for the best ghost story. Here, too, the evening ends in boisterous enjoyment. All kinds of games, surprises, and jokes are prepared, and the old games are played, such as "cutting flour" and "catching apples." In the latter, an apple is either hung on a string from a door frame or swims in a bowl of water. People must try to catch it with their mouths. This is great fun (1913a, 114–6).*§

The custom of lighting bonfires on November 1 (holowe'en) was widespread in America, and stemmed from the Celtic Druids in England (1896a, 54).*§

In several towns of New Hampshire, children parade through the streets on November 5. They carry lanterns made of pumpkins, play loud music, ring doorbells, and light a bonfire (1896a, 53–4).*§

Labor Day

On Labor Day, members of various trades celebrate with a joint parade. Afterwards people sit down in some suitable place in the open air to drink and to listen to speeches of praise from popularity seeking politicians or crafty labor leaders (1905b, 58).*‡

Lynching

Lynching was common and Knortz talks about its origins extensively (1900b, 42–4), then gives two examples which he found in recent newspapers under the same date.

Tarring and Feathering

Hutchinson, Minnesota, June 30, 1898. Two vagrants bathed in hot oil here to get rid of a coat of tar and feathers which they got from the citizens in this town. Both had asked farmer Austin Cook for a meal. One of them, who was drunk at the time, had the impudence to curse Cook, who immediately knocked him down. Since people were still very agitated about the murder of Sheriff Rogers, committed by transients, they got hold of the two men and tarred and feathered them thoroughly.

Montrose, Michigan, June 30, 1898. People in this town are highly excited about the fact that William Davis, who lives two miles from here, was tarred and feathered. A year ago, Davis found employment with farmer William Bailey. By and by, he fell in love with the latter's wife and threw the husband out of the house. When the citizens here heard of it, they hurried to Bailey's house, broke the windows, dragged Davis out of bed, and tarred and feathered him. All through the incident he prayed and asked his tormentors for mercy. Then he was given a week to leave the area (1900b, 46).*§

Ladies' Choice

In some states of the Union, especially in Pennsylvania, every unmarried lady has the right to invite a man to a dance or another festivity during a leap year. She is then obliged to pick him up at his home, to see to it that he has enough to eat and drink, and to be sure that he gets home again safely (1900c, 343).*§ (In *Nachklänge germanischen* [1903, 82–3], Knortz adds that if she proposes to him on this occasion, he will not be surprised).*§

May Day

Certain children's games are played only on special occasions. The May Dance, which was known by the Romans and Greeks and was danced in honor of Ceres and Flora, is retained mainly in England and a few areas of the states of New York and Pennsylvania. This dance is regarded as a spring festival, which certainly is its original meaning. Formerly it was danced by young people of both sexes; now it lives on only as children's amusement. But from year to year, less is left of it (1896a, 27).§

In Indianapolis, children in public schools celebrate a May festival outdoors every year. Beneath a big tree a stage is set up, where the queen—in a white dress—and her maid of honor sit down. Both are students. All the children surround them and sing and recite. A high pole decorated with flowers and long ribbons represents the historic Maypole and the children dance around it, weaving and unweaving the ribbons (1900b, 108-9).*§

New Year

In Virginia and North Carolina, where people often burn a yule log, a twig of mistletoe—in England frequently called kissing bush—is fastened to the ceiling on New Year's Day. The girl who "happens" to step beneath it and is kissed by one of the men present will be married within one year (1902b, 166).*

The Blacks on plantations in Louisiana regard New Year as their most important festival of the year. Early in the morning, old and young go out to wish each other happiness and to receive gifts, usually a big piece of ox meat and a suit. Women get a brightly colored handkerchief in addition. In the afternoon they eat, dance, and play games. The most common instrument is a barrel covered with cowhide, on which the rhythm of a short song is beaten with hands or sticks (1900c, 45).*

As a rule, only German-Americans still celebrate New Year's Eve, feasting and drinking with their friends. But they, too, have begun to pass this time quietly and to be content sending colored greeting cards with tender verses to their friends and neighbors, wishing them much luck in the new year. Since it has become a custom to ask God's blessing for one's friends on Christmas Day, the always practical American recently had the idea to manufacture a greeting card for both holidays. Now the well wisher can kill two birds with one stone and thus save time and money (1903, 74).*§

On New Year's Eve there is much shooting in America, not to chase away witches and other evil spirits but simply to make noise. Every self-respecting American kid who intends to become President of the United States one day naturally has his own revolver, and if he shoots off some of his fingers on New Year's Eve or the Fourth of July, well, he suffers the loss quietly; after all, he has fulfilled his patriotic duty (1903, 74-5).*§

In New York and Philadelphia, the Chinese often display a red flag with white fringes on New Year's Day. To the middle of it are attached symbols of strength and long life and the inscription "Obey the heavens and act rightfully" (1900c, 47).*§

Shrove Tuesday

On Shrove Tuesday, the Pennsylvania Dutch bake a special kind of doughnut, and they dance and joke to make sure that "the flax grows" (1902b, 66).*§

Spooning Parties

In some areas of the United States, so-called "spooning parties"... are among the favorite evening entertainments for young people of both sexes. Guests are asked to bring along spoons dressed up in male or female clothes. A committee decides, according to certain characteristics, which should be matched, and their owners then spend the evening together (1907a, 31).*§

In Harvard College the most popular student is given a wooden spoon. This "wooden spoonman" is very proud of the honor (1907a, 32).*

Strawberry Harvest

In Quakertown, Connecticut, the strawberry harvest is a busy and happy time. At sunrise women and young girls go to pick the delicious fruit .... In Quakertown, a man who has not more than an acre of strawberry land is regarded as poor; whoever possesses more than five acres belongs to the rich. Of course, a family, even if it is very numerous, cannot pick the strawberries on a five-acre lot themselves. That is why young people from neighboring villages are invited to come and help pick the fruit. Laughter and jokes lighten the work, and for many of them it is an opportunity to find a spouse (1900b, 60).*

Sweetheart's Rings

Recently, young Americans of both sexes, who sometimes try to spend their extra money in a romantic way, started giving each other so-called "Sweetheart's Rings," engraved with the name of the respective young man or young girl and set with a precious stone. The acceptance of the ring is no obligation to marry, only to engage in pleasant courtesy and entertainment, in short, in "flirtation," which a Frenchman called "attention without intention." When the young people are no longer interested in each other, they return the rings and this is the end of it (1903, 89–90).*§

Thanksgiving Day

Thanksgiving Day is the oldest American national holiday . . . . Every American thinks it is his duty to have a turkey that day, even if he has to steal it or to borrow the money to buy it (1905b, 57).*‡

Valentine's Day

On Valentine's Day (February 14), it has become customary among young people in America to send their beloved a card or a slip of paper which tells of the lover's feelings towards the recipient (1903, 75).*§

Weddings

Nowadays, if an American girl marries, she often gets a broom as a wedding present from a girl friend. It is usually accompanied by this verse:

If ever you get married,
A broom to you I'll send,
In sunshine use the brushy part,

In storm the other end (1900c, 349),*ᴇ§ (1913a, 152).

Recently the custom, or rather the bad custom, of throwing rice on the bride in the church after the wedding ceremony has been adopted in America. It comes from India. Sometimes this ritual becomes so violent that the priest must call the police for protection (1903, 86).*§

[Among the Pennsylvania Dutch], if the wedding took place in a church, bride and bridegroom often were stopped on their way to it by a rope across the street. They could not go on until the bridegroom had given the people a present consisting of money or wine. A similar custom still exists in several places in Cook County in the state of Illinois (1902b, 64).*§

In the German settlements in Pennsylvania, a bridal procession on its way to church is often stopped by ropes or poles, which are only taken away when the bridegroom agrees to give a barrel of beer or some bottles of wine to the people who set up the barrier (1903, 88).*§

In New York a shoe is used to amuse the wedding guests. All marriageable girls are lined up, and a shoe is thrown as far as possible. The girl who gets hold of it first will be the next bride. Then the young men stand together and the lucky girl throws the shoe among them. The one she hits will be the next bridegroom (1900c, 198).*†

In the countryside in many of the United States, there is a charivari for the young couple on the evening of their wedding. Loud music is played on long tin horns, and noise is made with old watering cans, stove pipes, and kettles, until the bridegroom appears and gives the conductor of the concert money for a barrel of beer (1903, 97).*§

Appendices

·Appendix A·

A BIBLIOGRAPHY OF
KARL KNORTZ'S WORK

1865. Geschichte, Wesen und Literatur der Stenographie [History, nature, and literature of stenography]. *Deutsch-Amerikanische Monatshefte.* Mai: 385–396.

1871a. a)*Märchen und Sagen der nordamerikanischen Indianer* [Tales and legends of the North-American Indians]. Jena, Costenoble.

b) *Skazky severo-amerických Indiánů,* české mládeži. Vypravuje Václav Petru. Prague: Hynek, 1882. [Czech translation.]

c) More recent edition: *Märchen und Sagen der Indianer Nordamerikas.* München: Borowsky.

1871b. Longfellow. *Evangeline.* Trans. by Knortz. Der deutsche Pionier. April.

1872a. *Lieder und Romanzen Alt Englands* [Songs and romances from old England]. Trans. by Knortz. Cöthen: Schettler.

1872b. Longfellow. *Der Song von Hiawatha* [The song of Hiawatha]. Ed. and trans. by Knortz. Jena: Costenoble.

1873. *Little Snow-white and the Dwarfs.* Cincinnati. [Dramatization.]

1874a. Die fonographische Literatur in den Vereinigten Staaten Nordamerikas [The phonographic literature in the United States of America]. *Panstenographikon* 1: 3–4, 279–303.

1874b. Longfellow. *Die Brautwerbung des Miles Standish* [The courtship of Miles Standish]. Trans. by Knortz. Leipzig: Reclam.

1875a. *Gedichte* [Poems]. Leipzig: Reclam.

1875b. *Schottische Balladen* [Scottish ballads]. Ed. and trans. by Knortz. Halle: Waisenhaus.

1876a. *Amerikanische Skizzen* [American sketches]. Halle: Gesenius.

1876b. *An American Shakespeare Bibliography*. Boston: Schoenhoff & Moeller. Reprint 1877, Leipzig: Kittler.

1877. *Humoristische Gedichte* [Humorous poems]. Baltimore: Rossmässler u. Morf. 3d ed. 1912, Berlin) W. Kästner.

1878. *Epigramme* [Epigrams]. Lyck: Wieüe.

1879a. *Longfellow: Literarhistorische Studie* [Longfellow: a study in literary history]. Hamburg: Grüning.

1879b. Whittier. *Snow-Bound*. Trans. by Knortz.

1880a. *Aus dem Wigwam. Uralte und neue Märchen und Sagen der nordamerikanischen Indianer* [From the wigwam. Very old and new tales and legends of the North-American Indians]. Leipzig: Spamer.

1880b. *Kapital und Arbeit in Amerika* [Capital and work in America] (lecture). Zürich: C. Schmidt.

1880c. *Modern American Lyrics*. Ed. by Knortz and O. Dickmann. Leipzig: Brockhaus.

1882a. *Aus der transatlantischen Gesellschaft. Nordamerikanische Kulturbilder* [From the Transatlantic Society. Pictures from North American culture]. Leipzig: Scheicke.

1882b. *Mythologie und Zivilisation der nordamerikanischen Indianer* [Mythology and civilization of the North-American Indians]. Zwei Abhandlungen. Leipzig: Frohberg.

1882c. *Shakespeare in Amerika. Eine literarhistorische Studie* [Shakespeare in America. A study in literary history]. Berlin: Hofmann.

1882d. *Staat und Kirche in Amerika* [State and church in America] (lecture). Gotha: Stollberg.

1883. *Amerikanische Gedichte der Neuzeit* [Modern American poems]. Trans. by Knortz. Leipzig: Wartig.

1884a. *Amerikanische Lebensbilder. Skizzen und Tagebuchblätter* [Pictures of American life. Sketches and pages from a diary]. Zürich: Schabelitz.

1884b. *Neue Epigramme* [New epigrams]. Zürich: Verlags-Magazin.

1884c. *Neue Gedichte* [New Poems]. Glarus: Vogel. 2d ed. 1893, Glarus: B. Vogel.

1885a. *Eines deutschen Matrosen Nordpolfahrten. Wilhelm Ninde-mann's Erinnerungen an die Nordpolexpedition der "Polaris" und "Jeanette"* [A German sailor's voyages to the North Pole. Wilhelm Ninde-man's recollections of the North Pole expeditions with the ships *Polaris* and *Jeanette*]. Zürich.

1885b. *Goethe und die Wertherzeit. Ein Vortrag. Mit dem Anhange: Goethe in Amerika* [Goethe and the time of Werther. A lecture. With the appendix: Goethe in America]. Zürich.

1885c. *Representative German poems, ballad and lyrical; original texts with English versions by various translators.* Ed. with notes by Knortz. New York: Holt; Boston: Schoenhof.

1886a. *Brook Farm and Margaret Fuller* (lecture). New York: Bartsch. 2d. ed. 1900, Hamburg: Rudolph.

1886b. *Gustav Seyffarth. Eine biographische Skizze* [Gustav Seyffarth. A Biographic Sketch]. New York: Steiger.

1886c. *Irländische Märchen wiedererzählt* [Irish Tales Retold]. Trans. by Knortz. Zürich: Verlagsmagazin.

1886d. *Walt Whitman* (lecture). New York: Bartsch.

1887a. *Lieder aus der Fremde* [Songs from a foreign country]. Trans. by Knortz. Glarus: Vogel. 2d. ed. 1899, Oldenburg: Schulze.

1887b. *Nokomis. Märchen und Sagen der nordamerikanischen Indi-aner. Wiedererzählt* [Nokomis. Tales and legends of the North American Indians. Retold]. Zürich: Verlagsmagazin.

1888. *Hamlet und Faust* [Hamlet and Faust]. Zürich: Verlagsmagazin.

1889a. *Die deutschen Volkslieder und Märchen* [The German folksongs and folktales](2 lectures). Zürich: Verlagsmagazin.

1889b. *Whitman, Walt. Grashalme. Gedichte* [Whitman, Walt. Leaves of grass. Poems]. Trans. by Knortz and T. W. Rolleston. Zürich: Verlags-magazin.

1889c. Knortz, Karl and O. Thanet. *Amerikanische Kriminal-Erzählun-gen* [American detective stories]. Berlin: Zehnpfennig Bibliothek Verlag.

1889d. *Deutschlands Bilder und Balladen. Originaltexte mit englischen Übersetzungen von verschiedenen übersetzern* [Germany's pictures and bal-lads. Original texts with translations by different translators]. New York.

1891a. *Der amerikanische Sonntag. Kulturhistorische Skizze* [The American Sunday. A sketch in cultural history]. Zürich: Schabelitz.

1891b. *Das deutsche Volkslied* [The German folksong]. In *Gedenkblätter*. Verein für Kunst und Wissenschaft.

1891c. *Geschichte der nordamerikanischen Literatur* [History of Northern American literature]. Berlin: Lüstenröder.

1891d. *Rom in Amerika* [Rome in America]. Lecture. Zürich: Schabelitz.

1892a. *Der amerikanische Schutzzoll* [The American protective duty]. Zürich: Schabelitz.

1892b. *Aus der alten und neuen Welt. Bunter Kram* [From the Old and the New World. All kinds of Bagatelles]. München: Poessl. 2d ed. 1895, München: Poessl.

1892c. *Die christlich-kommunistische Kolonie der Rappisten in Pennsylvanien und neue Mitteilungen über Nikolaus Lenau's Aufenthalt unter den Rappisten* [The Christian-communist colony of the Rappites and new information about Nikolaus Lenau's stay among the Rappites]. Lecture. Leipzig: Wiest.

1892d. *Kulturhistorisches aus dem Dollar-Lande* [Cultural-historical information from the country of the dollar]. Basel: Verlagsdruckerei.

1892e. *Eine Weltanschauung in Citaten* [A philosophy of life in quotes]. Leipzig: Spohr.

1893a. *Aus der Mappe eines Deutsch-Amerikaners. Frommes und Gottloses* [From the files of a German-American. Things religious and irreligious]. Bamberg: Schneider.

1893b. *Sich selbst verbannt. Amerikanischer Kriminalroman nach J. Hawthorne* [Self-exiled. An American criminal novel after J. Hawthorne]. Mannheim: J. Bensheimer.

1894a. *Deutsches und Amerikanisches* [Things German and American]. Glarus: Vogel.

1894b. *Wie kann das Deutschtum im Auslande erhalten werden?* [How can the German culture be preserved in a foreign country?] Bamberg: Handelsdruckerei.

1895. *Der fröbelsche Kindergarten und seine Bedeutung für die Erhal-

tung des Deutschtums im Auslande [The Kindergarten, as developed by Froebel, and its importance for the preservation of German culture in a foreign country]. Glarus: Schweizerische Verlagsanstalt.

1896a. *Folklore. Mit dem Anhang: Amerikanische Kinderreime* [Folklore. With the appendix: American children's rhymes]. Dresden: Glöss.

1896b. *Lesebuch für deutsch-amerikanische Volksschulen* [A reader for German-American schools]. Boston: Heintzemann.

1896c. *Parzival. Literaturhistorische Skizze. Mit dem Anhang: Der Einfluss und das Studium der deutschen Literatur in Nordamerika* [Parzival. A sketch in cultural history. With the appendix: the influence and study of German literature in North America]. Glarus: Schweizerische Verlagsanstalt.

1896d. *Die wahre Inspirations-Gemeinde in Iowa. Ein Beitrag zur Geschichte des christlichen Pietismus und Communismus* [The true inspirational community in Iowa. A contribution to the history of Christian Pietism and Communism]. Leipzig: Wigand.

1897a. *Individualität. Pädagogische Betrachtungen* [Individuality. Pedagogic studies]. Leipzig: Mayer.

1897b. *Das Nibelungenlied und Wilhelm Jordan. Mit dem Anhange: Richard Wagner in Amerika* [The Nibelungenlied and Wilhelm Jordan. With the appendix: Richard Wagner in America]. Glarus: Schweizerische Verlagsanstalt.

1897c. *Die plattdeutsche Literatur Nordamerikas* [The Low-German literature in North America].

1898a. *Das Deutschtum der Vereinigten Staaten* [The German way of life in the United States]. Hamburg: Verlagsanstalt A. G.

1898b. *Friedrich Nietzsche und sein Übermensch* [Friedrich Nietzsche and his Übermensch]. Zürich: Verlag von Stern's literarischem Bulletin der Schweiz.

1898c. *Plaudereien eines Deutsch-Amerikaners* [Chats of a German-American]. Basel: Kattentidt.

1898d. *Über den Einfluss und das Studium der deutschen Literatur in Amerika* [About the influence and the study of German literature in America]. Glarus.

1899a. *Ein amerikanischer Diogenes (Henry Thoreau)* [An American Diogenes (Henry Thoreau)]. Hamburg: Verlagsanstalt A. G.

1899b. *Walt Whitman, der Dichter der Demokratie. Mit den Beilagen Neue Übersetzungen aus "Grashalme" und 13 Original-Briefe Whitman's* [Walt Whitman, the poet of democracy. With the addition: new translations from *Leaves of Grass* and 13 original letters of Whitman's]. 2d.ed. Leipzig: (Fleischer) R. Voigtländer.

1900a. *Kindeskunde und häusliche Erziehung* [Pedagogics and education at home]. Altenburg: Tittel.

1900b. *Was ist Volkskunde und wie studiert man dieselbe?* [What is Volkskunde and how do you study it?]. Altenburg: Tittel.

1900c. *Folkloristische Streifzüge* [Folkloristic excursions]. Oppeln und Leipzig: Maske.

1902a. *Poetischer Hausschatz der Nordamerikaner* [Poetic family treasures of North Americans]. Ed. by Knortz. Oldenburg and Leipzig: Schulze.

1902b. *Streifzüge auf dem Gebiete amerikanischer Volkskunde. Altes und Neues* [Excursions in the domain of American folklore. Old things and new ones]. Leipzig: Hoppe.

1903. *Nachklänge germanischen Glaubens und Brauchs in Amerika. Ein Beitrag zur Volkskunde* [Aftereffects of Germanic belief and custom in America. A contribution to folklore]. Halle: Peter.

1904a. *Die amerikanische Volksschule* [The American elementary school]. Tübingen: Laupp'sche Buchhandlung.

1904b. *Der Handfertigkeitsunterricht. Ein amerikanisches Gutachten* [Instruction in manual dexterity. An American expertise]. Arnsberg: Stahl.

1904c. *Römische Taktik in den Vereinigten Staaten* [Roman tactics in the United States]. Berlin: Schwetschke.

1905a. *Schiller der Dichter der Freiheit* [Schiller, the poet of freedom]. Lecture. Evansville, Indiana.

1905b. a) *Zur amerikanischen Volkskunde* [A contribution to American folklore]. Tübingen: Laupp'sche Buchhandlung.

b) American Folklore. *The Folklore Historian* 5, no. 1, 1–43. Middletown, PA (1988) [English translation].

1906a. *Deutsch in Amerika* [German in America]. Leipzig: Hirschfeld.

1906b. *Nietzsche's Zarathustra*. Halle: Peter.

1907a. *Amerikanische Redensarten und Volksgebräuche. Mit dem Anhang: Folkloristisches in Longfellow's "Evangeline"* [American sayings and customs. With the appendix: fokloristic data in Longfellow's "*Evangeline*"]. Leipzig: Teutonia.

1907b. *Die Vereinigten Staaten von Amerika* [The United States of America]. Berlin: Hillger.

1908a. *Das Buch des Lebens. Sprüche der Weisheit für Freie und Unfreie* [The book of life. Aphorisms of wisdom for free and unfree people]: Leipzig, Klinkhardt & Biermann.

1908b. *Sudermanns Dramen* [The drama of Suderman]. Lecture. Halle: Grosse.

1909a. *Christentum und Kirchentum* [Christianity and the church]. Lecture. Leipzig: Teichmann.

1909b. *Fremdwörterei* [The way of using foreign words]. Lecture. Hannover: Hahn.

1909c. *Friedrich Nietzsche, der Unzeitgemässe* [Friedrich Nietzsche the unseasonable]. Annaberg: Grafer.

1909d. *Der menschliche Körper in Sage, Brauch und Sprichwort* [The human body in legends, customs, and proverbs]. Würzburg, Kabitzsch.

1909e. *Die Notwendigkeit des religionslosen Moralunterrichts in der Volksschule. Ein amerikanisches Gutachten* [The necessity of moral education without religion in elementary school. An American expertise]. Leipzig: Teichmann.

1909f. *Der Pessimismus in der amerikanischen Literatur* [The pessimism in American literature]. Wien: Lumen.

1909g. *Religiöses Leben in den Vereinigten Staaten. Ein unerbaulicher Bericht* [Religious life in the United States. An unsavory report]. Jugenheim: Sueviaverlag.

1909h. *Washington Irving in Tarrytown. Ein Beitrag zur Geschichte der nordamerikanischen Literatur* [Washington Irving in Tarrytown. A contribution to the history of North American literature]. Nürnberg: Koch.

1910a. *Die Insekten in Sage, Geschichte und Literatur* [Insects in legends, history, and literature]. Annaberg: Graser.

1910b. *Die Notwendigkeit einer Organisation der Freidenker* [The necessity for an organization of freethinkers]. Milwaukee, Wisconsin: Verlag des Bundes-Vororts.

1910c. *Robert Owen und seine Weltverbesserungsversuche* [Robert Owen and his attempts at changing the world for the better]. Leipzig: Demme.

1911a. *Macbeth. Eine Shakespeare-Studie* [Macbeth. A Shakespeare study]. Essen: Literatur-Verlag.

1911b. *Reptilien und Amphibien in Sage, Sitte und Literatur* [Reptiles and amphibians in legends, tradition, and literature]. Annaberg: Graser.

1911c. *Walt Whitman und seine Nachahmer* [Walt Whitman and his imitators]. Leipzig: Heichen.

1911d. *Der Weltfriede. Ein amerikanisches Gutachten* [World peace. An American expertise]. München: O. T. Scholl.

1913a. *Amerikanischer Aberglaube der Gegenwart* [American superstition of the present]. Leipzig: Gerstenberg.

1913b. *Hexen, Teufel und Blocksbergspuk in Geschichte, Sage und Literatur* [Witches, devils, and spooks on the Blocksberg]. Annaberg: Graser.

1913c. *Nietzsche und kein Ende* [Nietzsche and no end]. Torgau: Druck- und Verlagshaus Gmbh.

1913d. *Die Vögel in Geschichte, Sage, Brauch und Literatur* [Birds in history, legends, customs, and literature]. München: Seybold.

1914. *Das amerikanische Judentum* [American Jewry]. Leipzig: Engel.

1915. *Die Deutschfeindlichkeit Amerikas* [American hostility toward Germans]. Leipzig. Gerstenberg.

1920. *Die Nackten in Sage, Sitte, Kunst und Literatur* [The naked in legends, customs, art, and literature]. Berlin: Neukölln: Freisonnenland Verlag.

·Appendix B·

BOOKS OR ARTICLES USED BY
KARL KNORTZ AS REFERENCES

Knortz interspersed in his books referrals to works he had used. In most cases he gave no bibliographic information in the index—if there is one at all—and he seldom wrote down his sources in footnotes. The following list contains some of the more important works he mentions. Among those, only books dealing with American folklore and a few of general interest are included. The place where Knortz quoted his source, and the folkloric genre or detail he associated with it, are bracketed. Since the material translated in this book refers mainly to data collected by Knortz himself, many of the bracketed items will not have been included, since there is no indication he collected them orally.

Alger, A. 1897. *In Indian tents.* Boston: Roberts Brothers. [1913d, 115; raven, Am. Ind.]

Annual report of the bureau of ethnology. 1881. Washington: Govt. Printing office.

Annual report #2. 1882–83. [1910a, 113; spider, mound builders]

Annual report #14. 1895–96. [1913d, 161; eagle, Am. Ind. (J. Mooney)] [1913b, 165; mouse, Am Ind.]

Annual report #15. 1896–97. [1911b, 27; snakes, Am. Ind.]

Annual report #16. 1897–98. [1913d, 56; duck, Am. Ind.] [1913d, 57; duck, Am. Ind.]

Annual report #18. 1899–1900. [1913d, 86; swallow, Eskimo]

Annual report #19. 1900–01. [1910a, 126; katydid, Am. Ind.] [1910a,

129; cricket, Am. Ind. (J. Mooney, Myths of the Cherokee)] [1913d, 32; goose, Am. Ind.] [1913d, 138; owl, Am. Ind.]

    Annual report #23. 1904–05. [1913d, 137; owl, Am. Ind.]

    Annual report #26. 1907–08. [1910a, 94; fly, Am. Ind.] [1910a, 141; butterfly, Am Ind.] [1911b, 87; lizard, Am. Ind.] [1913d, 159; eagle, Am. Ind.]

    Antiquities of Ohio. 1877. Final report of the Ohio State Board of Centennial Managers. Columbus, Ohio. [1900b, 17]

    Bailey, C. S. 1907. *Firelight stories.* Springfield, Mass.: Milton Bradley Co. [1911b, 52; frogs, Blacks] [1913b, 165; mouse, Am. Ind.]

    Baker, Theodor. 1882. *Über die Musik der nordamerikanischen Wilden.* Leipzig: Breitkopf & Härtel. [1902b, 270; Am. Ind. songs]

    Bancroft, Hubert Howe. 1874–75. *Native races of the Pacific states of North America.* New York: D. Appleton and Co. [1882a, 249; flood stories] [1900c, 101; raven] [1913a, 56]

    Baraga. 1850. *A theoretical and practical grammar of the Otchipwe language.* Detroit: J. Fox.

    ———. 1853. *A dictionary of the Otchipwe language.* Cincinnati: J. A. Heman [1876a, 308] [1882a, 25] [1907a, 51]

    Baring Gould, S. 1866. Story Radicals. In Henderson, *Folk lore of the northern counties of England and the Borders.* London: Longmans, Green, and Co. [1900b, 29]

    ———. ND. *Myths of the Middle Ages.* [1896a, 8]

    Bassett, Fletcher. 1885 and 1888. *Legends and superstitions of the sea and of sailors.* Chicago: Belford, Clarke & Co. [1911b, 19; snakes] [1913d, 38; goose]

    Bergen, Fanny D. 1896. *Current superstitions.* Boston: Houghton, Mifflin and Co. [1913a, 7; superst.] [Knortz seems to have used Bergen's collections extensively]

    ———. 1899. *Animal and plant lore.* Boston: Houghton, Mifflin and Co. [1913a, 7; superst.]

    Boas, Franz. ND. *Indianermärchen der Nord Pacific-Küste.* [1910a, 116; spider]

    Böttger, H. 1891. *Sonnenkult der Indogermanen.* Breslau, [1902b, 15]

Bolton, H. C. 1888. *The counting-out rhymes of children*. New York: D. Appleton and Co. [1902b, 270]

Bourke, John G. 1891. *Scatologic rites of all nations*. Washington: W. H. Lowdermilk & Co. [1900c, 338; means to win love] [1909d, 80; eye/devil]

Brinton, D. G. 1870. *The national legend of the Chahta-Muskokee Tribes*. Morissania, New York: Holt and Co. [1909d, 238; bones, Am. Ind.]

———. 1876. *Myths of the new world*. New York: Holt and Co. [1903, 117]

———. 1885. *American languages, and why we should study them*. Philadelphia: Lippincott. [1900b, 34]

Browne, W. H. 1878. *Witty sayings*. Philadelphia. Reprint, *Witty sayings by witty people*. New York: Arno Press, 1974. [1902b, 209; riddles]

Campbell, J. F. 1860–62. *Popular tales of the West Highlands*. Edinburgh: Edmonston and Douglas. Reprint, 1890–93, London: A. Gardner. [1889a, 72; solar myth]

Carr, L. 1883. *The Mounds of the Mississippi Valley historically considered*. Frankfort, Kentucky: Yeoman Press. [1900b, 76]

Charades and responses. 1874. Philadelphia. [1902b, 209; riddles]

Chestnuth, Chas. W. 1899. *The conjure woman*. Boston: Mifflin and Co. [1913a, 71; superst., voodoo]

Conant, A. J. 1879. *Foot-prints of vanished races in the Mississippi Valley*. St. Louis: C. R. Barnes. [1900b, 76]

Culin, St. 1898. *Chess and playing cards*. Washington: Govt. Printing Office. [1900b, 82]

Curtin, Jeremiah. 1889. European folk-lore in the United States. *JAF* 2: 56–59.

Deans, James. 1889. Raven Myths of the Northwest Coast. *American Antiquarian and Oriental Journal*. Sept. [1900c, 100; raven]

Drake, S. A. 1884. *A book of New England legends*. Boston: Roberts Brothers. [1913b, 36; witches] [1913b, 35; witches]

———. 1900. *The myths and fables of to-day*. Boston: Lee & Shepard. [1913a, 7; superst.] [1913a, 74; ghost]

Dresslar, F. 1907. *Superstition and education.* Berkeley: University of California Press. [1913a, 48; superst., medicine]

Dunn, John. *History of the Oregon Territory.* London: Edwards and Hughes. [1900c, 147; spittle, Am. Ind.]

Eaton, Ch. B. 1885. *Riddles and their answers.* New York. [1902b, 209; riddles]

Fisher, H. L. 1885. *An historical sketch of the Pennsylvania Germans.* Chicago. [1902b, 58]

Fortier, A. 1894. *Louisiana folk-tales.* Boston: Houghton, Mifflin and Co. [1913a, 7; superst.]

———. 1894. *Louisiana studies.* New Orleans. [1900c, 408; Hallowe'en]

Gatchet, A. S. 1890. *The Klamath Indians of southwestern Oregon.* Washington: Govt. Printing Office. [1910a, 115; spider] [1902b, 265; Am. Ind. songs]

———. 1891. *The Karankawa Indians.* Cambridge, Mass.: Peabody Museum of American Archeology and Ethnology. [1902b, 264; Am. Ind. songs]

Gibbons, Phebe Earle. 1872. *Pennsylvania Dutch and other essays.* Philadelphia: J. B. Lippincott. [1902b, 57; Amish]

Gittée, A. 1888. *Vraagboek tot het Zamelen van Vlaamsche Folklore of Volkskunde.* Gent: J. Vuylsteke. [1900b, 33; general]

Grinnell, G. B. 1889. *Pawnee hero stories and folk-tales.* New York: Scribner's. [1902b, 261; Am. Ind. songs]

———. 1892. *Blackfoot lodge tales.* New York: Scribner's. [1902b, 262; Am. Ind. songs]

v. Hahn, J. G. 1864. *Griechische und albanesische Märchen.* Leipzig: W. Engelmann. [1900b, 29; tale types] [1902b, 44; chain sentence]

Haldeman, S. S. 1872. *Pennsylvania Dutch.* Philadelphia: Reformed Church Publication Board. [1902b, 58; Pa. Dutch]

Hale, Horatio. 1883. *The Iroquois book of rites.* Philadelphia: D. G. Brinton. [1902b, 263; Am. Ind. songs]

Harris, Chandler. 1889. *Nights with Uncle Remus.* New York:

Houghton and Mifflin. [1896a, 20; rabbit, Blacks] [1896a, 41; tales] [1913a, 66; rabbit foot among Blacks]

Higginson, T. W. 1870. *Army life in a Black regiment.* Boston: Fields, Osgood & Co. [1902b, 241; Negro spirituals]

Hoffman. 1889. Folk-Medicine of the Pennsylvania Germans. *Proceedings of the American Philosophical Society.* [1902b, 56]

Ingalls, H. 1895. *The Boston charades.* Boston: Lee and Shepard. [1902b, 209; riddles]

Jiriczek, Otto. 1894. *Anleitung zur Mitarbeit an volkskundlichen Sammlungen.* Brünn. [1900b, 33; general]

Jones, J. A. 1830. *Traditions of North American Indians.* London: H. Colburn and R. Bentley. [1900c, 193; legend about fingernails]

Jones, J. 1876. *Exploration of the aboriginal remains of Tennessee.* Washington: Smithsonian Institution. [1900b, 76]

Johnson, Clifton. 1896. *What they say in New England.* Boston. Reprint 1963. Edited by Carl Withers. New York: Columbia University Press. [1900c, 327; superst., wedding, others] [1902b, 45; chain sentence] [1910a, 31; bee] [1911b, 33; frog] [1913a, 7; superst.] [1913b, 16; witches]

Johnson, Elias. 1881. *Legends and traditions of the Six Nations.* Locksport, New York: Union Printing. [1913d, 162; eagle, Am. Ind.]

Journal of American Folklore (JAF). (No vol.) [1913a, 7; superst.]

JAF 3, 4, 8, 13. [1902b, 45; chain sentence]

JAF 1. [1900c, 69; Cherokees, stag] [1913b, 38; witches]

JAF 2. [1896a, 9; Will o'the Wisp, Pa. Dutch] [1896a, 40; song, Blacks] [1900c, 90; fairy tale about bees] [1900c, 139; spittle, (Bergen)] [1902b, 67; Pa. Dutch, witches] [1902b, 70; Pa. Dutch, cure] [1909d, 222; bones, Am. Ind.] [1911b, 79; toad, frog, turtle, Am. Ind.] [1913d, 50; duck, Am Ind.] [1913d, 163; eagle, Am. Ind.]

JAF 2: 33. [1896a, 9; Jack o'Lantern]

JAF 3. [1896a, 31; children's games] [1900c, 110; raven, Am. Ind.] [1900c, 264; games (Newell)] [1900c, 252; ball game, Am. Indians] [1902b, 45; chain sentence] [1913a, 72; witch in children's game]

JAF 4. [1896a, 31; children's games] [1900c, 100; raven, Am. Ind.]

[1900c, 139; spittle (Starr)] [1902b, 45; chain sentence] [1913d, 163; eagle, Am. Ind.]

JAF 5. [1910a, 120; grasshopper, Am Ind.] [1913b, 158; mouse, Am. Ind.]

JAF 6. [1896a, 42; wren] [1911b, 24; snakes, Am. Ind.] [1913d, 57; duck, mosquito, Am. Ind.]

JAF 7. [1900c, 165; beans, Am. Ind.] [1902b, 267; Am. Ind. songs] [1910a, 126; cricket] [1910a, 135; mosquito, Ainu] [1911b, 5; snake, Ainu] [1913b, 8; witch] [1913d, 115; raven, Eskimo] [1913d, 164; eagle, Am. Ind.]

JAF 8. [1902b, 45; chain sentence] [1910a, 114; spider, Am. Ind.] [1913d, 166; eagle, Am. Ind.] [1913d, 209; rooster, Blacks]

JAF 9. [1903, 66; thief]

JAF 10. [1911b, 26; snakes, Am. Ind.]

JAF 11. [1903, 9–10; turtle, Blacks] [1910a, 139; glow worm, Am. Ind] [1913d, 167; eagle, turtle, Blacks]

JAF 12. [1903, 63; witch, Blacks] [1913d, 33; goose, Eskimo]

JAF 13. [1902b, 45; chain sentence] [1910a, 140; butterfly, Am. Ind.] [1913d, 166; eagle, Blacks]

JAF 15. [1913d, 161; eagle, Am. Ind.]

JAF 16. [1913d, 33; goose, Eskimo]

JAF 17. [1910a, 150; ant] [1911b, 87; cures, Am. Ind.]

JAF 18. [1910a, 88; fly, Am. Ind.] [1911b, 52; frog]

JAF 19. [1910a, 115; spider, Am. Ind.] [1911b, 23; snakes, Am. Ind.] [1913d, 33; goose, Am. Ind.] [1913d, 137; owl, Am. Ind.] [1913d, 280; white bird, Am. Ind.]

King, Edward. 1875. *The great South*. Hartford, Conn.: American Publishing Co. [1902b, 241; Negro songs]

Leland, Ch. G. 1884. *Algonquin legends*. Boston: Houghton, Mifflin, and Co. [1900c, 161; "Gluskap"] [1902b, 262; Am. Ind. songs] [1903, 18; Am. Ind.; similarities with Edda] [1913b, 19; witches]

Longfellow, Henry Wadsworth. 1855. *The song of Hiawatha*. Boston: Ticknor and Fields.

———. 1858. *The courtship of Miles Standish and other poems*. Boston: Ticknor and Fields.

———. 1867. *Evangeline*. Boston: Ticknor and Fields. [e.g. 1874b]

Lunt, G. 1873. *Old New-England traits*. New York: Hurd and Houghton. [1900c, 264; games]

Mallery, Garrick. 1880. *Introduction to the study of sign language among the North American Indians*. Washington: Govt. Printing Office. [1900b, 39]

Mannhardt, W. 1875–77. *Der Baumkultus der Germanen und ihrer Nachbarstämme*. Vol. 1 of *Wald-und Feldkulte*. Berlin: Gebrueder Borntraeger. [1900c, 389; witches]

Monseur, E. 1891. *Questionaire de Folklore*. Liege: La Société du Folklore Wallon. [1900b, 33; general]

Mooney, James. ND. The ghost-dance religion and the Sioux outbreak of 1890. *14th annual report of the Bureau of American Ethnology*.

———. 1900. Myths of the Cherokee. *19th annual report of the Bureau of American Ethnology*. Washington.

Mother Goose nursery rhymes, tales and jingles. London and New York: F. Warren & Co. [1902b, 44; chain sentence] [1907a, 21] [Knortz writes about Elizabeth Goose and the beginnings (1719) of her *Songs for the nursery; or Mother Goose's melodies for children* in 1896a, 14]

Müller, Daniel. 1903. *Pennsylvania German*. Reading. [1913a, 102]

Newell, William Wells. 1883. *Games and songs of American children*. New York: Harper & Brothers. [1896a, 19, 28, 31, 32] [1900c, 264] [1902b, 45] [1902b, 270]

Owen, Mary A. 1893. *Voodoo tales*. New York: Putnam. [1898c, 32, 1913a, 71; voodoo] [1900b, 184; skunk] [1900c, 93; bees] [1902b, 255; witches] [1910a, 26; honey] [1911b, 15; snakes, Blacks]

Peef, St. D. ND. The tribal record in the effigies. *The American antiquarian* 15, no. 2. [1900b, 76]

Peet, St. 1905. *Myths and symbols or aboriginal religions in America*. Chicago: Office of the American Antiquarian. [1910a, 113; spider, mound builders]

Pennsylvania Dutch and other essays. 1872. Philadelphia: J. B. Lippincott. [1900c, 404; Halloween] [1902b, 57]

Phillips, H. 1888. *First contribution to the study of folklore of Philadel-*

phia and its vicinity. [1902b, 63; rice at wedding]

Pollard, J. G. 1894. *The Pamunkey Indians of Virginia.* Washington: Govt. Printing Office. [1900b, 35; name, Am. Ind.]

Powell, John W. 1877. *Introduction to the study of Indian languages.* Washington: Govt. Printing Office. [1900b, 33]

Powers, Stephen. 1877. *Tribes of California.* Washington: Govt. Printing Office. [1882a, 253; flood stories, Am. Ind.]

Rand, S. T. 1894. *Legends of the Micmacs.* New York, London: Longmans, Green, and Co. [1900c, 161; "Gluskap"] [1903, 18; Am. Ind.; similarities with Edda]

Riggs, Stephen R. 1869. *"Tahkoo wah-kan."* Boston: Congregational Publishing Society. [1889a, 79; Indian god, Am. Ind.]

Schoolcraft, Henry Rowe. 1856. *The myth of Hiawatha.* Philadelphia: J. B. Lippincott & Co. [1876a, 139]

Simrock, K. J. 1855. *Handbuch der deutschen Mythologie, mit Einschluß der nordischen.* Bonn: A. Marcus. [1903, 58]

Slave songs of the United States. 1867. New York: A. Simpson & Co. [1902b, 241; Negro songs]

Strong, J. C. 1893. *Wah-Kee-nah and her people.* New York: G. P. Putnam. [1913a, 99; fingernails]

Swan, J. 1869. *The Indians of Cape Flattery.* Washington. [1909d, 238; bones, Am. Ind.]

Thomas, C. 1887. *Work in mound exploration of the Bureau of Ethnology.* Washington: Govt. Printing Office. [1900b, 76]

———. 1889. *The circular, square and octogonal artworks of Ohio.* Washington: Govt. Printing Office. [1900b, 76]

———. 1889. *The problem of the Ohio mounds.* Washington: Govt. Printing Office. [1900b, 76]

———. 1891. *Catalogue of prehistoric works east of the Rocky Mountains.* Washington: Govt. Printing Office. [1900b, 17]

Trumbull, H. C. 1899. *Covenant of salt.* New York: Charles Scribner. [1910a, 92; fly]

Upham, C. W. 1867. *Salem witchcraft.* Boston: Wiggin and Lunt. [1913b, 33; witches]

Vining, E. P. 1885. *An inglorious Columbus*. New York: C. Appleton and Co. [1900b, 8; name, Am. Ind.]

Wilson, T. A. 1890. *Study of prehistoric anthropology*. Washington. [1900b, 33]

Wilson, T. A. *Prehistoric art*. Washington. [1900b, 76]

Whitman, Walt. 1855. *Leaves of grass*. Brooklyn. [And subsequent editions.]

Wuttke, A. 1869. *Der deutsche Volksglaube der Gegenwart*. 2d. ed. Berlin: Wiegand & Griegen. [1903, 44]

Yearbook of the Pennsylvania Society of New-York. 1910. [1913b, 106; witches]

Friedrich Ziegler. 1692. *Heilige Seelen-Vergnügungen im Grünen*. Leipzig: Caspar Lamitius.

BIBLIOGRAPHY

Abbreviations for Journals:
FFC: Folklore Fellows Communications
JAL: Journal of American Literature

Aarne, Antti. 1910. Verzeichnis der Märchentypen, *FFC*, no. 3. Helsinki, Suomalainen Tiedeakatemia.

Appleton's cyclopaedia of American biography. Vol. 3. 1887. New York: D. Appleton and Co.

Assion, Peter. 1988. Karl Knortz and His Works. *The Folklore Historian* 5, no.1: 2–12.

Bach, A. 1960. *Deutsche Volkskunde*. 3d ed. Heidelberg: Quelle & Meyer.

Bancroft, H. 1883. *Native races of the Pacific states*. Vol. 5. San Francisco: Bancroft & Co.

Baring Gould, S. 1866. Story Radicals. In *Notes on the folklore of the northern counties of England and the borders,* by W. Henderson. London: Longmans, Green, and Co.

Bassett, F. S. 1885. *Legends and superstitions of the sea and of sailors*. Chicago: Belford Clark & Co.

———. 1892a. The Chicago Folk-Lore Society. *The Folk-Lorist* 1, no. 1 July: 5–12.

———. 1892b. *The folk-lore manual*. Chicago: Folk-Lore Society. Reprint 1973 Darby, Penn.: Norwood Editions.

———. 1898. The Folk-Lore Congress. *International Folk-Lore Congress of the World's Columbian Exposition* 1: 17–23.

Bergen, Fanny D. 1896. *Current superstitions*. Boston: Houghton, Mifflin Co.

———. 1899. *Animal and plant lore*. Boston: American Folklore Society.

Boas, F. 1891. Dissemination of Tales among the Natives of North America. *JAF* 4: 13–20.

———. 1896. The Growth of Indian Mythology. *JAF* 9: 1–11.

———. 1902. The Foundation of a National Anthropological Society. *Science* 15: 804–09.

———. 1909. The History of Anthropology. *Science* 20: 513–24.

Brinton, Daniel. 1876. *The myths of the new world: a treatise on the symbolism and mythology of the red race of America*. 2d ed. New York: Holt & Co.

———. 1895. The Aims of Anthropology. *Proceedings of the American Association for the Advancement of Science* 44: 1–17.

———. 1897. *Religions of primitive people*. New York: G. P. Putnam's Sons.

———. 1902. *The basis of social relations: a study in ethnic psychology*. Edited by Livingston Farrand. New York, London: G. P. Putnam's Sons.

Bronner, Simon J. 1986. *American folklore studies, an intellectual history*. Lawrence: University of Kansas Press.

The Frank C. Brown collection of North Carolina folklore. 1952–1964. 7 vols. Durham, North Carolina: Duke University Press.

Brümmer, F. 1913. *Lexicon der deutschen Dichter und Prosaisten vom Beginn des 19. Jahrhunderts bis zur Gegenwart*. 6th ed. Vol. 4. Leipzig: Philipp Reclam.

Brunvand, Jan Harold 1968. *The study of American folklore; an introduction*. New York: Norton & Company.

Child, Frances James. 1881. A Circular of Child. Filed in Harvard Library.

Cox, G.W. 1878. *The mythology of the Aryan nations*. 2 vols. London: Green.

Cronau, R. 1909. *Drei Jahrhunderte deutschen Lebens in Amerika; eine Geschichte der Deutschen in den Vereinigten Staaten*, Berlin: Reimer.

Deutsch-amerikanisches Conversations-Lexicon. Mit specieller Rücksicht auf das Bedürfniß der in Amerika lebenden Deutschen. Vol. 6. 1872. New York: Steiger.

Deutsches Literatur-Lexikon. 1981. Edited by Wilhelm Kosch. 3d ed. Vol. 8, columns 1430–1432. Bern and München: Francke Verlag.

Deutscher Litteratur Kalender. 1901. Edited by Joseph Kürschner. Leipzig: Walter de Gruyter.

Der Deutsche Pionier. 1874. March, 35–37.

Die deutschsprachige Presse der Amerikas. 1973. Vol. 1, München: Verlag Dokumentation.

Dorson, Richard. 1959. *American folklore.* Chicago: University of Chicago Press.

Dresslar, Fletcher Bascom. 1920. *Superstition and education.* University of California Publications in Education, vol. 5, no.1. Berkeley: University of California Press.

Dundes, Alan. 1964. Robert Lee J. Vance: American Folklore Surveyor of the 1890s. *Western Folklore.* 23: 27–34.

———. 1965a. The Study of Folklore in Literature and Culture: Identification and Interpretation. *JAF* 78, no. 2: 136–142.

———, ed. 1965b. *The study of folklore.* Englewood Cliffs, New Jersey: Prentice-Hall.

Frenz, Horst. 1946. Karl Knortz, Interpreter of American Literature and Culture. *The American-German Review.* 13, no. 2: 27–30.

Gomme, G. L., ed. 1890. *The handbook of folklore.* London: David Nutt.

Handwörterbuch des deutschen Aberglaubens. 1987. Edited by H. Bächtold-Stäubli. Berlin, Leipzig: Walter de Gruyter & Co.

Hartert, Wilhelm. 1976. Karl Knortz. 'Der Weise von Tarrytown.' *Garbenheim 776–1976. Ein Heimatbuch.* Garbenheim: Gemeinde Garbenheim.

Henderson, William. 1866. *Folk lore of the northern counties of England and the borders.* London: Longmans, Green, and Co.

Johnson, Clifton. 1963. *What they say in New England.* Edited by Carl Withers. New York: Columbia University Press.

Kürschner, Joseph. 1901. *Deutscher Litteratur Kalender.* Vol. 23, p. 731. Leipzig: Walter de Gruyter.

Lang, Andrew. 1906. *Myth, ritual and religion.* 2 vols. London: Longmans, Green, and Co.

————. 1897. *Modern mythology.* New York: Green and Co.

Longfellow, Henry Wadsworth. 1855. *The song of Hiawatha.* Boston: Ticknor and Fields.

————. 1858. *The courtship of Miles Standish and other poems.* Boston: Ticknor and Fields.

————. 1867. *Evangeline.* Boston: Ticknor and Fields.

Mannhardt, Wilhelm. 1858. *Germanische Mythen.* Berlin: Ferdinand Schneider.

Mc Neil, William K. 1980. *A history of American folklore scholarship before 1908.* 2 vols. Ph.D. diss., Indiana University.

Mason, Otis. 1891. The Natural History of Folklore. *JAF* 4: 10.

Menges, Franz. 1980. Knortz, Karl, Schriftsteller, Kultur- und Literarhistoriker. *Neue Deutsche Biographie.* 12: 226–27.

Meyers Großes Konversations-Lexikon. 1907. Vol. 11, p. 191. Leipzig and Vienna: Bibliographisches Institut.

Müller, Max. 1856. Comparative Mythology. In *Oxford essays.* London: J. W. Parker.

————. 1862. *Lectures on the science of language.* 2d ed. London, New York: C. Scribner.

————. 1867. *Chips from a German workshop.* London, New York: C. Scribner.

————. 1897. *Contributions to the science of mythology.* 2 vols. London: Longmans, Green, and Co.

The national cyclopaedia of American biography. 1900. Vol. 10. New York: James T. White & Co.

Neue Deutsche Biographie. Vol. 12. Berlin: Duncker and Humblot.

The New Schaff-Herzog Encyclopedia of Religious Knowledge, Embracing Biblical, historical, doctrinal, and practical. 1908–1914. 13 vols. New York: Funk and Wagnal Co.

Newell, William Wells. 1883. *Games and songs of American children.* New York: Harper and Brothers.

——. 1888a. On the Field and Work of a Journal of American Folk-Lore. *JAF* 1: 3–7.

——. 1888b. Necessity of Collecting the Traditions of Native Races. *JAF* 1: 162–63.

——. 1888c. Notes and Queries. *JAF* 1: 79–81.

——. 1890a. Additional Collection Essential to Correct Theory in Folk-Lore and Mythology. *JAF* 3: 23–32.

——. 1890b. The Study of Folk-Lore (abstract). *Transactions of the New York Academy of Sciences* 9: 134–36.

——. 1891a. Review of *The handbook of folklore*, by Gomme. *JAF* 4: 184–86.

——. 1891b. Review of *The Sabbath in Puritan New England*, by A. Morse Earle. *JAF* 4: 356–58.

——. 1892a. Folk-Lore at the Columbian Exposition (notes and queries). *JAF* 5: 239–40.

——. 1892b. Lady Featherflight. *International Folk-Lore Congress: Papers and Transactions*. London: D. Nutt.

——. 1900. Early American Ballads. *JAF* 13: 105–22.

——. 1906. Individual and Collective Characteristics in Folk-Lore. *JAF* 19: 1–15.

William Wells Newell Memorial Meeting. 1907. *JAF* 20: 61–66.

Priest, Josiah. 1834. *American antiquities*. 2d. ed. Albany, New York: Hoffman & White.

Riedl, N. 1965. Folklore vs Volkskunde. *Tennessee Folklore Society Bulletin*. 31: 47–53.

Riehl, Wilhelm Heinrich. 1935. Die Volkskunde als Wissenschaft (reprint of the lecture). In *Die Volkskunde als Wissenschaft*. Berlin, Leipzig: Herbert Stubenrauch.

Rush, Benjamin. 1789. *An account of the manners of the German inhabitants of Pennsylvania*. Reprint 1910, Lancaster: Pennsylvania-German Society.

Simrock, Karl Joseph. 1855. *Handbuch der deutschen Mythologie, mit Einschluß der nordischen*. Bonn: A. Marcus.

Starr, Frederick. 1892. Anthropological Work in Europe. *The Popular Science Monthly* 31(May): 54–72.

Taylor, Archer. 1951. *English riddles from oral tradition*. Berkeley: University of California Press.

Thompson, Stith. 1928. The Types of the Folktale. *FFC* 74.

———. 1932. *Motif-Index of Folk-Literature*. 6 vols. Bloomington: Indiana University Presss.

Tylor, Edward Burnett. 1871. *Primitive culture*. 2 vols. London: John Murray.

Vance, Lee J. 1893. Folklore Study in America. *The Popular Science Monthly*, 43: 586–98.

———. 1896–97. The Study of Folk-Lore. *Forum* 22: 249–56.

Wer ist's? Unsere Zeitgenossen. 1906. Vol 2. Leipzig: H. A. Ludwig Degener.

Who's who in America? A biographical dictionary of living men and women of the United States. Vol. 1. Chicago: A. N. Marquis.

Wuttke, A. 1869. *Der deutsche Aberglaube der Gegenwart*. 2d ed. Berlin: Wiegand & Griben.

Zumwalt, Rosemary Levy. 1988. *American folklore scholarship, a dialogue of dissent*. Bloomington and Indianapolis: Indiana University Press.

INDEX